A MOST FORCEFUL
ARGUMENT

When Athena bluntly told the Earl of Glencairn exactly what she thought of his title, he merely smiled and said, "If I wish to avoid becoming a traitor to my class, I must avoid talking with you. You are very persuasive."

His mockery was too much. "I have kept you too long, Lord Glencairn," Athena said.

But the earl made no move to leave. Instead he said, "God in heaven, you are so damnably beautiful." He caught Athena to him, crushing her in a tight embrace and capturing her mouth in a passionate kiss.

Athena was so startled that she did not protest. Indeed, filled with an intense longing, she returned his kiss with surprising fervor.

"I want you," the earl said, "and you want me, too."

"No, my lord," said Athena. "You have misjudged me."

"I don't think so," returned the earl . . . and for the first time in her life, Athena feared she was in a debate she might not win.

Midwestern native M[...]
history, and journalism in college. The a[...]
novels, she lives in northern Illinois with her Welsh corgis, Morgan and Mally. Miss Summerville enjoys romantic poetry, painting, gardening and vegetarian cookery.

My Lord Tyrant

by

Margaret Summerville

A SIGNET BOOK

SIGNET
Published by the Penguin Group
Penguin Books USA Inc., 375 Hudson Street,
New York, New York 10014, U.S.A.
Penguin Books Ltd, 27 Wrights Lane,
London W8 5TZ, England
Penguin Books Australia Ltd, Ringwood,
Victoria, Australia
Penguin Books Canada Ltd, 10 Alcorn Avenue,
Toronto, Ontario, Canada M4V 3B2
Penguin Books (N.Z.) Ltd, 182-190 Wairau Road,
Auckland 10, New Zealand

Penguin Books Ltd, Registered Offices:
Harmondsworth, Middlesex, England

First published by Signet,
an imprint of New American Library,
a division of Penguin Books USA Inc.

First Printing, June, 1993
10 9 8 7 6 5 4 3 2 1

 REGISTERED TRADEMARK—MARCA REGISTRADA

Printed in the United States of America

1

It WAS fortunate that Athena Blair had the ability to
ignore the noise and chaos about her, for the atmosphere
of the offices of the *Clarion Voice* was not conducive to
meditation. A weekly newspaper that expressed contro-
versial views on political and literary subjects, the *Voice*
attracted a number of opinionated persons to its door.
Athena had long become accustomed to the confusion of
the place—the hurried bustling of employees and visitors and the loud, often heated conversations that constantly took place there.

In addition to the internal distractions, there was a
constant clamor from the street because the *Clarion
Voice* was located on a busy thoroughfare near the center
of London. On a spring day when the windows were
open, the sound of carriages, carts, and wagons could be
very disruptive.

Yet as she sat writing at her desk in the cluttered, busy
office, Athena seemed unaware of her surroundings.
Having long ago developed the ability to screen out the
noises about her, she worked diligently at her desk,
scribbling rapidly and pausing only to dip her pen in ink.
After a time Athena paused to read what she had written.

Then appearing satisfied, Athena put the work aside
and rather reluctantly took up a slim vellum-bound book
of poetry she was to review. Athena dreaded this task for
she had already read the book and had found it ap-
pallingly mediocre. While most reviewers relished the

task of savaging a work they found repellent, Athena did not enjoy the prospect. As an author herself, she was only too aware how devastating the criticism of others could be.

Athena turned from the poetry to look across the room where her fellow workers, Mr. Pike and Mr. Ashton, were engaged in a loud discussion that appeared to be turning into an argument. The two men did not usually get along very well despite similar political views. Pike tended to be scornful of his fellow writer Ashton, who was a quiet, unassuming young man. They bickered constantly, much to Athena's annoyance.

Eying them with disapproval, Athena decided it best to ignore them and reluctantly returned to her work. However, a welcome diversion appeared in the form of a well-dressed young gentleman who appeared at her desk. "Good morning, Miss Blair."

"Good morning, Mr. Sheffield."

A good-looking man in his middle twenties, Sheffield smiled. "It appears that Ashton and Pike are quarreling again."

Casting a glance in their direction, Athena nodded. She noted that Ashton was very red in the face and that Pike was scowling. "Is it not tiresome?" she said. "One should like to take them by the scruffs of their necks and shake them like willful puppies."

Sheffield laughed. "I hope you will leave that to your father, Miss Blair. Is he here?"

Athena regarded the young man indulgently. He was devoted to her father, Baldwin Blair, who was editor and publisher of the *Clarion Voice*. "I am sorry, Mr. Sheffield, my father is not here at present. I do not know when he will return, for he is at Parliament, witnessing the debate on the new Corn Laws." As she said this, Athena hoped that it was true. Her father was not at the office as much as might be expected. And although Baldwin was supposed to be listening to parliamentary debate, one could not be certain of his whereabouts. Had he met one of his numerous friends along the way, he might be sitting in some public house exchanging stories.

It seemed that lately more and more responsibility for the weekly newspaper was falling to Athena. Sometimes, she reflected, she felt far older than her twenty-two years, and sometimes her responsibilities on the *Clarion Voice* seemed decidedly onerous. As time went on, Baldwin wrote fewer and fewer pieces, preferring to spend his time discussing social problems, politics, literature, and philosophy with his friends and colleagues.

Although it was a heavy burden for a young lady, Athena usually relished her duties on the *Voice*. Knowing very well that few women had the opportunity to do such work, she considered herself very fortunate that her father was an unusually enlightened and open-minded man. Indeed, Baldwin was a man of such revolutionary views that he believed that the female of the species had a brain and ought to be allowed to use it.

"I fear I do not have time to wait for Mr. Blair," said Mr. Sheffield, his voice expressing his disappointment. Athena suppressed a smile. Baldwin Blair had a good many devoted admirers and Thaddeus Sheffield was one of the most faithful.

Baldwin inspired devotion for he was a man of passionate and forceful opinions. A talented writer and compelling orator, Baldwin Blair was particularly fond of rejecting commonly held views and shocking those of more traditional persuasions. He was quite radical politically, and he was not afraid to express unpopular anti-monarchist opinions and frequently spoke of the superiority of the American and French systems. However, since Britain was at war with France and its relationship with the United States was at present very strained, Baldwin's opinions were hardly popular. He was also very concerned with social problems and had come up with a number of utopian models for righting them.

An idealistic young man, Sheffield thought Baldwin Blair the greatest man of the age. Since Sheffield had inherited a prosperous shipping business, he was occupied much of the time, but he tried to see Baldwin whenever he had the opportunity. "I must go, Miss Blair. Would you tell your father that I was here?"

"Indeed I shall, Mr. Sheffield."

Sheffield smiled. He hesitated a moment. "And Miss Blair, you look very pretty today." Athena's face registered faint surprise. It was unlike the shy Mr. Sheffield to give compliments. "I must be off then. Good day, Miss Blair."

With an amused expression she watched him go. Athena was not unaccustomed to compliments. She was, after all, an exceedingly pretty girl. Tall and elegant, she had been blessed with fine classical features and an excellent figure. Her remarkable light blue eyes and deep auburn hair were widely admired. When she smiled— and she smiled often—few could resist her girlish dimples and animated expression.

Yet while many had paid her compliments, Athena was sure that such words did not come easily to Mr. Sheffield. She hoped that he was not falling in love with her. A number of the intense young men who admired her father had thought themselves in love with Athena. Indeed, since she was fifteen, she had been the object of numerous infatuations. Yet no matter how handsome the young man or how heartfelt the sentiments expressed to her, Athena had not fallen in love with any of them.

It was not that Athena was indifferent to love and romance. On the contrary she always hoped that one of the young men she met might kindle passionate feeling within her. However, while she was fond of a number of gentlemen, no one had come close to inspiring the kind of emotion that Athena knew to be love.

She was, therefore, content to work at the *Clarion Voice* where she could help express her father's principles and address the evils of society. She felt that her writings were very important although the readership of the newspaper was certainly not as sizable as they might have wished.

Blair had started the *Clarion Voice* two years ago, using much of his modest inheritance to finance the endeavor. At that time Athena had begged her father to allow her to write an article or two. Baldwin had agreed, and within a few months Athena found herself the author of many of the articles in the *Voice*. As time went by, Baldwin had been quite willing to relinquish much of his editing and reviewing responsibilities to his very capable daughter. He had also very happily allowed her to write most of the numerous tracts published by the Blair printing press, although most of these were published under Baldwin's name.

Immensely proud of his daughter's accomplishments, Baldwin had no reservations about allowing her to take on increasing responsibility. Indeed, Athena's talents and hard work allowed Baldwin time for his favorite activity, socializing with friends and trying to convert strangers to his views. Baldwin's many friends and acquaintances were apt to show up at the office and stay for a morning or afternoon.

Athena, of course, loved and respected her father although she was not at all blind to his faults. Most times Athena did not appear bothered by what more critical observers might have considered to be Blair's shirking of his responsibilities. This was because she was happy to be allowed free rein at the *Clarion Voice*.

After noting that Pike and Ashton had returned to their desks, Athena sat pondering what to write in her review. So intent was she on her reflections that she scarcely noticed that another gentleman had entered the office. Looking up from her desk, she was surprised to see a tall, redheaded young man standing near the door. Gangling and unprepossessing, the newcomer was dressed in an ill-fitting, old-fashioned suit of clothes. He clutched a worn beaver hat and stood there awkwardly looking about. When his eyes met Athena's, a broad smile of recognition came to his face, and he hurried toward her.

"Miss Athena Blair, I'll warrant," he said, grinning. Athena noted he spoke with an accent, rolling his *r*'s in the distinctive way of a Scotsman.

Athena looked up with a puzzled expression. "I fear you have the advantage of me, sir."

"Och, ye dinna know me, lass? Why I know ye, even though ye've grown tae be a lady, and ye talk like an Englishwoman now." When Athena looked blankly at him, he laughed. "Why, 'tis your own cousin, Robert Blair, come frae Scotland."

"Robert? Is it really you?" cried Athena, rising from her desk.

"Aye, it is, Athena, your own cousin." Robert enfolded her in a hearty embrace.

Finally extricating herself from her enthusiastic visitor, Athena urged him to take a seat. She then sat down to survey her cousin with great interest. Athena had last seen Robert Blair when she was eight years old and living in Scotland. She and Robert were exactly the same age, and they had been excellent friends when Athena was a child in the Highlands. When Athena had left Scotland, she had cried and cried at the idea she was leaving her cousin and playfellow.

Athena noted that Robert looked like a poor relation in his well-worn clothes, yet she knew that Robert's father, Lord Blair, a Scottish baron, was a wealthy man. Robert sat there smiling broadly. He was not a handsome young man. Gaunt and long in the face, Robert had bushy red eyebrows, overly prominent front teeth, and numerous freckles. Yet his cheerful smile and amiable demeanor helped one overlook the deficiencies of his countenance.

"This is a wonderful surprise, Robbie," said Athena. She had always called her cousin "Robbie," only resorting to Robert when she was annoyed with him. "I cannot believe you are here! Why did you not write us?"

"Och, I had nae time, Athena. I left in such a hurry as soon as I had my inheritance."

"Your inheritance? You cannot mean that my uncle Malcolm . . . ?"

"Nae, lass, my father is fit as always. 'Tis an inheritance frae my mother's uncle, John Hamilton. He left me twenty-five thousand pounds!"

Athena's eyes grew wide. "Twenty-five thousand!"

"Aye," said Robert, grinning again. "I couldna believe my good fortune. But Uncle John was a rich man, and now I am rich. Sae I told my father I was off tae London, for I wouldna stay in Kinlochie one day longer than necessary. My father was nae happy at my going, but I am now my own master sae here I am."

"It is so wonderful to see you, Robbie," said Athena. "I am so happy for you. Do you plan to stay in London?"

Robert nodded. "London is the center of things, Cousin, and here is where Robbie Blair will make his home. 'Tis time I made my mark on the world."

Athena suppressed a smile, for Robert did not look at all like someone who was about to make his mark on the world. "Then you have plans, Robbie?"

"Aye, Cousin. I'm going tae take my place in London society."

"Society?" Athena regarded him with surprise. "Oh, Robbie, why on earth would you wish to do that? Society is filled with idle, thoughtless persons who contribute nothing. As my father says, they are the drones of the hive."

"Idleness looks verra good tae me," said Robert. "I have been a slave tae my father too long. Who is it that

looks after the planting and the harvest? Who is out
sweating away in the fields like a hired man day in and
day out? Who is it who is at his beck and call day and
night like a servant? And yet I am the laird's son! Robert
do this and do that, and never a word of thanks do I get
frae him. Nae, Athena, 'tis time I had some fun. I'll nae
be young forever. I want tae be a proper gentleman, nae
a bumpkin frae the Highlands. Aye, London society is
for me."

Athena shook her head. "I cannot imagine what my
father will say to that."

"What Uncle Baldwin will say does nae concern me,"
said Robert with a smile. "I am my own man and will do
as I please. I will be happy tae see Uncle Baldwin. He is
a famous man, though my father says he is woefully
misguided."

Athena laughed. "There are many who would agree
with your father, but it is they who are misguided. Your
uncle should be back presently, Robbie. And I know he
will be very pleased to see you."

Robert nodded and looked around the office. "So this
is where my uncle writes? I had nae trouble discovering
where he might be found. I had but tae ask a gentleman
at the hotel if he knew of Baldwin Blair. Indeed he had
and he asked another fellow and he consulted another
and soon I knew tae come here. But I did nae expect tae
find you here, Athena. What is a lady doing about such a
place as this?"

"I work here, Robert. I write for the *Clarion Voice*."

Robert looked shocked. "My uncle allows that?"

"He does have advanced views, Robbie."

"Indeed, he must," said Robert, rubbing his chin
thoughtfully. "But are ye nae married, Athena?"

"No I am not."

"Ye must have suitors. Ye are a bonnie lass, Cousin.
Ye've grown to be a very pretty young woman."

"I should prefer, Robbie, not to discuss my suitors or

lack of them. But what of you? Did you bring a wife with you to town?"

"Nae, Cousin, I've had nae time for courting. And there was nae lass in Kinlochie who struck my fancy. I thought I'd take a look at the London girls. They say they are the prettiest in the world. Aye, I thought I'd find an English lass."

"I daresay my uncle Malcolm will not take a liking to that."

"Och, nae. He wants me tae marry one of Sir Charles Graham's pudding-faced daughters. I'll have none of that. I'll find my own wife here in London."

"I see you know exactly what you want, Robbie," said Athena. "And you intend to find a bride in London society?"

"Aye. I want an English bride, a rich one."

"What a mercenary fellow you are, Robbie," said Athena, her eyebrows arched in amusement. She doubted that her cousin's appearance and way of speaking would cause heiresses to flock to him. And while twenty-five thousand pounds was a goodly fortune, that and the prospect of becoming a Scottish baroness would hardly be enough to entice a wealthy London lady to follow him to a remote place like Kinlochie. However Robert apparently did not think that finding a rich English bride would be difficult at all.

"I'm nae mercenary, Athena," he said, laughing. "But a man can love a rich wife as well as a poor one."

Athena was about to chide her cousin for his unabashed intent upon fortune hunting, but she was prevented by the appearance of her father. Baldwin entered the office. He was an impressive-looking man of middle years, tall and carefully dressed. He possessed good regular features and the same remarkable blue eyes that were so striking in his daughter. Baldwin's brown hair was sprinkled with gray, giving him a distinguished appearance. Amiable as always, he greeted Ashton and

Pike. Seeing an unknown young man with Athena, he made his way to them and then looked expectantly at his daughter for an introduction. "Papa, you will never guess who this young man might be."

Baldwin looked puzzled for a moment and then smiled broadly, "Not Robert Blair!"

"Indeed so, Uncle!" said Robert, delighted that Baldwin recognized him.

"I'll be damned!" said Baldwin, taking his nephew's hand and pumping it vigorously. "I should never have expected to find you here!"

"Aye, Uncle. Who would think that Robbie Blair would be in London?"

"Not I," said Baldwin. "And how is my brother? Is he in town as well? And your sisters? I hope they are well."

"My father is fine, but nae, Uncle. My father wouldna come tae the land of the hated English for all the gold in the kingdom. And my sisters are in good health. Mary wed Sir Duncan Gilmour of Kinlochie. They have three wee bairns. Agnes married Ronald Maxwell but two months ago. He's a good man."

"So your sisters are well situated," said Baldwin. "I am glad to hear it. But tell me, Robert, what did your father think of your coming to London?"

"He didna want me tae come, but I am my own man now." Robert grinned again. "I've got twenty-five thousand pounds frae my uncle, John Hamilton."

"My hearty congratulations," said Baldwin. "Why, we should celebrate your arrival, my dear Robert. Athena, let us go at once to the White Willow Coffeehouse."

"As dearly as I would wish that, Papa," said Athena, "there is so much work to do and so little time."

"Poppycock!" cried Baldwin. "The work will wait. This is an occasion, my dear girl."

Athena nodded. "Indeed it is. Very well."

Athena went to fetch her bonnet. When she returned, Baldwin was introducing his nephew to the others in the office. The three Blairs then left to make their way along the crowded sidewalk to the White Willow Coffeehouse.

The White Willow was one of Baldwin's favorite haunts. Scarcely a day went by that he did not frequent this thriving establishment, for the coffeehouse was a popular meeting place for writers and intellectuals.

Ladies, however, were not welcome at the White Willow, although an exception was made for Athena when she accompanied her father there. It was rare that Athena disturbed the masculine company of the White Willow, a fact much appreciated by the coffeehouse's proprietor. That gentleman was well aware of Athena Blair's intellectual and literary standing but, nevertheless, preferred to keep his business a masculine refuge.

When they entered the White Willow, they found it largely deserted since most of the regular customers arrived later in the day. Baldwin glanced about, looking for friends and acquaintances. "Why, there is hardly a soul about," he said.

"It is a relief," said Athena. "If your friends were here, we would scarcely have any opportunity to talk with Robbie."

"Aye, that is true," said Baldwin, ushering them to his usual table. They were seated and Baldwin ordered some refreshments.

" 'Tis marvelous being in London," said Robert. "And seeing ye after sae many years."

"I cannot say how very glad I am to see you, my boy," said Baldwin. "Now tell us. How long will you stay?"

"Why, Uncle, I have come tae stay here. I'll nae go back tae Scotland."

"And what does my brother think of that?"

"He does nae like it, Uncle. We've had a falling out, ye might say. Just as ye did sae many years ago."

"I see," said Baldwin, frowning at the memory of his estrangement with his brother. Although he and Robert's father had never gotten along even as children, it always pained Baldwin that they had feuded and vowed never to speak to each other.

"Och, dinna worry, Uncle," said Robert. "We are better apart. He never approved of me. There was nothing I could do tae please him. He'll be happier without me. But let us nae talk of my father. I wish tae talk of London. Ye've become a Londoner, Uncle. Why, ye hardly sound like a Scotsman at all."

Baldwin shrugged. "It seems a very long time ago, almost another life. Yet at times I think of the Highlands and miss Kinlochie very much."

"Ye nae can mean that, Uncle," cried Robert. "Kinlochie! Och, what a sad, wee place it is."

"I miss it, too, sometimes," said Athena thoughtfully. "I remember how beautiful it was."

"Ye'd have your fill of it very soon should ye find yourselves there," said Robert.

"But you don't think you'll be homesick, Robbie?" said Athena.

Robert regarded her incredulously. "Homesick? Nae I."

"So you plan to stay in London, Robert?" said Baldwin.

"Aye, that I shall," said Robert.

Athena smiled mischievously at her cousin. "Robbie, you must tell my father of your plans. Papa, Robbie is to enter London society."

"What!" cried Baldwin, regarding his nephew as if he were a chucklehead. "Society! Why, society consists of the most iniquitous lot of parasites ever to inhabit this island! Society! What a gathering of idle, silly, witless knaves! By heaven, you must avoid society at all costs. But we will introduce you to our society—the society of intellectuals, artists, and liberal thinkers."

Robert arched his thick eyebrows and shook his head. "That is all well for ye, Uncle—intellectuals and the like—but nae for me. As I have told Athena, I've a mind tae have some fun. I'm not the bookish sort, Uncle, and what would I have tae say to such scholarly fellows as would be your friends? Nae, Uncle, I wish tae see what society is like. I'm nae a man tae scorn something until I've had a look at it. Perhaps I shall scorn society as well, but I must find out for myself. I'd like tae meet all the fine sporting gentlemen and the great ladies. Why, I might even meet the Prince Regent himself."

"The Prince Regent!" cried Baldwin. "That degenerate lackwit!"

"Now, Papa," said Athena. She smiled at Robert. "Papa does not like His Royal Highness overmuch. I advise you not to mention him."

"Then I shall nae do so, Uncle. I didna know ye disliked the man sae much."

"Then it is apparent that Robbie does not read the *Clarion Voice*, Papa," said Athena, winking at her father.

Baldwin laughed. "Well, we'll change you to our way of thinking in time, my boy. But how do you intend to enter society? Do you have letters of introduction? One does not simply burst into the drawing rooms of the English aristocracy uninvited. One must have connections."

"I know that," returned Robert, nodding. "But I have ye and Athena."

This remark caused both Baldwin and his daughter to burst into laughter. "My dear Robert," said Baldwin, "you are sadly mistaken if you think that we can assist you. We are as far removed from society as one can be. No, lad, I am not the sort of fellow who is welcomed into the homes of titled ladies. I am a revolutionary after all."

Robert looked very disappointed. "Have ye nae friends in society, then, Uncle?"

"Indeed not. I should think I have a good many enemies though, but that will not do you any good at all."

"I am sorry tae hear that, Uncle, but I'll nae be deterred. I shall take a house in a fashionable neighborhood. Ye must advise me on where a gentleman of substance should live."

"A man of substance would reside a good distance away from our rooms on Threadneedle Street to be sure," said Athena. "I fear we live very modestly, Robbie."

"Then I shall take a very fine house, and ye will come and live with me. I shouldna wish tae live alone. 'Twould be much better tae have my kin tae keep me company."

Athena smiled. "That is good of you, Robbie, but my father and I are very happy where we live."

"I should not say completely happy," said Baldwin. "The rooms are very small, but we are very close by, and it is convenient for us."

"Well, I shall take a house and then we will see. But ye must tell me all about London. I must know everything."

"It would take some time to do that, Robbie," said Athena. "Why don't you tell us about Kinlochie? Is it the same as I remember it?"

"Kinlochie? Why, there is little tae tell. 'Tis nae changed at all. 'Twas always a dull sort of place, but now with the clearances, 'tis dismal and grim."

"The clearances?" said Athena. "What do you mean?"

"Och, ye dinna know about that? Why, the Earl of Glencairn has turned many of his tenants frae the land. They have nae place tae go. Many were made homeless, some of them burned out sae that they barely escaped with their lives."

"What!" cried Athena. "That is monstrous!"

"Aye," said Robert. "Glencairn owns nearly all the land around Kinlochie save for my father's estate. He wants the land for sheep sae he can make a profit. The tenants are a nuisance, ye see. 'Tis a pitiful state of affairs, for many of the families have lived there for generations. My father for all his faults would nae do such a thing."

"What sort of man would be capable of that?" said Athena indignantly.

"Och, I've nae idea," said Robert with a shrug. "I dinna know the man. He's nae set foot in Scotland. He was born in England. He is a powerful man."

"And rich as a nabob," said Baldwin. "He is one of the Prince Regent's cronies. You have heard of him, haven't you, Athena? He was the one who spent ten thousand pounds on a racehorse."

"Yes, of course. That is disgraceful. He is one of the Carlton House set. Indeed, I can believe anything of such a man."

"Ten thousand on one horse," said Robert, rather impressed at this information. "He must be a verra rich man, and it must have been a verra good horse."

"For ten thousand it might have been Pegasus himself," said Athena. "What disgraceful extravagance!"

"Well, there is no one more hated in the Highlands than Glencairn," said Robert. "He is thought tae be a ruthless tyrant."

"That is indeed what he is," said Athena. She was accustomed to hearing of how rich and powerful men abused their positions in society, but it outraged her to find yet another example of the ill-treatment of the poor and powerless.

"This is what comes of our feudal system," said Baldwin. "A man has wealth and a title and may lord it over everyone else. We must work to eliminate such absurd relics left from the Middle Ages."

Robert nodded solemnly, but, as he was heir to a barony, he did not think the feudal system altogether bad.

"Tell me more about the clearances, Robbie," said Athena. "I should think it might be a good subject for the *Clarion Voice*."

"An excellent idea," said Baldwin. "We too often ignore our homeland. Yes, Robert, you must tell us everything you know about it."

Robert shrugged again. He would have much preferred changing the subject, but since his cousin and uncle seemed so intent on hearing about the evil Earl of Glencairn, he was more than happy to oblige.

2

ALEXANDER MONCRIEF, sixth Earl of Glencairn, was in a devilish bad temper as he entered the dining room. Noting his lordship's scowl, the footmen in attendance prepared themselves for the worst. Accustomed as they were to the earl's foul moods, they had reason to dread their master's ill humor. He was seldom in a good mood at breakfast, and that morning seemed even worse than usual.

As the earl approached the table, one of the footmen rushed to pull out the chair for him. Glencairn sat down and put a hand to his forehead. He had slept badly and now had a splitting headache. He had risen earlier than was his custom, for it was only eleven o'clock. Since he had gone to bed after five o'clock, this was an early hour indeed.

Observing their master's evident distress, the footmen tread carefully, trying to be as quiet as possible. One of the servants approached nervously with a silver platter laden with ham and bacon. "Get that out of my sight," snapped the earl. "Take all the food away. I want nothing but tea and toast."

The butler, who had been supervising the operation, motioned to the footmen, who hurried to remove the plates of food. Glencairn frowned as a footman hastened to bring the tea and buttered toast.

Not very hungry, the earl nibbled only a piece of toast. The hot tea did seem to improve his mood a little. As he put his cup down on the linen tablecloth, he frowned again. By all the gods, he told himself, he felt miserable. But then how did one expect to feel after carousing all night, gaming and drinking until nearly dawn?

As usual the earl had rather hazy memories of the night's activities. Every evening was virtually the same, however. He would begin by dining at his club, or at the home of one of his acquaintances. Then he and some of the gentlemen would be off for one of the gaming houses that also featured the celebrated beauties of the demimonde.

The earl picked up his cup and stared glumly into space. At times his life seemed tedious and entirely pointless. But today, at least, he was to investigate buying a new racehorse. He had heard of an outstanding two-year-old, a son of the famed Pericles, and he was to see the animal that day. The thought cheered him considerably, for he loved horses more than anything in the world.

After finishing his tea, the earl quitted the dining room, retreating into the drawing room to peruse the morning newspapers. His headache was somewhat better by that time, and his mood was improving as he thought of the horse he might be adding to his renowned racing stables.

Caring little for political news, Glencairn skipped many items in the newspaper. He did read about Napoleon's continued knavery, muttering a "Damn him!" every so often. He also read everything relating to society and court, for oftentimes the earl would be mentioned as accompanying the Prince Regent.

However, of late his lordship had fallen to some degree from the prince's favor. Glencairn did not mind this overmuch for, in truth, the prince was beginning to bore him. Prinny could be a most amusing and charming companion, but at other times he could be maddeningly petty and irksome. The earl was also so accustomed to being the master that the role of royal courtier did not suit him very well.

While engaged in reading the newspaper, the earl scarcely noticed the entrance of his butler. The servant cleared his throat, causing Glencairn to look up from his reading. "Yes, Evans?"

"I beg your pardon, my lord, but Master Peter is here."

"Here? What do you mean, Evans? Master Peter is at Oxford."

"He was indeed, my lord, but he is here now, and he wishes to see your lordship. I told him I was certain that you did not wish to be disturbed."

"And you were damned right," muttered the earl. "I cannot imagine what the whelp is doing here. But send him in, Evans."

The butler bowed and retreated, leaving the earl to speculate about his brother's presence. Soon the doors were opened again, and in walked the Honorable Peter Moncrief.

Anyone observing the two brothers would have immediately noted that they could hardly have been more dissimilar in appearance. Peter Moncrief was a slightly built young man with blond hair, delicate features, a pale complexion, and cool gray eyes. Eighteen years old, Peter was very handsome, but boyish and almost frail-looking.

In contrast the earl was tall and broad-shouldered with unruly black hair and brown eyes. Nearly nine-and-twenty, his rugged countenance featured a square jaw, cleft chin, thick dark eyebrows, and wide brow. Although not handsome in the classical sense, his lordship possessed a masculine attractiveness that many women found hard to resist.

One dog-loving family acquaintance had described the brothers as being as different as a whippet and a mastiff, Glencairn being the mastiff, of course. They also differed radically in temperament, and many observers thought it hard to believe that they were brothers at all. In actuality they were half brothers, both sons of the late fifth earl, but having different mothers. Glencairn's mother had been the earl's first wife, the former Lady Anne Harley, a lady of illustrious family and formidable personality. Peter's mother was of more modest lineage, the daughter of an impoverished baronet.

Almost eleven years in age separated the brothers, causing Glencairn to regard Peter with paternalistic condescension. He adopted a stern fatherly pose as his brother approached. "Good morning, Glencairn," said Peter. "I am sorry to disturb you. Evans said you were occupied."

"Sit down," said the earl, motioning toward a chair beside him. He could tell that the young man seemed ill at ease.

"I do hope you are well, Brother," said Peter after he had seated himself on one of the earl's elegant upholstered chairs.

"Shall we dispense with the polite inquiries into each other's health, Peter? I think you should explain what you are doing here when you are supposed to be at Oxford. I am expending a good deal of blunt keeping you there. I do hope you are not going to tell me you have been sent down."

"Indeed not," said Peter rather indignantly. "I have left." He paused a moment and then bravely continued. "And I am not going back. There is nothing you can do that would make me go back."

Glencairn frowned ominously. "Explain yourself. Why do you not wish to return?"

"I do not belong there," said Peter. "I cannot bear it! Those of my college hate me."

"That is nonsense," said the earl.

"Indeed it is not," said Peter. "All they care about is

drinking and whoring. If one is not like them, they make life a total misery."

The earl frowned again. He had been at Oxford and did not dispute that drinking and whoring were principal occupations of most of the students, especially those of noble families. While at university, Glencairn had behaved as wildly and irresponsibly as any of his fellows. Indeed, he had thoroughly enjoyed himself.

Why his brother would be miserable bewildered the earl. The young man had a handsome allowance and could not want for anything. The earl's headache was beginning to grow worse again, and his lordship was becoming increasingly annoyed with his brother. "I cannot understand why you wish to leave Oxford. You have your friends there."

Peter shook his head. "I wish to leave university. I ask you to allow it. If you refuse, I shall defy you."

"So you wish to leave? And you think you may do as you please?"

"*You* may do as you please," said Peter resentfully, "but then you are Lord Glencairn."

Glencairn bristled at the remark. "You may be surprised to learn that no one does as one wishes at all times, even if one is Lord Glencairn. I have had enough of this, my lad. You are going back to Oxford. You will face whatever is troubling you like a man. I'll have no mewling kittens hanging about here."

Peter stood up. "I have told you that I will not go back. I ask you to understand. I beg you to understand."

His brother's words were so anguished that Glencairn was taken aback. Despite his gruff demeanor, the earl was not without affection for his only brother. "God in heaven," said the earl. "You are overtired. Go to your room. We will talk of this later."

Peter looked as if he was about to say something else, but then decided to accept his elder brother's dismissal. "Very well, sir," he said. He directed a formal and, to

Glencairn's mind, ironical bow toward his brother and then retreated.

The earl shook his head. He wished that he and Peter got on better. They were always at loggerheads when they were together, and his lordship was usually glad that they saw so little of each other.

The earl rose from his chair and walked across the room to the window. There he stood staring out at the never-ending progression of vehicles that passed along the cobblestone street in front of his elegant town house on Regent's Square.

A smart high-perch phaeton pulled by two high-stepping bay horses pulled up at the curb in front of the house. Recognizing the driver, Glencairn smiled. There was only one person in the world that he felt like seeing now, and that individual had arrived at his doorstep, his good friend Edward Lyttleton.

Glencairn laughed as Edward got down from the ridiculously high seat of the phaeton. Rather stout and not in the least athletic, Edward had to receive a good deal of assistance from his groom. Once firmly on the ground, he smoothed his many-caped coachman's coat, straightened his beaver hat, and proceeded to the earl's door.

Evans the butler was always eager to announce Mr. Lyttleton, for he knew that the gentleman was one person whose visits always seemed to cheer the earl. "Mr. Lyttleton is here, my lord."

"Yes, yes, I know," said the earl. "Bring him here, Evans."

When the visitor arrived in the drawing room, he greeted Glencairn with a hearty handshake. "Good day, Alex, I feared I would find you still abed."

"I should have stayed there, Ned," said the earl. "My dear friend, I pray you will take care descending from the heights of Olympus."

Edward looked blankly at him for a second and then

burst into laughter. "So you have been spying on me. 'Pon my honor, it is a trifle awkward getting down from there. I'm not a very nimble fellow."

"That I know. I used to play cricket with you, Ned."

Edward laughed again. He was a good-natured man with bright red hair and a ruddy round face. Always having a tendency toward stoutness, Edward had lately been increasing his girth substantially, a fact he attributed to his excellent French chef.

"Your new phaeton is quite bang up to the nines, Ned."

"I am so glad you like it. It is a ridiculous extravagance, but marvelous fun. Fanny thought me quite mad."

"She is not mistaken," returned the earl. "But every man must be allowed a folly. Now sit down, Ned. I have not seen you for days."

"Indeed, I have been too occupied. My sister Clarissa is having her first season, and my wife has taken her under her wing. Fanny has decreed that I am to find Clarissa a husband, and I must scrutinize an endless stream of bachelors."

"I am a bachelor. What about me?"

"Egad, Alex, I had not thought of it. Are you thinking of marrying this season?"

"I suppose I must marry one day."

"An excellent idea. Marriage is a fine institution no matter how it is maligned by fashion. Why, Fanny and I are so very happy."

"But you are one in a thousand, Ned," said Glencairn with a frown.

"Perhaps. Fanny is one in a thousand to be sure." He paused. "Clarissa is a very nice girl. She is no beauty, but not bad to look at. And she is very pleasant and cheerful."

"So you would be happy with me as a brother-in-law, Ned?"

Edward eyed his friend, wondering if he was serious.

It was often hard to tell with Glencairn. The earl burst into laughter. "Do not worry, Ned. I am only quizzing you. I should hardly wish to destroy our friendship by making your sister miserable as my wife. No, I shall marry the sister of one of my enemies."

Edward laughed. "I should know that you are never serious about such things. Then I shall have to find someone else for Clarissa."

"I do not doubt that if she is like most females, Ned, she will find her own husband without any assistance from her brother."

"No doubt." Edward sighed. "It is very difficult being the elder brother."

"How well I know that," said Glencairn.

"Have you heard from Peter then?"

"Heard from him? Why, at this moment he is in the house, moping about in his rooms. He has left Oxford."

"Not sent down?"

"No, he has left. Evidently it is not to his liking. I cannot understand why. He claims everyone hates him."

"Why, he seems a likable enough lad. He is very polite and well-mannered. But university is not the place for everyone."

"Hang it, Ned. Do not be so confounded understanding. I do not wish him to abandon something at the first obstacle. Oh, I know well that there are those who delight in making the lives of others miserable. They seek out the weaker links in the chain and make mischief. But Peter must stand up to them."

Edward nodded. "I am sure you are right, but it is not easy if you are a 'weaker link.' As you may recall at Eton, I was perhaps the weakest link of them all. You remember that bully, Darlington? He was forever plaguing me."

"You did not run away from school."

"My dear Alex, that was only because you nearly beat him to death for tormenting me."

"Oh, yes," said the earl, with a smile.

"So do not be hard on the lad."

"Are you so indulgent with your children, Ned?"

"I fear I am. I spoil them. But I shall be very strict when they are older. But come, Alex, I wish to take you for a ride. I am becoming a dashed respectable whip."

Glencairn raised his dark eyebrows. "Indeed, Ned? If you promise I shall not be killed in a disastrous collision, I shall go with you. Indeed, you may take me to see Colonel Kingsley. He is selling a fine two-year-old."

"The son of Pericles out of Queen Mab? By God, Alex, it will take a fortune for Kingsley to part with that one. And I have heard that Prinny is interested."

"Then we must make haste, Ned. I must get the horse before His Royal Highness has the opportunity."

"He will not forgive you very soon."

Glencairn smiled. "Good," he said. They both laughed and left the drawing room.

3

ATHENA and Baldwin did not return to the offices of the *Clarion Voice* for several hours. They had lingered at the White Willow Coffeehouse for some time discussing the topic of the Earl of Glencairn's infamous conduct. Afterward a number of new subjects came up, mostly resulting from Robert's numerous questions about their life in London.

Baldwin had wanted Robert to stay with them in their lodgings, but the young man declined, saying that he had already settled into the Hotel Wilmot, a fine establishment that was frequented by the gentry. Athena had been relieved that Robert had other accommodations, for their rooms were cramped with little space for a guest.

She and her father spent the evening at home talking about Robert and his family and about life in the Scottish Highlands. It was hard to think of anything else, for Robert's arrival was a very interesting development.

When Athena retired to bed, she lay for a long time reflecting about her cousin and the things he had told them. It was remarkable that Robert had appeared so suddenly and unexpectedly, but Athena was very glad he had done so. As an only child, Athena had always wished she had some relations close by, but her father's and mother's families lived in Scotland.

Therefore Athena was very glad to become reacquainted with Robert. Perhaps he was rather silly about wanting to obtain a place in London society, but Athena thought him amusing and rather charming in a rough-hewn sort of way.

Although most of her life had been spent in England, Athena had not been indifferent to her Scottish origins. Indeed, she had often thought of visiting Scotland and seeing her relatives.

Of course Robert had also brought the disturbing story of the Earl of Glencairn's harshness and indifference. Before she fell asleep, Athena thought about what she would write on the subject in the *Clarion Voice*.

The following morning Athena and Baldwin arrived at the office early. Since it was the day of printing the weekly publication, there was a sense of urgency about getting the edition ready on time.

Athena was glad that her father seemed eager to take on the editing duties, for she had some writing to do. Still incensed over what Robert had told her about the Earl of Glencairn, she wished to have something appear about the subject in the new issue. Taking out a sheet of paper, Athena picked up her pen. "I shall tell all of London about Glencairn and what he is doing," she told herself. "The *Clarion Voice* will reveal the cruelty and greed of this man. I shall write a letter to Glencairn that all may read."

Dipping her pen into the ink, Athena gazed down at the blank sheet of paper. She then began to write.

To the Most Noble Lord, the Earl of G., My Lord Tyrant, There are those to whom loyalty, decency, and charity mean nothing. You, my lord, are such a man, a man who can ignore the pain and suffering of those poor and weak persons whom Providence has put under your care. You have cast out helpless souls from your Scottish Highland property, causing untold misery to blameless men, women, and children. You have ignored pleas for mercy and compassion, forcing your tenants from their ancestral homes. You have replaced these hard-working and virtuous farmers with sheep so that your lordship may increase your wealth at the expense of your fellow man. I wonder, my lord, that you can have no pangs of conscience as you squander your ill-gotten riches in a life of luxury and licentiousness—spending ten thousand pounds on a racehorse while your impoverished tenants have nothing. May the Higher Powers cause you to regret your disgraceful conduct and make restitution.

Once she had finished, she took the paper to her father, who read it and nodded his approval. Feeling satisfied, Athena turned her attention to the literary reviews.

By late morning all of the articles had been edited, and the *Voice* was ready to have its type set. Athena could breathe a sigh of relief. It would be an excellent issue, she told herself. As always, she was filled with pride and excitement at the idea of a new *Clarion Voice* appearing. It never ceased to be a thrill for her to see what she had written appear in clear black letters.

The printing of the weekly was done in the print shop behind the offices on the aged, but venerable printing press purchased by her father. The printers were reliable, capable men proud of their craft.

Athena always enjoyed watching the printing press at work and did not mind the pungent smell of ink and other chemicals that permeated the print-shop area. Athena found nothing more satisfying than seeing the newly printed sheets taken off the press.

The office was fairly quiet, for Pike and Baldwin had gone off to the White Willow with some other gentlemen who had stopped by. Athena was left with Ashton, who appeared busily engaged in writing.

Sitting down, Athena began to tidy her desk. Buoyed by the knowledge that another issue of the *Voice* would soon see the light, she felt very pleased with herself.

"Good day, Athena. Ye look verra happy."

Athena looked up to see her cousin. "Robbie! Yes, I

am happy. We've got another issue of the *Clarion Voice* ready for printing. It is a great relief. Do sit down."

Robert lowered his gangling form into the chair. Hardly a vision of sartorial elegance, he was dressed in an old black coat with brass buttons that was open to reveal a bright tartan waistcoat. "I shall look forward tae reading the *Clarion Voice,* Cousin. Of course, I am nae one for reading verra much, but I shall take a subscription."

"Good, we are in need of subscribers. You will be glad to know that I have written about Glencairn in this issue."

"Do ye think he will see it?"

Athena smiled. "He is hardly one of our subscribers. But I shall have a copy sent to him."

" 'Tis very good of ye," said Robert with an amused expression. "But I must tell ye my news. I've taken a house."

"Robert! You have found a house so quickly?"

"Aye, Robbie Blair is nae a man to shilly-shally. 'Tis a fine town house with all the furnishings on Regent's Square. The last fellow who lived there has fled tae the Continent. Debts, ye see. His name was Hewlett. They say he was once called the nonesuch."

"Not Fitzwilliam Hewlett, the arbiter of fashion?"

"Ye've heard of him?"

"Indeed, who has not heard of him? They say the Prince Regent could not tie his cravat without consulting him."

"And now I have his house," said Robert. "It seems Mr. Hewlett was what my father would call an improvident fellow. What a grand house it is, Athena."

"And would not your father call you an improvident fellow, Robbie? Such a house must be ruinously expensive."

"Your cousin is a canny Scot," said Robert with a smile. "I've nae paid a shilling more than I've had tae.

Now ye and Uncle must come and live with me. I'll insist upon it."

"Indeed not, Robbie. We are very content where we are. It is far better to be but a short walk from here."

"There is nae point in arguing with me, Cousin. Ye and my uncle will live with me. I need ye about me. I am sure that my uncle will wish tae live on Regent's Square."

Athena laughed. "I daresay that considering how my father feels about royal George, he should not wish to have such an address." Robert smiled and changed the subject, but he was firmly resolved that his uncle and cousin would share his splendid residence.

4

PETER MONCRIEF sat in his bedchamber and reflected upon how bad the world had treated him. Many would have found the gentleman's gloomy reflections surprising, for most would have considered him a very fortunate young man. Born to wealth and privilege, Peter had had every material advantage.

Yet Peter had been unhappy throughout much of his short life. He had not known his mother, for she had died shortly after giving birth. His father had had little interest in his second son, handing him over to the care of a series of nurses and nursery maids.

When Peter thought of his childhood, it was not with the fond reflections of so many of his class. He had spent his early years in the country at one of his father's estates in Sussex. Ridgefield was a beautiful place, but Peter had been lonely and isolated there. He had had no playfellows, for his father had thought the children of the local gentry of insufficient consequence to be suitable companions.

When Peter had gone off to Eton, his life had become even more miserable. Shy and bookish, he had not gotten on well with the other boys. He had not excelled at sports and was apt to get the worst of it in the rough-and-tumble play that was commonplace there. He had preferred to spend his time reading or writing poetry.

Peter had hoped that Oxford would make a positive change for him. Yet he had soon found that he had liked

it no better than Eton. He had made some good friends
among the more modest and scholarly young men of less
illustrious families. Yet he had not gotten along at all
with his peers, the sons of the nobility, who had thought
him priggish and a cold fish. Some of the young bucks
had taken to playing practical jokes on him, and he had
been the object of cruel taunts and relentless teasing.

Peter thought of Oxford as he sat glumly paging
through a book of poetry. He knew that his brother,
Glencairn, would never understand the sort of agony he
had endured.

A frown crossed Peter's face as he reflected on his
elder brother. It seemed that Glencairn and he were vir-
tual strangers. Glencairn had gone off to school when
Peter was still a baby. They had seen little of each other,
for Glencairn had spent much of his school holidays
with his mother's family. By the time Peter had started
Eton, Glencairn was an adult. With a host of friends and
nearly unlimited resources, Glencairn had been too busy
enjoying himself to think much about his young half
brother.

When Peter's father had died three years ago, his
brother had become earl and head of the family. He continued to treat Peter as a child on the infrequent occasions when the brothers were together. Peter always
sensed that the earl appeared to be vaguely disappointed
in him. Their relationship was formal and somewhat remote, more like distant cousins who did not get along
very well but endured each other's presence at family
gatherings.

It was difficult for Peter to view his brother with anything but resentment, for the earl seemed totally inca-
pable of understanding or sympathizing with him. Since
Glencairn had been so happy at Oxford, it seemed incon-
ceivable to him that anyone else would not be equally as
happy. That someone would dislike the things Glencairn

enjoyed seemed absurd and decidedly wrongheaded to his lordship.

The day after Peter had come down from Oxford, Glencairn had scarcely talked to him. Shortly after rising, he had gone off to see the new horse he had bought, returning only to dress for the evening. After exchanging a few words, the earl had hurried off again, leaving Peter to dine alone and then spend the evening reading by the drawing-room fireplace.

Now it was midmorning of the third day of Peter's return. Glencairn had not risen in time to join Peter for breakfast. After dining, the young man had returned to his bedchamber where he now sat brooding.

After a time Peter grew bored and restless. Leaving his room, he made his way to the drawing room. The butler, who had always been fond of young Master Peter, asked if there was anything the young gentleman might require.

"No, thank you, Evans," returned Peter. "I think I shall read the newspapers."

"His lordship's newspapers are there, sir," said Evans, gesturing toward a finely crafted cherry table. "And this has just arrived by messenger. I do not believe it is one of the master's regular newspapers. Shall I include it with the others, Master Peter?"

Peter took the periodical from the servant and glanced at it. "The *Clarion Voice*?" said Peter. "Good lord, Evans! I cannot believe my brother would read this!"

"Shall I take it then, sir?"

"No, indeed," said Peter. "I should like to read it myself."

The young man sat down upon the sofa and viewed the *Clarion Voice* with eager anticipation. He was acquainted with the publication, knowing it to be the work of the radical theorist Baldwin Blair. Peter admired Blair tremendously. Indeed, he considered Blair's treatise, *Of*

Justice and the Rule of Free Men a wonderful and inspiring work.

A smile appeared on Peter's face as he thought of another work of Baldwin Blair, a pamphlet entitled "On the Abolition of Titles of Nobility." His brother would be most interested to read that, thought Peter.

His spirits uplifted by the prospect of reading the *Clarion Voice*, Peter continued to smile. He thoroughly enjoyed the scathing criticism of the government contained in the newspaper, and he laughed at a rather nasty caricature of the Prince Regent. There was also an excellent, though rather reserved, review of a book of poetry by Mr. Harold Osgood. Peter did not approve of Mr. Osgood's work, so he was happy to see the reviewer shared his opinion.

After reading a number of pieces, Peter's eye alighted on the words "To the Most Noble Lord, the Earl of G., My Lord Tyrant." He began to read. When he came to the end, the reference to paying ten thousand pounds for a racehorse made him experience a jolt of recognition. It referred to his brother!

When he had finished reading the letter several times, Peter shook his head. Could it be true? Was his brother a villainous character, heartlessly abusing his powerless and impoverished tenants?

While Peter pondered this unpleasant possibility, Glencairn arrived at the drawing-room door. He was in a decidedly good humor. Few things had pleased him more than his purchase of the outstanding young racehorse two days ago. The tall chestnut colt was unquestionably a wonder. That he had had to pay a king's ransom for the animal did not in the least diminish Glencairn's delight in his new acquisition.

As the earl strode into the room, he did not seem to note the serious expression on his brother's face. "Good morning, Peter," he said with unusual cheeriness. "It is a fine day."

Peter would usually have been encouraged by his lordship's rare good humor, but he was too preoccupied. "Good morning, Glencairn."

The earl raised an eyebrow at the young man's sullen greeting, but decided to overlook it. He was feeling particularly agreeable, so agreeable that he was willing to tolerate his younger brother's bad temper. Indeed, Glencairn was feeling oddly conciliatory. Perhaps he had been too hard on the boy, he had told himself. He would make amends and try to understand the lad.

"I am going to see the new horse, Peter. Tucker will be training him. There is not a better man in the kingdom than old Tucker. And Vulcan is a right one, Peter. And what a beauty! There's much of Pericles in him. If he has his sire's heart, he'll be unstoppable."

Much to his lordship's surprise, Glencairn's enthusiastic remarks only provoked a frown from the younger man. The earl regarded him with a puzzled expression. When Peter made no reply, Glencairn found his good humor changing quickly to irritation.

"I am sure your new horse is a fine specimen," said Peter finally, "but if I cannot be as happy about him as you, sir, you must forgive me." He held out the copy of the *Clarion Voice*. "I have been reading something in this, which I have found most unsettling. It is about you, sir."

"About me?" said the earl, reaching out and taking the newspaper. "What the devil is this? Why, it is one of those foul rabble-rousing sheets written by traitors. What is it doing in my house?"

"It was delivered here. I daresay the writer wished you to read it. It is there on the third page.'To the Most Noble Lord, the Earl of G.'"

Glencairn looked down at the newspaper distastefully before opening it. As he scanned it, his frown grew deeper. "Scurrilous lies," he said finally, tossing the offending paper to the floor "'My Lord Tyrant' indeed! What knave has written such things? I shall sue the wretches for libel. They'll not speak of me in such an infamous way with impunity!"

"Then you have not tossed these Highland farmers from their land?"

"Highland farmers? God in heaven! I know nothing of Highland farmers. I have never once set foot in the accursed place. How could I have done anything to these farmers?"

"But what of your men at Glencairn?"

"Good God, how can I know what my men in Glencairn do?"

"Then they might have done this. Your agents may have driven these persons from the land. Surely they would not do it without your approval."

"So you think I am a cruel, greedy tyrant, do you?" snapped the earl. "By God, it does not surprise me that you are willing to believe the worst of me. But I tell you, my dear brother, I will not allow those rogues to spread such calumnies about me. Who wrote such drivel?" He picked up the newspaper from the floor and looked once again at the article. "It is signed 'B.' I will know who this B. is, and he will rue the day he was ever born. That these fellows think they can write anything however scurrilous will not be borne!"

"I cannot imagine that Mr. Blair would have written this unless there is some basis in fact."

The earl regarded his brother with a startled look. "You cannot mean that you know the man who wrote this?"

"I have no personal acquaintance with him," replied Peter. "But I do know his work. Baldwin Blair is a brilliant man, a great man."

"Oh, is he?" said Glencairn, glowering at brother.

Peter rose from his chair. "You admit you know nothing of what is happening at your estate in Scotland. Not that you would care if you found that your agents were hanging and drawing and quartering the tenants for sport! Indeed, you care nothing for anyone or anything but your precious racehorses and your own pleasure!"

Glencairn could scarcely believe the words that had issued forth from his brother's mouth. Peter had sometimes been stubborn and uncooperative, but he had never been so insultingly defiant. Mustering all his self-control, the earl managed to speak in an even tone. "You are to go to your room, Peter. I will not hear one more word from you."

"So you send me to my room again like a schoolboy?"

"As long as you act like a moonling, I shall do so. And I will not have you reading such drivel as this! Now get out of my sight!"

Peter hurried from the room. Glencairn crumpled up the *Clarion Voice*. He would see to his troublesome brother later. Now he would deal with the author of these malicious and defamatory words. The earl rang for a servant and angrily called for his carriage.

Since the address of the *Clarion Voice* was conveniently listed on the second page, the earl wasted no time in making his way toward the newspaper office. A renowned whip, he expertly guided his perfectly matched black horses through the busy traffic. In a short time he pulled his curricle up in front of the office. Jumping down, he motioned to a boy who was gaping at the magnificence of the earl and his stylish vehicle. "Watch my horses, lad," he said, tossing the youth a coin.

"Right, guv'nor," said the boy, grinning at his unexpected good fortune.

The earl strode resolutely into the office, which was deserted except for a nondescript young man seated at a desk near the door. Mr. Ashton looked up in surprise to see a tall, well-dressed gentleman before him, holding a crumpled paper in his hand, an angry expression on his face. "Was this loathsome rubbish produced here?" demanded the earl, tossing the crumpled paper onto Ashton's desk.

To his credit Ashton very calmly took the paper and unfolded it. "Yes, sir, this is the office of the *Clarion Voice*," he said. Having worked at the *Voice* since its start two years ago, Ashton was not unaccustomed to irate persons appearing at the office. Hardly a week went by that some disgruntled individual did not show up to vent his spleen.

Ashton's bland look irritated Glencairn. "I wish to see this fellow Blair."

"I fear Mr. Blair is not here, sir," said Ashton.

"God in heaven!" shouted the earl, pounding his fist on Ashton's desk. "Where is the damned scoundrel?"

Cowed by this violent gesture, Ashton managed to reply, "I do not know, sir."

Glencairn scowled. He was growing impatient. "Dammit! I will not go until I see the rogue!"

Ashton was unable to reply, but at that moment Athena came from the back print shop. Having heard the loud voice, she wondered what was wrong. "Might I assist you, sir?" she said, hurrying to Ashton's aid.

Not expecting to see a woman, Glencairn regarded her in surprise. He could not help but notice that she was very attractive. Eyeing her appraisingly, the earl took note of Athena's rich auburn hair and splendid figure. Attired in a simple morning dress of pale green muslin with long sleeves and high neckline, she looked undeniably lovely. "I am Glencairn," he said. "I wish to see Blair."

Athena tried not to allow her feeling of surprise to register on her face. So this was the Earl of Glencairn, she thought, regarding him with great interest and some trepidation. So he had read the *Clarion Voice*! Athena felt oddly gratified, although at the same time rather dismayed.

Meeting the earl's gaze, Athena noted that he had very dark eyes beneath his dark brows. She found herself thinking that he was younger than she had expected. He appeared to be a very formidable personage, tall and broad-shouldered with an arrogance in his bearing that was at once intimidating and irksome.

"My father is not here, my lord," said Athena with admirable composure.

"Then I suggest you send for him. He has written some libelous drivel concerning me."

"And I fear you are mistaken, sir. My father did not write anything about you." She fixed her blue eyes upon him. "It is I who wrote the article."

"You!" said the earl, regarding her incredulously. He found it quite surprising that the young woman before him was the author of the offending letter. Even more surprising was the fact that she stood there before him, calmly admitting it.

Meeting her pale blue eyes, the earl felt oddly disconcerted. Glencairn was hardly a stranger to pretty women. Indeed, he had had liaisons with some of the great beauties of the day. While he appreciated feminine charms, he had never been one to lose his head over a pretty face. Still, the young lady before him seemed different from anyone he had ever met. She had an almost regal dignity and self-possession. She appeared completely unintimidated by him, which, despite his irritation, rather intrigued him. "You are the author?" said the earl.

"I am," returned Athena. "So you may speak to me if you found anything objectionable about it."

"Objectionable?" said Glencairn. "By God, madam, I found a good deal objectionable. I have been addressed as if I am some sort of wicked scoundrel! You had best thank Providence that your sex protects you, madam. I had fully intended to give the author of this scurrilous calumny a sound thrashing."

"I am so sorry to have deprived you of that pleasure, my lord," said Athena scornfully. "And if I address you as a scoundrel, I daresay your lordship's actions have warranted it. To have driven so many from their homes! It is shameful!"

"You are speaking nonsense," said Glencairn angrily. "I have not knowingly done anything of the kind."

"Not 'knowingly'?" said Athena.

"God in heaven! How can I know what happens in some godforsaken Highland wilderness? I have many estates. I cannot say what goes on at all of them."

Athena frowned. "I should think it your duty to be aware of what is happening on your estates."

Glencairn bristled. He was not accustomed to having someone take him to task. Indeed, he had grown so used to being treated with obsequious deference that Miss Blair's obvious disapproval seemed quite astonishing.

Still, there was something about the young lady who stood before him that made his lordship curb his temper, and he found himself thinking that her blue eyes were quite remarkable. He also knew that, for some inexplicable reason, he wanted her good opinion of him. "You are doubtlessly right, Miss Blair," he said with unusual mildness. Having expected angry indignation, Athena regarded the earl curiously. He continued, "Had you written to me directly, I should have investigated the matter."

As he said these words, the earl fastened his brown eyes upon Athena with such intensity that she was rather taken aback. Her admirable composure faltered a bit. "You would have investigated it? Will you not do so now?"

Glencairn shrugged. "Perhaps." Seeing her upraised eyebrows, the earl nodded. "Oh, very well. I shall look into it if you cease calling me tyrant in this *Clarion Voice* of yours."

"I shall be happy to do so, my lord . . . if the title is undeserved."

A slight smile appeared on the earl's countenance. Athena eyed him warily for a moment and then smiled in return. Glencairn regarded her intently, thinking that she had the most dazzling smile he had ever seen. "I shall take my leave of you then, Miss Blair," said the earl. "Good day."

"Good day, my lord," replied Athena. He tipped his hat and turned to go, leaving Athena to regard him with a somewhat perplexed look.

Returning to his curricle, Glencairn gave another coin to the young man who had watched his horses. Then jumping up into the vehicle, he took up the reins and drove away. As he skillfully maneuvered his vehicle through the traffic, the earl puzzled over his encounter with Baldwin Blair's daughter.

It rather unnerved him that a young lady could have made such an impression on him. He had known acquaintances to become completely besotted upon first sight of a pretty woman, but he had always thought himself immune. Yet apparently he, too, had fallen victim to a female's spell. That the woman who so evidently enthralled him was a strong-willed bluestocking seemed quite preposterous.

As he continued on, the earl tried to direct his attention to other matters, but he could think only of Baldwin Blair's daughter. He knew that he wanted to see her again. Indeed, he wanted her in his bed. This realization caused his lordship's mind to engage in some delightful imaginings that were interrupted by a close brush with a tradesman's wagon.

Trying to keep his attention on the street, Glencairn drove on, proceeding to his club. Although he rarely entered the privileged portals of White's so early, the earl was too agitated to return home. Entering the elite establishment, his lordship was glad to see his friend Edward Lyttleton seated in a leather chair and reading a newspaper.

"Ned," said Glencairn. "I'm damned happy to find you here." He sat down in an armchair next to his friend.

"Alex," said Edward, delighted to see the earl. "What good luck. I am in need of your company after spending the morning with Fanny and my sister. Good God, Alex, how they carry on about the damnedest silly things. I made the mistake of taking them to the linen drapers. How they agonized over what to buy for Clarissa's new dress! It took hours! It is such a relief to find refuge here." Edward paused and regarded his friend with interest. "You are here early. Is something amiss?"

The earl shrugged. "I have had an interesting day, Ned." Taking a rumpled paper from his breast pocket, Glencairn handed it to his friend.

"The *Clarion Voice*?" said Ned. "What is a good Tory like you doing reading that?"

"I would not have read it had my brother not waved it in my face. It is about me."

"About you? Baldwin Blair has written about you?"

"Good God, you know of this Blair?"

"Of course, Alex. Surely you must have heard of him. He is quite famous. You would be particularly interested in a pamphlet he wrote. Let me see. What was it called? Oh, yes, 'On the Abolition of Titles of Nobility.' "

"Damnation!" cried the earl. "It sounds treasonous."

Edward smiled. "He made a very good argument for it, you know. Now do allow me to read this."

Glencairn sat impatiently for a few moments as his friend scanned the paper. "Can you imagine that she would write such nonsense?" he said.

"She?" said Edward, looking up.

"Blair's daughter."

"His daughter?" said Edward, very much interested. "Athena Blair?"

"Athena?"

"That is her name, the same as the goddess of wisdom. Really, Alex, you should keep upbreast of such things. Everyone knows of Baldwin Blair and his daughter. They say she is a very scholarly lady of prodigious ability."

"I cannot abide bluestockings," said the earl, speaking

without conviction. "She appeared to be a vexatious creature."

"Appeared to be? You mean that you met her?"

Glencairn nodded. "I went to the *Clarion Voice* demanding to see this Blair fellow, but he was not there. His daughter informed me that she wrote this absurd tripe."

"So you met Baldwin Blair's daughter? What is she like?"

"What is she like?" said the earl. Nothing his friend's keen interest, he shrugged and tried to appear indifferent. "I cannot say."

"What does she look like?"

"I suppose one might say she is tolerable good-looking," he said gruffly. "But did you read what she wrote? It was as if I am some sort of Caligula."

Edward nodded. "Highland farmers being driven from their homes?"

"I know nothing about that. God in heaven, Ned, you know I have always said I care nothing about Scotland. I have given my agent free rein there. If he is abusing his authority, I shall rectify the matter. It was quite infuriating that this Miss Blair did not come to me directly with this. Instead she writes this scurrilous piece. Thank God no one I know would read it, except my brother, of course."

"And what of your brother? Is he back at Oxford?"

"No, indeed. He is at home, thinking himself ill-used. He was all too eager to think the worst of me. I am half considering having my servants take him back to university—bound and gagged if necessary."

Ned grinned. "In light of Miss Blair's printed remarks, I should not advise that. It would be decidedly tyrannical."

The earl smiled in return and ordered the club waiter to bring them wine.

5

LATER that afternoon Athena sat at her desk, reading an article by Mr. Pike on the recent antics of Parliament. Pike had a satirical pen, and his article presented the august members of government as a bunch of chuckle-heads and buffoons. Although Athena usually thought such ridicule of politicians amusing and well-deserved, this time she found herself wondering if Pike's portrayal was too harsh.

It was no coincidence that the Earl of Glencairn's visit to the *Clarion Voice* had provoked such editorial doubts in Athena. Ever since Glencairn's departure from the newspaper office, she had wondered if she had been too hasty in publishing her article branding him as a heart-less tyrant. If it was true that the earl knew nothing about the clearances on his Highland estate, she had been un-just in presenting him as such a monster to the world.

Pushing Pike's article aside, Athena sighed and thought again of her meeting with Glencairn. Certainly the earl did not appear to be such an ogre. Although he had at first seemed the arrogant lord, he had agreed to investigate what was happening on his Scottish lands. She felt instinctively that he would be true to his word.

Athena found herself thinking of Glencairn's dark eyes and the slight smile that had appeared on his face before he took his leave. She could not deny that there was something strangely appealing about him.

Shaking her head, Athena chided herself. Surely she

could have no interest in such a man—a wealthy lord who was an intimate of the Prince Regent. After all, she shared her father's aversion to the excesses of the aristocracy. Indeed, while it was not common knowledge, Athena was actually the author of the well-known pamphlet attributed to Baldwin, "On the Abolition of Titles of Nobility."

Athena disliked noblemen on principle, and, from what she knew of Glencairn, he was typical of his class. But it was ridiculous to think about the man, she told herself. After all, it would be unlikely that they would ever meet again.

"You appear serious, my dear," said a voice, and Athena looked up to see her father standing in front of her desk.

"Papa, I didn't hear you come in."

"No, you seemed deep in thought." Baldwin Blair looked down at the paper on her desk. "So what has put you in such a pensive mood, Daughter, Ashton's article on the Corn Laws?"

"Oh, no. It is Mr. Pike's article on Parliament."

Baldwin looked surprised. "What? Such a long face for one of Pike's articles? Don't tell me the fellow has lost his touch." He picked up the paper and began to read it. Soon Baldwin was chortling in glee. Finishing the article, he grinned over at his daughter. "Pike has properly skewered them!"

"You do not think he was a trifle . . . hard on them?"

Baldwin cocked a quizzical eyebrow at her. "Hard, my girl? I daresay he is being too kind."

She smiled. "I am certain you are right, Papa."

He pulled up a chair next to her. "My dear, you look tired. I fear you have been working too hard. You must take some time to enjoy yourself."

"I enjoy my work here, Papa," Athena protested.

"Yes, yes, but it *is* work, my girl. You are too young to

be spending all of your time in this dreary office. I have been allowing you to take on too many responsibilities."

"Nonsense, Papa."

"Indeed I have. I have been lax in my duties here. When one has such a capable and talented daughter, it is too easy to stand aside and leave all to her. But it is not fair to you. I promise to do better. Yes, I shall insist that you rest more."

"Papa, you are speaking bosh. I am thoroughly enjoying myself. But I must tell you of our illustrious visitor."

"Illustrious visitor?"

"The Earl of Glencairn."

Baldwin regarded her in amazement. "Good lord! Glencairn! You cannot mean that he saw the article in the *Voice*?"

"Yes, and he was quite furious that we had published it."

"Furious, was he? By God, I wish that I had been here."

"I am glad you were not, Papa," said Athena with a smile. "His lordship was under the impression that you had written the article, and he said that he intended to give you a thrashing. By the look of him, he was quite capable of it."

Baldwin grinned. "Then I am fortunate to have been absent. But it appears the fellow did not intimidate you. What a brave girl you are."

"Oh, he did not remain furious for long. Indeed, he became quite civil to me, even after I told him that I was the author of the article." She paused. "He insisted he did not know about the clearances, Papa."

"Of course. Scoundrels always claim ignorance."

Athena frowned. "But he seemed sincere. And he said he would have the matter investigated."

"Did he? Well, we shall see."

"You seem skeptical, Papa."

"I am eternally skeptical, my girl, especially of men of

Glencairn's ilk. I doubt our noble lord will give another moment's thought to the matter."

"I don't know, Papa," said Athena. "I cannot say why, but I felt that Glencairn will do as he says. He is not nearly so villainous as I had thought."

"That may be what he wanted you to think, my dear. Do not mistake civility for decency. I have seen enough of such men to know that they cannot be trusted. I shall hope that he is as you say, for I should like nothing better than these clearances to be stopped. But I thought of an idea for an article while at the White Willow. I must get to work before it has flown from this addled pate of mine."

Baldwin surprised his daughter by sitting down at his desk and diligently writing. Athena tried to forget about Glencairn as she, too, attempted to work. She realized that the earl was not a person she could easily remove from her thoughts. He seemed to loom there as an unsettling and disturbing presence.

Some time later Baldwin stopped working and announced to Athena that it was time they both went home. Although it was earlier than usual, Athena did not argue. She felt rather tired, and the idea of going home seemed appealing.

They completed the short walk to the residence on Threadneedle Street in a few minutes. "What is that wagon doing there?" said Athena, noticing that a large conveyance pulled by two draft horses was positioned in front of their lodgings. In front of the wagon stood a fine phaeton pulled by two dappled gray horses.

Baldwin shook his head. "I do not know. Perhaps we are getting a new neighbor. If that is his carriage, he must be a wealthy man." As they approached, two men were loading a heavy oak table into the wagon.

"Is that not our table?" said Athena in surprise. "Why someone is stealing our furniture!"

"What the deuce!" cried Baldwin, rushing toward the

men. "What is going on here? What are you doing with that table?"

"Loading it into this wagon, sir," replied one of the men as they hauled it up and shoved it to the back of the wagon.

"But that is my table!" said Baldwin.

The man paused to wipe his brow with a handkerchief. "I have orders from Mr. Blair to load the furniture."

"Mr. Blair?" cried Baldwin. "*I* am Mr. Blair!"

The workman scratched his head. "It is young Mr. Blair."

"Young Mr. Blair?"

"Aye, sir, the Scottish gentleman."

Athena and her father exchanged a glance. "Robert!" said Athena.

"Mr. Blair is in the house, sir," said the workman.

"Is he?" said Baldwin. "Well, come Athena, we will get to the bottom of this."

Entering the house, Baldwin and Athena walked upstairs to their rooms. There they found Robert giving orders to two other men.

"Robert!" said Athena. "What are you doing!"

Robert turned and grinned. "Och! Ye're home early! I'd hoped tae surprise ye."

"You have succeeded in that, Robert," said Baldwin. "Do explain yourself."

"I am moving all of your things, Uncle. Ye and Athena are tae live with me at Regent's Square. I told your landlady ye are moving. Ye will love the house. 'Tis very fine."

"You must be mad, Robert," said Athena. "I cannot believe you would do such a thing."

"What else was I tae do?" said Robert. "Why, ye said ye would nae come live with me. I had nae choice but tae take all your things sae that ye would have tae come."

"Your cousin is a determined young man, Athena," said Baldwin. His surprise had by now turned to amusement. "I do admire your audacity, lad, but you have gone too far."

"Indeed you have, Robert," said Athena severely. "You will have our things put back at once."

"I'll nae do it," said Robert. "How can I live in a fine house while my only family in all of London lives like this?"

"There is nothing wrong with these rooms," said Athena.

"They're nae for a Blair," said Robert. "Ye must come and live with me. Ye must try it, at least for a fortnight. Aye, if ye dinna like it after a fortnight, ye may come back."

"That is an idea," said Baldwin, considering the matter. "Perhaps we should do that, Athena. We would keep Robert company."

"Papa! You cannot mean it."

"Indeed I do. I must say I have felt very guilty about the poor home I have given you, Athena. You deserve far better. Why it is always so cold and damp and the roof leaks."

"But spring is here, Papa, and it is not a very bad leak," protested Athena. "And we are so close to the *Clarion Voice*. It must be miles to Robert's house."

" 'Tis scarce over three miles," said Robert. "And I have a carriage. Did ye nae see it outside? I can take ye here every morning and come for ye."

"It is quite out of the question, Robert," said Athena.

Robert turned to his uncle. "Ye canna object tae staying with me for a time. I should be sae lonely without ye."

"Oh, Robert, that is balderdash," said Athena.

"Now, my dear," said Baldwin. "It is a very logical idea going to live with Robert. There is no reason why we cannot stay with him. Do not argue with me, Athena. We will go to live with your cousin."

Robert grinned triumphantly. "Ye will nae regret it, Uncle. And Athena, ye will love the house. Ye will see!"

Athena frowned and reflected that her cousin was a very stubborn and entirely brazen young man.

Although she thought it most inconvenient to be leaving their lodgings on Threadneedle Street, Athena softened considerably upon getting her first view of Robert's town house. It was one in a row of elegant Georgian residences that lined the cobblestone streets of Regent's Square. The square itself was a lovely park filled with stately elm trees. Its well-manicured lawn and garden were a delight to behold.

"A very fine house," declared Baldwin as the carriage pulled up in front.

"Aye, that it is," said Robert, eyeing the residence proudly. "Do ye nae think it a lovely house, Athena?"

"It is indeed," she replied, "but it must have been terribly expensive."

"Now, Cousin, I will nae have ye chiding me for squandering my fortune. I've nae ruined myself, I've got a real bargain. Ye're nae tae worry about that."

Athena cast a disapproving glance at her cousin, but said nothing. Robert helped her down from the carriage and eagerly escorted Athena and her father to the door. They were met there by Robert's servant, Jock Stewart, who opened the door wide and appeared very pleased to see them. At Stewart's heels was a large gray deerhound who wagged its tail enthusiastically.

"Do ye nae remember Jock Stewart?" said Robert. "He's come with me frae Scotland. I've made him my butler. He'll be a good one." Pleased by this expression of confidence in his abilities, Jock happily took the gentlemen's hats. "And this is Mally. Come here, girl."

The dog came eagerly to Robert, who caught her

shaggy head between his hands and rubbed her ears affectionately. "What a beautiful dog," said Athena, who was very fond of all animals. "Did you bring her from Scotland?"

"Aye, I couldna part with her. But poor Mally misses the Highlands. Do ye nae miss your home, lass?" The dog fixed her brown eyes upon her master and cocked her head as if trying to understand the question. "Aye, she does," said Robert. "Poor wee homesick lass."

Mally wagged her tail and, in Athena's view, did not look in the least homesick. When Robert released her, she went first to Athena, who petted her and pronounced her a fine dog indeed. She then turned to Baldwin, who made a great fuss over her. "I had a dog very much like her when I was a boy," said Baldwin, stroking the deerhound's neck. "How I loved that dog."

"I can see ye'll be spoiled badly, Mally," said Robert approvingly. He grinned at Athena and Baldwin. "But come, ye must see the drawing room. It is very grand." They followed Robert to the drawing room with the deerhound close behind. " 'Tis as Mr. Hewlett left it," said Robert. "Is it nae splendid?"

Athena viewed the room with wide eyes. Decorated in a Chinese motif, the wallpaper was bright red and emblazoned with gold and green dragons. The furniture was also Chinese with chairs and tables decorated with elaborate carvings. A large screen painted with peacocks was a focal point in the room. Chinese lanterns, lacquered cabinets, and potted palms completed the picture.

"I must say it is dramatic," said Athena, not quite sure whether she admired or detested the room's decoration.

"Well, I think little of Mr. Hewlett's taste in wallpaper," said Baldwin.

"Och, 'tis only that ye're nae yet used tae it, Uncle. Now ye must see the rest of the house!" Robert led them about, excited as a child at showing off his new acquisition.

The other rooms were equally as magnificent although considerably more traditional. As they went from room to room, Athena and Baldwin expressed their admiration much to Robert's great satisfaction. Of particular interest to both Athena and Baldwin was the library. Prominently displayed was a large Egyptian-style table set upon a sphinx pedestal. There were also comfortable chairs and an entire wall of bookshelves.

Athena and her father set about perusing the collection. "It appears Mr. Hewlett was a learned man," said Athena, pulling out a volume and examining it with great interest.

"He was if he read any of these," said Baldwin. "This is a dashed fine library. We will make good use of it."

Although Robert was pleased that his cousin and uncle were so obviously thrilled with the library, he grew rather impatient as they lingered among the books. It was some time before he was able to lead them away to see the rest of the house.

When the tour was completed, Baldwin praised the house enthusiastically. "But I daresay I cannot imagine what you will do with the furniture from our lodgings, Robert," he said.

"Och, that will go tae the servant's hall," replied Robert. When Athena raised her eyebrows at this, Robert grinned. "But dinna worry, Cousin. I shall return it tae ye if ye should decide tae go somewhere else."

Now that they had seen the entire residence, Athena retired to her room, a second-floor bedchamber that was spacious and airy. There was an elegant canopied bed and magnificent Queen Anne–style wardrobe. From the windows one had an excellent view of the square. As Athena gazed out upon the street and park, she reflected that it would be hard not to like living there, inconvenient or not.

6

AFTER leaving his club, the Earl of Glencairn proceeded toward Regent's Square. As he drove past a row of shops, the sign on a bookseller's establishment caught his attention. The earl was not an avid reader and rarely picked up a book. He was woefully ignorant of the latest novels and knew nothing of the works of essayists and scholarly authors. Although bookstores did not usually interest his lordship, that afternoon he decided to stop.

The proprietor of the bookshop knew at once from the earl's clothes and manner that he had a gentleman of quality at hand. Quickly excusing himself from another more modest customer, the bookseller hurried to the earl. "Might I assist you, sir?"

"Do you have any books by Baldwin Blair?" said his lordship.

The bookseller tried to hide his surprise. He had never expected the well-dressed man before him to request the works of the radical Mr. Blair. "Yes, sir," returned the shop owner. "We have *Of Justice and the Rule of Free Men* and *Discourse on Achieving a New Society*."

"And what of his pamphlet called 'On the Abolition of Titles of Nobility.'?"

"I do have that as well, sir," said the bookseller.

"I shall take them all," said the earl.

"Very good, sir," said the man, quite pleased with his sale. He motioned to his assistant to fetch the books and wrap them neatly in brown paper.

After paying for his books, Glencairn returned to Regent's Square. He was in a cheerful mood as he entered his house. Books in hand, the earl went to the drawing room. There he found his brother, Peter, sitting near the fireplace and reading. Seeing the earl, Peter rose to his feet.

"Good afternoon, Peter," said his lordship, placing his parcel of newly acquired books on the table.

"Have you bought books, Glencairn?" said Peter, his curiosity making him overlook his irritation with his brother.

"Yes, you know what a bookish fellow I am," returned the earl amiably. "But do sit down, Peter."

"I thought you would wish me to go to my room."

Glencairn shook his head. "No, I was angry before, but I am quite in the best of moods at present."

Peter was relieved at his brother's surprising affability. "Did you see Baldwin Blair?"

The earl lowered his tall frame into a chair. "No, I did not have that pleasure. But I did meet his daughter, Miss Blair. It was she who was the authoress of the article, not Blair. I assured the lady that I knew nothing of what she was accusing me. She will doubtless regret her hastiness in painting me as such a villain. So you see, I have gotten over my fit of temper. One sometimes says things at such times he later regrets."

Peter looked over at his brother. "Indeed, one does. I am sorry, Glencairn."

The earl nodded, accepting his brother's apology. "My friend Lyttleton believes I am too hard on you. Perhaps I am. If you are determined not to return to Oxford, I shall not insist you do."

"Oh, Glencairn!" said Peter. "I am so grateful to you!"

"Is there anything you would wish to do? Would you like a commission in the army? I could purchase one for you."

"That is very good of you, Glencairn," said Peter, hiding his revulsion at the thought of entering the army, "but I do think I am ill-suited to a military career."

"Very well. You will be well occupied here in town for the season. There are no end of functions you might attend." The earl became serious and paternalistic. "Yes, you may take your place in society. But I caution you that I shall expect you to keep respectable company. There are far too many wild young bucks rushing about town getting into scrapes. You will choose your friends wisely from the best families. And I will not countenance excessive gaming. You have a very generous allowance; you must make do with that."

That Glencairn was issuing such orders to his brother would have struck the earl's friends as amusing. After all, his lordship had spent his youth reveling in the most dissolute company while Peter, on the other hand, was a quiet young man who was considered dull and excessively virtuous by his acquaintances at Oxford. Still, the earl thought he had best not allow Peter to think that he was being given carte blanche to do as he pleased.

"I have far more money than I can spend, Glencairn," replied Peter. "I thank you for your generosity. But, sir, I must admit that I have no desire to spend much time in society. I do not enjoy hovering about young ladies, asking for a dance or listening to insipid conversations. In truth, I think such things are frightfully dull."

Although the earl himself disliked most society functions, he nevertheless frowned at this remark. "Then how do you think you will occupy your time?"

Peter hesitated. "I have an occupation that will keep me very busy."

"An occupation?" said the earl.

"Yes, I am a poet. Or I should like to be one. I have been writing poetry for years. It is what I wish to do."

"A poet?" said the earl.

"There is no nobler profession than that of a poet," said Peter fervently.

His lordship frowned again, but did not reply at once. Having only scorn for literary pursuits, the earl hardly thought poetry a proper occupation for anyone, let alone a gentleman of rank. That his brother would waste his time scribbling silly verses seemed utterly ridiculous. Noting his brother's earnest countenance, Glencairn stopped himself from expressing the opinion that only an addlepated ninny would wish to devote himself to poetry when there were such gentlemanly diversions as horse racing, hunting, and bouts of fisticuffs available.

"You may do as you please," said the earl. "I have been accused of being a tyrant. I shall demonstrate that I am nothing of the kind."

Peter smiled, relieved at his brother's newfound tolerance. "Indeed you are not," said the young man. "You are the best of brothers, Glencairn."

Rather embarrassed by this effusive remark, the earl changed the subject, suggesting that Peter accompany him to see his new racehorse. The young man was only too happy to do so, and the brothers left the drawing room together in complete harmony.

7

WHEN Athena awoke after her first evening at the house on Regent's Square, she looked around the room, taking in the elegant furniture and the hand-painted French wallpaper. It was lovely, thought Athena. She lay there for a time, luxuriating in the soft feather bed as sunlight peeked through the opening in the curtains.

After a time Athena rose from bed and pulled open the curtains. The park in the center of the square looked green and fresh in the morning light. It appeared to be a very fine day with bright sunshine and billowy white clouds decorating the sky.

It was hard not to feel happy on such a day, and Athena felt particularly cheerful as she opened the door to her wardrobe to survey her clothes. Although many other young ladies might have felt dismay that so few dresses were hanging there, Athena seemed unconcerned. Selecting a morning dress of printed muslin, she placed it on the bed and began to dress.

Athena arrived in the dining room some time later. There she found Robert and her father already seated at the table. They rose as she entered. "Good morning, Cousin. How lovely ye look," said Robert.

"Athena always looks beautiful," said Baldwin. "It is her curse."

"You are utterly ridiculous," said Athena with a smile. She did think she looked well although her dress was several seasons old. It was a simple blue and white creation with a high waist and tight-fitting long sleeves. The garment's high neck was trimmed with a small white ruff.

After selecting breakfast from a wide and delectable variety of food on the sideboard, the three sat down at the table. "I must turn my attention tae my clothes," said Robert, slicing a sausage with his knife and spearing the piece with his fork. "I'll nae be taken seriously in this old suit."

"I am happy to recommend my tailor," said Baldwin brushing off the lapel of his coat. "He does excellent work."

"Aye, Uncle, ye look verra handsome, but I've discovered that Mr. Hewlett's tailor was Mr. Warriner. As Mr. Hewlett was a tulip of fashion, I shall visit his tailor."

"My father has never claimed to be a tulip," said Athena, directing a wry smile at Baldwin.

"No, it is better not to aspire to such distinction," said Baldwin with mock seriousness.

"Ye both may scoff if ye wish," said Robert good-naturedly, "but if one is tae succeed in society, one must pay attention to one's clothes."

"I fear, Athena," said Baldwin, "that your cousin has ambitions to become a dandy. He'll not want to be seen with us once he has been transformed by Mr. Warriner."

"Yes," said Athena, "you'll soon regret having us about, Robbie. We'll disgrace you. Everyone will say, 'Who are those drab old things with splendid Mr. Blair?'"

Robert grinned. "Aye, that is what they'll say, but I'll take nae notice."

Baldwin grinned. "That is good of you, my boy."

When they had finished breakfast, Athena and Baldwin announced that they had to go to the offices of the *Clarion Voice*. Robert obligingly called for his carriage to be brought round. Instructing a servant to drive his uncle and his cousin to their destination, he assured

Athena and Baldwin that the carriage would call for them promptly at five o'clock.

There was much to do at the office. Baldwin seemed to be making good his pledge to take his responsibilities more seriously. He worked industriously at his desk throughout the morning. When his friend Sheffield and another gentleman of his acquaintance arrived in the afternoon, Baldwin did accompany them to the White Willow. However Athena noted that the gentlemen were gone for less time than usual. Baldwin returned to work some more, although he was again distracted by the arrival of some visitors to London who wished to call and express their admiration for Mr. Blair.

Robert and his carriage arrived at five o'clock to take them back to Regent's Square. Robert hurried out to gallantly assist his cousin into the phaeton. Then once he and Baldwin were settled in the vehicle, he called to his driver to be off.

Robert was in the best of moods, having had an excellent day. He had spent much of his time visiting the renowned tailor, Mr. Warriner. While the tailor was very selective about taking new clients, he had accepted Robert. Rather reluctant at first to take on the rawboned Scotsman, Mr. Warriner had been influenced in Robert's favor when the young Scotsman had produced a number of bank notes, saying that he was only too happy to pay in advance. Since the accounts of a number of Mr. Warriner's illustrious clients were dreadfully in arrears, the tailor decided that a paying customer was not to be sneezed at.

After hearing far more than they wished about Robert and his tailor, Baldwin remarked to his nephew, "My friend Sheffield has invited us to dinner, Robert. While Sheffield is not a member of society's inner circle, I believe he is wealthy and respectable enough for you. And more important, he sets a very fine table. There is al-

ways interesting company at Sheffield's. You will enjoy
the evening."

"I should like that, Uncle," said Robert.

"I must beg to be excused," said Athena. "I shall not
be missed, and I am quite exhausted. I should much prefer staying at home this evening."

"We could not leave ye alone," protested Robert.

"Nonsense," said Athena. "I shall read and retire
early. Do say you will not mind if I do not go to dinner
at Mr. Sheffield's, Papa."

After trying unsuccessfully to get her to change her
mind, Baldwin acquiesced, saying that Athena may stay
at home if she wished and that while they would go to
Sheffield's, they would not be late.

Arriving back at Robert's town house, the gentlemen
dressed in their evening clothes while Robert's cook prepared Athena a cold supper. After Robert and Baldwin
had gone, Athena ate her meal. She then retired to the library where she browsed through the bookshelves. Finally taking up a history of Tudor England, Athena
settled herself onto the sofa near the fireplace. In the
quiet library Athena reflected how rare and pleasurable
it was to have some time alone. After a while a footman
came in.

"Excuse me, Miss Blair. I was looking for the dog."

"Mally? She is not here," replied Athena. "Is she not
in the house?"

The footman shrugged. "I do not know, Miss Blair.
Mr. Stewart thought she was in the kitchen, but she's not
there now. I'm looking for her. She probably found a
place in the master's rooms to sleep. I'll go see."

"Do bring her here when you find her," said Athena, a
trifle unsettled at the idea of the deerhound being gone.
She knew how Robert doted on the animal, and even
upon such a short acquaintance, Athena had grown at-
tached to the hound as well. After the footman left,
Athena returned to her reading.

* * *

As usual, Mally had devoured her meal of scraps in a few seconds. She then had curled up in the corner to sleep. Mally had determined that the kitchen was her favorite location when her master, Robert, was absent, for she had found the cooking smells irresistible. The hound had quickly come to know the servants, who were always ready to give her a pat or a tidbit.

No one had taken much notice of the big gray dog asleep in the corner. The kitchen servants had been too busy gossiping to see Mally raise her head as one of the footmen entered the kitchen with a bucket of coal. As usual, he had propped the door to the garden open. Mally had sniffed inquiringly as the scents of the outdoors wafted into the room. Wagging her tail, she had risen to pace quickly to the open door and freedom.

The Earl of Glencairn slowed his two spirited black horses as his curricle turned onto Regent's Square. It was nearly eight o'clock, and his lordship was due at Carlton House. He would be late, he knew, and the Prince Regent would be vexed with him. He would have to hurry and change and leave as soon as possible.

Just as his lordship was urging his horses onward, a gray shape dashed from nowhere into the path of his horses. "What the deuce?" cried the earl, pulling sharply on the reins to stop the curricle. The horses reared up at the large gray shape that Glencairn saw to be a dog. There was a thud as one of the horses' hooves hit the animal. The dog bounced back away from the horses, landing in a heap near the curb. "Damnation!" cried the earl, jumping down from the vehicle.

A large deerhound was lying motionless on the ground. Since Glencairn's love of dogs equaled his love of horses, he was very upset. He hurried to the dog's side, but there was no sign of life. "Poor fool," said the earl, kneeling down beside the stricken animal. As he touched the animal's shaggy side, he felt the dog breathing. Running his hands expertly along the dog's back, sides, and legs, he was relieved to find no broken bones.

Suddenly the deerhound raised her head and turned her luminous brown eyes upon his lordship. "So you're alive, my girl?" said the earl. "Can you get up?"

As if understanding this question, Mally tried to get to her feet. Terribly shaken, she slumped down again. By this time two of Glencairn's servants had come out from his house. One took charge of the curricle while the other man came alongside the earl. "Is the dog dead, my lord?"

"No, Harry," returned Glencairn. "I cannot say how badly she is hurt. I am hoping that she only had the wind knocked out of her. She's a beautiful dog."

" 'Tis the bitch belonging to the gentleman who has moved into Mr. Hewlett's house, my lord," said the servant, pointing toward Robert's town house.

"He must be a great idiot to allow her to run about like this," said the earl testily. Mally by this time seemed to be regaining her senses. She rose to stand unsteadily on her thin legs.

Glencairn stroked her comfortingly. "You will be fine, my girl," he said. "We'll take you back to your master."

"Shall I take her then, my lord?"

"No, Harry, I'll take her myself." To the servant's surprise the earl picked up the dog and started toward Robert's town house. He was very familiar with the former residence of Fitzwilliam Hewlett, having spent many amusing evenings there.

Mally seemed happy to be carried. She looked up at her rescuer and grinned a toothy smile. Weighing nearly seventy pounds, she was scarcely a lightweight, but Glencairn carried her easily. When he arrived at Robert's door, the earl lifted the door knocker and rapped it loudly. The door was quickly opened by Jock Stewart.

"Sae there she is!" cried the butler. "We were just about tae start a search."

"She was nearly killed," said the earl, entering the house and putting the dog down on the floor. Mally walked a bit unsteadily, but seemed unhurt. "She may have sustained injuries. I cannot say. My horses nearly ran her over." Glencairn frowned. "I should like to speak to your master."

"My master is nae at home, sir," said Stewart. "I shall fetch miss." Before the earl could protest that there was no need to do so, the butler hurried off. In a few moments he returned, followed by a young lady.

It was hard to know who was more shocked to recognize the other, but as Glencairn and Athena caught sight of each other, their faces registered astonishment. "Miss Blair!" said the earl. "What are you doing here?"

"I live here," said Athena.

"You live here?"

"My cousin, Robert Blair, has taken the house. My father and I have come to live with him. But *you* are the gentleman who has brought Mally?"

"My horses nearly killed her."

Athena looked away from the earl in some confusion. "Mally," she said, kneeling down beside the dog, "where did you go, you naughty dog? Are you unhurt?" The deerhound responded by licking her on the nose. "You bad girl, you have given us all a terrible fright." She looked up at Glencairn. "Were your horses injured?"

The earl shook his head. Staring down at Athena, he found the undeniable feelings of attraction surfacing again. She was very lovely there beside the dog, the candlelight putting coppery highlights in her auburn hair.

Athena rose from the floor. "My cousin is not at home. I do thank you for returning the dog. I am sorry for the trouble she caused you. It seems she left the house through an open door. No one knew that she was gone until but a moment ago."

Glencairn stood in the entry hall, regarding Athena intently. All thoughts of his engagement with the Prince Regent seemed to fly from his mind. He wanted only to stay with Athena Blair. "Perhaps you might offer me a glass of sherry," he said. "I carried your hound a good distance."

Athena hesitated. She was certain that it was not a good idea for her to invite the Earl of Glencairn into the drawing room. After all, it would be quite improper to do so, since she was alone. While Athena might have thought such attention to propriety ridiculous had the visitor been some other gentleman, Glencairn's presence set off alarms within her.

She eyes him curiously for a moment, considering the situation. "Stewart, his lordship would like a glass of sherry. Do come to the drawing room, my lord."

The butler nodded and led the way into the Chinese room. The deerhound followed him, her tail wagging. Athena sat down on the sofa. Glencairn would have liked to have taken the place beside her, but decided instead on an armchair next to her.

Steward poured the glasses. After placing them on a silver tray, he went first to Athena. "No thank you, Stewart."

The earl took his glass and stared over at Athena. "I must say, Miss Blair, that I did not expect that we would be neighbors."

"Nor did I, sir," said Athena, feeling rather uncomfortable at the earl's proximity.

"I must say I like the idea."

Stewart, who thought his young mistress in need of a chaperone, hovered about near the bottle of sherry. After a time he reluctantly left the drawing room, but stationed himself just outside the door in case the young mistress might call for him.

"I wanted to tell you," said the earl, "that I have written to my agent in Scotland. I have asked for an explanation about what is happening there. You have my promise that if I find anything amiss, I shall correct the matter."

"I am glad of it, my lord," said Athena. "There have been wrongs done. I do believe they are without your knowledge, but they are wrongs nonetheless."

"Yes, you are right, Miss Blair," said the earl, sipping his sherry. He looked around the room. "I must say that it is rather odd that Baldwin Blair is now residing in the house that was the home of Fitzwilliam Hewlett." Glencairn's dark eyebrows arched in amusement. "I have been reading your father's books."

"You have?" said Athena, very much surprised.

"I have only begun," said the earl. "I have purchased two books and a pamphlet. I have only had opportunity to read 'On the Abolition of Titles of Nobility.' "

Athena suppressed a smile at the idea of Glencairn reading a work that stridently condemned his way of life. She wondered what he would say if he knew that she had written it. "And what did you think, my lord? Did you not find the arguments worth considering?"

"I am no scholar, Miss Blair," said the earl, "and your father appears to be an erudite man. Yet I believe he is grossly mistaken in his opinions. Do you agree with him that titles of nobility are unjust?"

"Indeed I do, sir," replied Athena resolutely. "I do not believe that an accident of birth should give certain persons such great privileges." She looked over at the earl, expecting him to look insulted, but Glencairn only shrugged.

"I cannot say that you are wrong. When one is born and raised with something, he oftentimes gives little thought to it. I have been born to privilege. I do not deny it, nor do I deny that I enjoy it. But those of rank have obligations and responsibilities as well, although I do not say that all perform their duties as they should. Perhaps some day there will be no place for hereditary titles.

However, one does not turn a society on its head in a day. The example of the French proves that."

"You astonish me, my lord," said Athena, surprised at his serious and thoughtful answer. "You speak very sensibly . . . for an earl. I shall not despair that you may yet be converted to republicanism."

Glencairn smiled. "Lest that happen, perhaps I should desist from reading any other works by your father." Athena smiled in return. She found herself thinking that perhaps Glencairn was different from most of the empty-headed sporting gentlemen of his class. "And if I wish to avoid becoming a traitor to my class, I see that I must avoid talking with Miss Athena Blair. I believe that you are a very persuasive young woman."

The way in which these words were said and the expression on the earl's face as he gazed at Athena triggered a warning signal inside her head. She rose from the sofa, thinking that it would be prudent for the Earl of Glencairn to leave. "I have kept you too long, Lord Glencairn," she said.

The earl rose. "You could not keep me long enough, Miss Blair. I have no wish to go."

Athena avoided meeting his gaze. "I think you had best go, sir."

The earl made no move to take his leave. As he stood there, the urge to take Athena into his arms was overpowering. "God in heaven, you are so damned beautiful." Athena looked up into his eyes, a look of faint surprise and confusion on her lovely face. The earl could resist no longer. He caught Athena to him, crushing her in a tight embrace and capturing her mouth with his own in a passionate kiss.

Athena was so startled that she did not protest. Indeed, the earl's strong arms about her and the closeness of his body temporarily caused all reason to fly from her. Filled with an intense longing, she returned his kiss with surprising fervor.

What caused Athena to come to her senses was not readily apparent, but somehow the realization of her danger came to her. Managing to pull away, she stepped back from him. "You go too far, my lord," said Athena, looking down in confusion.

"Athena," said Glencairn, "do not resist me."

"I warn you, I shall call for the butler,' said Athena. "You mistake me for a light-skirt, sir. Now go at once."

Filled with almost unbearable desire, Glencairn shook his head in frustration. "I do not want to leave."

"Good night, my lord," said Athena.

At that moment the door to the drawing room was opened and in walked Baldwin and Robert. "Stewart said we had a guest," said Baldwin, eying the earl with unmistakable disapproval.

Robert was far more interested in his deerhound than in his titled visitor. "Mally, Stewart said ye had a mishap." Now completely recovered, the dog hurried to her master, wagging her tail furiously. "Ye silly old thing," said Robert, "ye must be more careful."

Robert's concern for his pet caused sufficient diversion for both the earl and Athena to compose themselves. "Father, this is Lord Glencairn," said Athena. "It seems he is our neighbor, for he lives across the square." She looked over at the earl. "My father, Baldwin Blair, and my cousin, Robert Blair."

Although unhappy at this untimely interruption, Glencairn nodded to Baldwin and Robert in a civil manner. Baldwin acknowledged the introduction coolly. Prepared to dislike all men of title, he had not been very happy to find the earl alone in the drawing room with his daughter.

Robert, however, viewed his lordship with interest. "I am frae Scotland, my lord," he said. "The town of Kinlochie. 'Tis near your lands at Glencairn. I've nae been in London verra long."

"Indeed," said Glencairn, realizing that Athena's cousin must have been the source of her information about his Highland estates. He studied Robert, noting his ill-fitting evening clothes and his unruly red hair. The earl's expression took on an aristocratic aloofness.

"I am grateful tae ye, for bringing Mally home," said Robert. "How I love that dog. Should anything have happened tae her, I wouldna know what I would do."

"I hope your servants will be more careful in the future," said Glencairn ill-humoredly. "I must take my leave of you, gentlemen, and Miss Blair." He looked pointedly at Baldwin Blair. "I am expected by His Royal Highness. Good evening." After bowing slightly to Athena and nodding to the men, the earl retreated from the drawing room.

"By all the gods, Athena," said Baldwin once Glencairn was gone. "Have you taken leave of your senses allowing that man in the drawing room when you are here alone? Thank heaven that we left Sheffield's at such an early hour. Such a man cannot be trusted. And what an arrogant fellow he is! 'I am expected by His Royal Highness' indeed! As if that would impress me."

"I suspect he was more interested in vexing you than impressing you, Papa," said Athena quietly.

"Sae that was the Earl of Glencairn. I shall write tae my sisters at once. They will want tae know all about the earl. 'Twill be interesting talk in Kinlochie."

"I hope the fellow does not think he will call upon us again," said Baldwin distastefully. "What ill luck that he is our neighbor. I should have known Regent's Square to be an unfortunate address."

"Och, Uncle," said Robert. " 'Tis not as if his lordship will be calling upon us. Ye'll nae see him again, I'll warrant."

Athena nodded absently. Her cousin changed the subject, speaking of their dinner with Sheffield and his guests, but Athena scarcely listened, for all she could think of was her disturbing encounter with the Earl of Glencairn.

8

IT WAS noon when the earl rose from bed. As often was the case when he had been up for most of the night and had drunk far more than he should have, Glencairn was in a foul mood. He suffered the ministrations of his valet with ill humor, snapping at the hapless servant at the least provocation. The valet was happy when he had completed his morning duty and his master left his dressing room attired with his usual care.

The earl went down to the dining room where his breakfast awaited him. "Where is Master Peter?" he asked one of the footmen.

"He has gone out, my lord," returned the servant.

Glencairn nodded and turned his attention to the sideboard. He eyed the assorted foods with indifference, taking only a small helping of kippers. Then seating himself at the table, Glencairn frowned.

He had had a miserable night. After his frustrating experience with Athena Blair, he had gone to Carlton House. The Prince Regent had seemed rather vexed with him. To show his displeasure, the royal gentleman had been barely civil to the earl, a fact that infuriated his lordship.

Glencairn had wanted to take his leave shortly after he had arrived, but a courtier was forced to stay as long as the prince required. Thus the earl had found himself enduring the company of men he now realized that he did not like very much. He spent most of his time drinking and playing hazard with some other titled acquaintances.

Never the best of card players, the earl had lost badly. A man of fabulous wealth, his lordship had not minded the loss of his money so much as the fact that the gentleman who had taken it from him had been a man he disliked intensely, Sir John Reynolds. Reynolds had seemed so pleased at Glencairn's bad luck that the earl had been tempted to plant him a facer. Fortunately his lordship had restrained himself, enduring Reynolds's smug expression with a grim visage.

Irritating as his experience at Carlton House had been, what was really bothering the earl was the thoughts of his meeting with Athena Blair. He had never wanted a woman as he had wanted her. As he sat at the breakfast table, he wondered how he could win Athena. Her response to his kiss had assured him that she was not indifferent. Indeed, he had sensed the passion stirring within her.

Remembering the softness of Athena's body against his caused the earl to experience irksome physical sensations. He slammed his fist against the table in frustration, causing the waiting footmen to jump in alarm. "Damnation!" muttered the earl.

"Is something wrong, my lord?" said one of the footmen, hurrying to him.

"No," said the earl curtly. The servant retreated to his station. Exchanging a glance with one of his fellows, the footman reflected that working for such a temperamental master could be very trying. He was very glad when the butler entered the room to announce Edward Lyttleton.

"You must forgive me for calling at this hour," said Edward, grinning broadly as he approached his friend. "I have just deposited my wife and Clarissa at Fanny's sister's. And since I was passing directly by, I could not resist stopping."

"Ned," said the earl, not bothering to rise from his chair. "Are you hungry? Do have some breakfast."

"I am always hungry," returned Edward. "Perhaps I shall have a little something." He went to the sideboard and piled a great quantity of food on his plate. He then sat down at the table across from Glencairn. "This does look good, Alex. And what a fine day it is! Fanny reminded me that I must insist on your coming to our ball. It is Thursday. It is Clarissa's first ball. Do not pretend you don't know about it. You had your invitation ages ago."

"Damn it, Ned, do not speak to me of balls. I cannot abide them. And do quit being so damned cheerful."

"Why, you are in a dashed fine mood, my lord," said Edward, taking a forkful of roast beef. I daresay it is this business with Reynolds. Pity to lose so much to the likes of him."

"And what do you know of that? I do not remember that you had the misfortune to be at Carlton House last night."

Edward laughed. "Why, my dear Alex, when I took Fanny and Clarissa this morning, her sister knew all about it. Her husband is Lord Mulgrave. He was there, of course."

"God," said the earl. "It never fails to amaze me how quickly gossip can travel. I do not doubt that you were also informed that our noble prince scarcely acknowledged my existence."

Edward nodded. "I should not worry. Prinny is a mercurial fellow."

"I am not worried, Ned," said Glencairn crossly. "If I am out of favor, I am glad of it. I do not enjoy being the prince's lapdog."

Edward laughed. "I doubt that His Royal Highness thinks of you as a lapdog, Alex." The earl allowed a slight smile to appear on his face. "I have heard he is vexed about your buying Kingsley's racehorse."

"Is he indeed? Then I am even more glad that I bought him." His mood somewhat improved, the earl returned to his kippers. "Ned, you will never guess who has taken Hewlett's house."

Edward looked at his friend. "I do not have the slightest idea."

"Baldwin Blair."

Edward laughed. "You are gammoning me, Alex. Baldwin Blair indeed!"

"I am perfectly serious. His nephew, a certain Robert Blair, is actually the one to have taken the house. He is a young Scottish fellow, quite the Johnny raw by the look of him. Baldwin Blair and his daughter have come to live with him."

"Why, I believe you do mean it," said Edward. "I cannot wait to tell Fanny. However did you find out?"

"I visited them last evening. I returned young Blair's dog to them."

"You visited Baldwin Blair? By God, that is extraordinary."

A sardonic smile appeared on the earl's face. "I fear it was not a success. I do not believe that the great man approves of me." Edward grinned and Glencairn continued. "Ned, what do you know of Athena Blair?"

"Athena Blair? Why, only what I have already told you. They say she is very learned and very charming. I should like very much to meet her."

"But . . ." The earl hesitated as if debating whether he should say anything more. "You seem to know about her. Has she suitors?"

Edward prudently refrained from smiling at this question. Apparently his friend was becoming interested in the lady. "I have heard that she has no end of suitors." Edward had the satisfaction of seeing the earl frown.

"And do you know anything else?"

"My dear Alex, if you want to know if she takes

lovers, I must disappoint you. I have heard that Athena Blair is a very virtuous lady."

"Quit being an ass, Ned," said the earl testily.

Edward suppressed a laugh and took another forkful of his food.

While his brother was conversing with Edward Lyttleton, Peter Moncrief walked briskly toward the offices of the *Clarion Voice.* Earlier that morning he had made an extraordinary decision. Encouraged by his newest poem, "Ode on Leaving Oxford," Peter had determined to try to have his work published. Although he knew that his brother would disapprove, Peter had decided to bring his poetry to Baldwin Blair. After all, the *Clarion Voice* had a reputation for encouraging new poets by publishing promising unknowns.

However, as Peter neared the newspaper office, his confidence began to falter. Stopping in front of the *Clarion Voice,* Peter glanced hesitantly down at the package he was carrying. He had never shown his poems to anyone before. What if they weren't any good? Mustering his courage, Peter walked over to the office and opened the door.

Once inside Peter stopped and looked around him. A young man sat at a desk in the front of the office, reading a newspaper. Two other men sat at desks in the back. Peter, feeling even more uncomfortable with his mission, approached the man at the front desk.

"Excuse me, sir."

Ashton looked up from his newspaper and regarded the young gentleman before him, noting his well-tailored and expensive clothes. "May I be of assistance?" he asked.

Peter paused, clutching his package closer to him. "Yes, I would like to see Mr. Blair."

"I'm sorry, sir, but Mr. Blair is not in."

Peter was momentarily crestfallen. "Oh. Well, then, might I see Miss Blair?"

Ashton eyed Peter curiously. "What would be your business with Miss Blair be?"

Peter reddened under the man's scrutiny. He wanted to tell the fellow it was none of his concern, but instead he answered meekly, "I have some poetry that I wondered if Miss Blair would read."

"I see," said Ashton. "Well, Miss Blair is rather busy at the moment, Mr. . . ."

"Moncrief."

"Mr. Moncrief. You can leave your poetry with me."

Peter shook his head. "No. I mean, I really must see Miss Blair myself."

Ashton eyed Peter speculatively for a moment and then got up. "Very well. I will go and ask Miss Blair if she can see you." Peter nodded gratefully and stayed rooted to the spot near Ashton's desk.

Making his way through the office to the back print shop, Ashton found Athena engaged in what appeared to be a rather serious discussion with one of the printers. "Excuse me, miss," said Ashton, and Athena looked over at him.

"Do not tell me there is another problem, Ashton," she said. "After all the problems with the printing press this morning, I am afraid one more thing will totally overset me!"

Ashton smiled at her. He doubted anything could overset the capable Miss Blair. "No, Miss Athena. There is a gentleman who wishes to speak to you."

Athena brushed a stray strand of auburn-colored hair from her face. "A gentleman?"

"Yes, miss. He appears to be an aspiring poet."

Athena made a comical face. "Oh, dear, Ashton. Not another aspiring poet?"

"I fear so, miss."

Athena sighed. The *Clarion Voice* attracted numerous

gentlemen with literary ambitions. Unfortunately, while most of them did not lack ambition, they did lack talent. And it usually fell to Athena to tell them that the *Voice* could not use their work.

Athena went to the door and peeked out into the office. She spied Peter and studied him with some interest. "He appears to be a very well-dressed aspiring poet," said Athena.

"Yes, miss," agreed Ashton. "That is why I thought you might wish to see him. The paper could use another wealthy benefactor."

Athena shook her head. "Mr. Ashton, are you implying that we should publish the man's poetry in an attempt to get another wealthy benefactor? Shame on you!" Ashton looked somewhat sheepish and Athena laughed. "I confess, the thought had also crossed my mind. Well, I suppose I should see him."

Ashton smiled. "The gentleman's name is Moncrief." Athena walked into the office and made her way toward Peter.

"Mr. Moncrief," she said, smiling at him. "I am Miss Blair."

Peter was momentarily speechless. He thought Athena was the most beautiful young lady he had ever seen. Even the smudge of ink on her cheek did not detract from the lovely vision Athena presented. The beginning of a sonnet was already beginning to flit through Peter's mind, but he somehow came to his senses.

"Miss Blair," he said. "I am very pleased to meet you."

"Please, come and sit down, sir," said Athena, leading Peter to a chair beside her desk. Once they were both seated, Athena continued. "Mr. Ashton informs me that you are a poet, Mr. Moncrief."

Peter nodded. "I have written some poetry, Miss Blair," he said modestly. He put the wrapped package on the desk. "I wondered if you might be so kind as to read some of my work. And . . ." Peter hesitated. "And if you might consider publishing it in the *Clarion Voice*."

Athena looked at the package with a sinking feeling. She had immediately liked Mr. Moncrief and hated to have to be the one to discourage him. She held out little hope that his poetry was any good since most of the poetry thrust upon her was utterly wretched. However she managed to smile at him. "Yes, I should be happy to read your poetry, sir. But I must warn you, I am by no means an expert—"

Peter interrupted her. "Oh, no, Miss Blair. I have every confidence in your judgment of my work."

Athena sighed inwardly and looked down at the bundle before her. She glanced back up at Peter and found he was watching her with some anticipation. Apparently he expected her to read his poetry then and there. Deciding she might as well get the business over with, Athena picked up the package.

"Do let me get the string for you," said Peter, quickly breaking it and unwrapping the package for her.

"It appears you have written a number of poems, sir," said Athena, somewhat dismayed at the large pile of papers.

"Oh, this is just a small sampling, Miss Blair," said Peter, who was torn between eagerness and apprehension in having her read his poems. Athena smiled at him and picked up the paper on top of the pile. She began to read the poem, a studious expression on her face. She looked up at him.

"Why, Mr. Moncrief, this is a wonderful poem!"

"Really, Miss Blair?" asked Peter hopefully.

Athena smiled. "Really, sir. It is excellent!" She picked up another paper and began to read. She looked again at Peter. "This is excellent, too, sir. The *Clarion Voice* would be happy to publish your poems."

"It would?" asked Peter.

"Yes," said Athena enthusiastically. "In fact, Mr.

Moncrief, perhaps there would be a possibility of our press publishing a book of your poetry."

Peter was dumbfounded. He never thought becoming a published poet would be so easy. He was about to reply when an impressive looking, middle-aged gentleman entered the newspaper office. Athena quickly got up from her desk. "Papa, you must come and meet Mr. Moncrief."

Baldwin Blair smiled at his daughter and made his way over to her desk. Peter hurriedly stood up to shake the hand Baldwin was extending to him. "Mr. Moncrief," said Athena, "this is my father, Baldwin Blair. Papa, this is Mr. Moncrief. He has just brought some of his poetry in, and it is quite remarkable."

"Has he? Well, Mr. Moncrief, if my daughter thinks your poetry remarkable, you must be a talented young man. Athena is a very perceptive critic."

Peter was somewhat dazed by everything that was happening to him. First, to hear the lovely Athena Blair praise his poetry, and then to come face-to-face with the famous Baldwin Blair! Peter shook the great man's hand and managed to speak. "Mr. Blair, it is such an honor to meet you! I am a great admirer of your work! I think *Of Justice and the Rule of Free Men* is one of the greatest writings of the age!"

Although Baldwin Blair was used to such high-blown tributes from his disciples, he never tired of hearing them. He smiled at Peter and decided he was a most discerning young gentleman. Baldwin could also not fail to note that Mr. Moncrief appeared to be a man of some means and as such, a valuable asset to the cause. "You are kind, sir," said Baldwin. "And I look forward to reading your poetry."

Peter was about to reply when another gentleman entered the newspaper office. He was a tall, lanky man who was dressed rather shabbily. "Uncle, Athena, I was nearby sae I thought I would come tae visit ye." He noticed Peter. "Oh, I didna mean tae disturb ye."

"That is all right, Robbie," said Athena. "Let me introduce you to Mr. Moncrief. Mr. Moncrief, this is my cousin, Robert Blair."

"How do you do, Mr. Blair?" said Peter, politely extending his hand.

"Pleased to meet ye, Moncrief," replied Robert. "Moncrief," he repeated. "There is a family of Moncriefs near my home in Scotland." Robert tactfully refrained from mentioning that the family was despised by every person in the vicinity. "Would ye by any chance be kin tae the Moncriefs of Glencairn?"

Peter hesitated. He was not sure how the Blairs would react to finding out that he was indeed kin to those Moncriefs and that his brother was the Earl of Glencairn. Surely the Blairs would not be happy to find that he was so closely related to a man whom the *Clarion Voice* had recently condemned as a tyrant. However, since he was an abysmal liar, Peter decided he had no choice but to tell the truth. "Yes, that is my family," he said, sounding somewhat regretful.

Robert regarded Peter with considerable interest. So the young gentleman was related to the detested Moncrief clan? Although Robert had little use for the family, especially for the present earl, he remained civil. "Then you must be related to the Earl of Glencairn?"

"Yes," said Peter, "I am Peter Moncrief, Glencairn's younger brother."

Athena regarded him in surprise. "You are the Earl of Glencairn's brother?" Peter nodded. Athena was momentarily taken aback. The two brothers were so different. Not only was the physical difference apparent, but Peter seemed a mild, quiet young man, quite in contrast to the brash earl. Athena again thought of the Earl's bold kiss and reddened slightly. Attempting to overcome her confusion, Athena smiled at Peter. "I have met your brother," she said, trying to sound nonchalant.

"We have all met the earl," said Baldwin Blair. Peter could not fail to note the tone of disapproval in his voice.

"You have met him, sir?" he said. "I was not aware of that. I knew that he had met Miss Blair. I read the article about my brother in the *Clarion Voice*. Indeed, it was I who brought it to Glencairn's attention. He has assured me he knew nothing about forcing tenants from the estate. He has written to the factor to find out about the matter. My brother is a man of honor."

"Humph," said Baldwin, who doubted very much that the earl was anything of the kind. However, Baldwin did not believe in holding one's family against one. Although he had little use for the aristocracy and especially the Earl of Glencairn, he had some sympathy for younger sons. "One can't be held responsible for one's family. I'd be in a devilish fix if I was held responsible for mine."

Robert laughed. "Aye, Uncle. I daresay my father feels the same way." Baldwin grinned at his nephew. Peter was somewhat relieved by the lack of enmity toward him. He began asking Robert about Scotland, and that gentleman was happy to describe the place and people of the area in considerable detail.

Athena found her mind wandering as her cousin spoke of his Highland home. She thought instead about the Earl of Glencairn, her mind lingering on memories of the night before. Peter, too, found his attention diverted from Robert's words, for he was far more interested in the beautiful Miss Blair.

9

Edward Lyttleton sat in his luxurious canopied bed, a silver breakfast tray before him. His wife, Fanny, a plump and pretty blonde, sat companionably beside him intent upon her own breakfast. Buttering a scone, Edward reflected upon how pleasant his life had become.

A man of considerable wealth and position in society, Edward also felt himself the most fortunate of men in having a wife he adored and three children whom he absolutely doted upon.

In addition to these blessings, Edward possessed the enviable quality of never being bored. A keen observer of the human condition, he was forever entertained by the foibles and follies of those around him. His prominent place in society guaranteed that he would never be at a loss for the diversion that other people provided for him.

Taking a bite of the scone, Edward turned his thoughts to the recent interesting developments involving his friend Glencairn. He smiled to himself as he considered his stolidly conservative friend's apparent interest in Baldwin Blair's daughter.

Edward's reflections were interrupted by his wife. "I daresay, Cook's marmalade is the best I've ever tasted. Don't you think so, darling?"

Edward looked at her. "Pardon, sweet, what did you say?"

Fanny smiled fondly at him. "You seem to be in the clouds, Ned."

Edward grinned. "Sorry, my dear. I was just thinking about Glencairn."

Fanny pushed a blond curl from her forehead and regarded her husband with a curious expression. "You really think he is interested in Baldwin Blair's daughter?"

Edward nodded. "I daresay, I might be barking up the wrong tree, but he did ask me about her."

Fanny shook her head. "Well, it certainly isn't unusual for Glencairn to be interested in a woman."

Edward laughed. "I know, Fan, my old friend is quite incorrigible when it comes to the ladies. But the idea of Glencairn and Baldwin Blair's daughter! It is quite funny. And what an astonishing coincidence that the Blairs have moved to Regent's Square. I think I should pay a call upon them today."

Fanny appeared surprised. "Call upon the Blairs?"

"And why not?"

"Indeed, my dear, they are not quite within our circle."

"Oh, but it would be so amusing meeting them. You must come with me."

"That is ridiculous, Ned. And even if I wished to make the acquaintance of these persons, I am far too busy to do so. I have to go with Clarissa to Lady Weston's today. But if you wish to call upon the Blairs, I shall be eager to hear all about it."

"I have it! I shall invite them to Clarissa's ball!"

"Oh, Ned!" cried Fanny. "You could not do that!"

"Any why not? It would be great fun! And I daresay it will be a way to get Glencairn to come. Do not be an old stick, Fanny! Having the Blairs will create a sensation."

Fanny paused to consider this. "I shall not object to your inviting them, but only if they seem presentable enough."

"You are a dear, Fanny," said Edward, leaning over to

kiss her on the cheek. Putting his tray on the table beside
the bed and then flinging away the blankets, he got up
and rang for his valet.

A short time later, Edward Lyttleton was dressed in
his usual sartorial splendor. Although his figure was a bit
too corpulent to do complete justice to his wardrobe, Edward still appeared very much the man of fashion in his
well-cut morning coat, nankeen pantaloons, and spotless
Hessian boots. Putting on his cape and beaver hat, he
called for his footman to bring his high-perch phaeton
around. After kissing his wife and children good-bye, he
was off.

It was a fine day, and Edward cheerfully raced his
horses down the familiar London streets toward what
used to be the establishment of Fitzwilliam Hewlett.
Pulling his horses up to the curb in front of the fashionable town house, Edward was assisted down from the
phaeton with some difficulty by his footman. Straighten-
ing out his coat, he glanced up at the red-brick residence.
He felt a sense of nostalgia, thinking about the merry
times he and his friends had had at Hewlett's house in
the past. He remembered a particular wild occasion
when a number of young actresses were present
and . . . Edward shook his head, smiling at the memory.
Of course he had been a mere youngster then, not the
staid family man he was now.

Walking up to the entrance, Edward knocked at the
door. It was quickly opened by an unlikely-looking butler, who stared at Edward with a rather dour expression.
"Is Mr. Robert Blair at home?" asked Edward, thinking
the fellow a poor excuse for a servant.

"Aye, he's at hame, sir," said the man in a Scots accent that amused Edward.

"Would you inform Mr. Blair that Mr. Edward Lyttleton wishes to pay a call on him?" asked Edward, produc-
ing a gilt-edged card for the butler.

Jock Stewart looked somewhat skeptically at the card.

"Aye, sir. I'll tell Mr. Blair that ye're wanting tae see him." The servant scurried away, leaving Edward standing on the doorstep. Stewart returned hastily. "Mr. Blair will see ye, sir," he said. "Follow me."

The butler led Edward into the elaborate Chinese drawing room that had been Fitzwilliam Hewlett's pride and joy. Relieved that the room had been left as it was without the addition of a country gentleman's hunting pictures or ghastly animal heads on the wall, Edward sat down on the modish oriental sofa.

"Mr. Lyttleton," came a voice, and Edward looked around to find a tall, ungainly red-haired gentleman hurry toward him. He was wearing such a hideous tartan waistcoat that Edward blenched at the sight. However he quickly regained his composure and stood up.

"Mr. Blair, I am very happy to meet you," said Edward.

The two men shook hands, and Robert motioned his guest back to the sofa. " 'Tis good of ye tae visit me, Mr. Lyttleton."

"I hope you don't mind the intrusion," began Edward.

"Och, nae," said Robert eagerly, "I am glad tae meet people. I am new tae town, ye know."

Edward smiled. "Why, yes, I had heard that you had moved into Fitz Hewlett's house so I thought I should pay you a call."

Robert appeared impressed. "Then ye knew Mr. Hewlett?"

"Oh, yes. I knew him quite well. I have raised many a glass with him in this very room." Edward shook his head sadly. "Poor old Fitz."

"I have heard that Mr. Hewlett ran into a spot of trouble," said Robert.

"More than a spot, I fear. Fitz was the unluckiest fellow at cards that you would ever hope to meet. He bankrupted himself and had to flee his creditors. The last I heard, he was in Italy."

"Och, 'tis a pity," said Robert, clicking his tongue. "I have been told he was a famous man who used tae tie the Prince Regent's cravat."

Edward smiled slightly. "Yes, fame does have its price and obscurity its recompense."

Robert was somewhat puzzled by this remark, but he nodded sagely. He decided to change the subject from the unfortunate Mr. Hewlett. "As I said, 'tis kind of ye to call on me. I have wanted tae meet some people in society, but have had little opportunity as of yet. Of course, I have nae been in town but for a short while."

"Yes, you are just come from Scotland are you not, Blair?"

Robert nodded. "Aye, that I am."

"And how do you like London?"

"Oh, 'tis a fine city tae be sure and quite different frae Scotland."

"I imagine it is," said Edward ironically.

"Then you have never been tae Scotland?" asked Robert.

"No, I fear I have not had that pleasure," said Edward, who had often expressed the opinion that Scotland was the last place on earth he would wish to find himself.

"Och, that is too bad. But do ye not have some Scottish blood?"

Edward Lyttleton regarded Robert as if he had not heard him correctly. "Scottish blood?"

"Aye, I thought with that red hair ye might be a Highland man, Mr. Lyttleton."

Edward smiled. "I am afraid not. The red hair is supposed to come from a tenuous family connection to the Tudors—strictly on the wrong side of the sheets, you understand."

Robert was appropriately awed to have a guest with such royal lineage. Suddenly remembering his role as host, he quickly said, "Och, would ye like some refreshment?"

"Thank you, but I really must be going."

Robert's face fell. He was quite enjoying the visit with Edward Lyttleton, who appeared to be a man of fashion and a tulip of the *ton*. Edward stood up and Robert hastily rose from the sofa.

"I was wondering, Blair, if you might be able to attend a ball at my house on Thursday. I know it is rather short notice . . ."

Robert jumped to the invitation like a fish to bait. "Oh, aye, I'd be happy tae attend."

"Good," said Edward. "And why don't you bring along your family as well? You do have family staying with you, do you not?"

Robert nodded. "Aye, my uncle and Cousin Athena."

"Splendid!" said Edward. "By all means, bring them along."

As Robert ushered his guest to the door, he could scarcely believe his good fortune. Wait until he told his uncle and Athena that they were to be included in such august company!

Edward Lyttleton also felt his visit was a success. He had found Robert Blair to be rather quaint and amusing, although in desperate need of a good tailor. Edward smiled. He was certainly looking forward to Clarissa's ball.

Soon after Edward Lyttleton's visit, Robert left the town house and did not return until much later. In fact, Baldwin and Athena had already come home from the *Clarion Voice* and were beginning to wonder what had become of him.

Robert burst into the drawing room where Baldwin and Athena were sitting. "Uncle, Athena. Och, I am sorry tae be sae tardy," he said, but his expression belied his words. Appearing to be in a jubilant mood, Robert grinned at them both.

Athena smiled at her cousin. "And what have you

been up to this day, Robbie? You look as happy as a grig."

"Yes, my boy," agreed Baldwin. "You do look particularly jolly this evening."

"Aye, I am that," declared Robert, sitting down next to Athena on the sofa. "I have had a grand day." He paused dramatically. "Ye will never guess who called on me today in this very room."

"I cannot imagine," said Athena curiously.

"Edward Lyttleton," pronounced Robert importantly. When both Baldwin and Athena looked blankly at him, he appeared disappointed. "Ye must have heard of him! Edward Lyttleton is a proper tulip and a prominent man in society! I asked several persons about him today and everyone knew of him. Why, he was a friend of Fitzwilliam Hewlett, and he is an intimate of the Prince Regent!"

"Humph," muttered Baldwin, "those are hardly recommendations for the fellow."

"But whyever did he come here?" asked Athena.

Robert appeared slightly offended by his cousin's remark. "And why should he nae come? He had heard I have taken Mr. Hewlett's house, and he was anxious tae meet me." Athena and her father exchanged glances, but Robert continued. "He was a fine gentleman and dressed all the crack! And the best of it is, he invited us all tae his house for a ball on Thursday." Both Athena and Baldwin looked surprised. "Aye," said Robert, pleased by their expressions, "it is a great honor."

"For whom?" asked Baldwin sardonically and Athena laughed.

Robert regarded his uncle with a perplexed expression. "But Uncle, aren't ye pleased at getting such an invitation? Mr. Lyttleton is a great man."

"A great man!" sputtered Baldwin. "Why is that, Nephew? Because the fellow dresses like a popinjay and is a sycophant to our degenerate prince?"

Robert looked shocked. "I hope, Uncle, ye will nae talk in such a manner at the ball."

"Who said I was going to attend this Lyttleton's ball?" said Baldwin sourly. "You know my opinion of society, Robert. I have no wish to waste my time on a bunch of idlers and featherheads!"

"But, Uncle, ye must go!" pleaded Robert and Baldwin hesitated. Despite his bluster, Baldwin was not totally averse to taking an opportunity to hobnob with the decadent aristocracy. It would no doubt provide plenty of fodder for the *Clarion Voice*.

Baldwin glanced over at Athena. "Well, I suppose I could go. I daresay, it might be interesting."

Robert smiled in relief. "Och, that is splendid, Uncle Baldwin! And, Athena, ye will go, won't ye?"

"Oh, I don't know, Robbie," she said. "I don't have any dress to wear to such an event."

"Nonsense!" said Baldwin. "You can wear your blue dress, my dear. It is dashed pretty."

Athena shook her head. "But it is several seasons old, Papa," she began.

Baldwin smiled. "I thought you didn't care a fig for fashion, my girl."

"I don't, but—"

"Of course, you don't! You have a brain, my dear. You don't care about such frippery matters."

Athena smiled. "Oh, very well. I see my once having said that I care nothing for fashion will condemn me to go about in the shabbiest of clothes without a whimper. What a ninnyhammer I am! But shabby or not, I shall go to the ball."

Robert beamed at them both and could hardly contain his excitement. With Edward Lyttleton's assistance, he was getting his entrance to elite society.

10

THE following day the earl asked his brother to accompany him to his racing stables. Pleased at the invitation, Peter was happy to accept. He had not yet told Glencairn his exciting news about getting his poetry published. He had been rather reluctant to do so, but seeing that the earl appeared amiable, Peter decided that he would venture to inform him.

As the two brothers rode in Glencairn's curricle, Peter bolstered his courage. "I must tell you that something wonderful has happened, Glencairn."

The earl, who was driving the vehicle, looked over at his brother. "Indeed, Peter?"

The young man smiled. "I am going to have some of my poetry published."

"Published?" said the earl.

"Yes," said Peter. "Is it not amazing? Now I hope you will not be angry when you hear the rest of it." Glencairn raised his eyebrows at this pronouncement but kept his attention on his horses. "My poetry is to be published in the *Clarion Voice*."

"Good God!" exclaimed his lordship. "The *Clarion Voice*! How did this come about?"

Peter noted that his brother did not look at all happy at this part of his news. "I know that the *Clarion Voice* is not the sort of publication that peers of the realm would be likely to approve. Indeed, considering the unfortunate business with Miss Blair's mistaking you for some sort of tyrant, I can see why you would not be happy about it. But one must not be concerned about the political positions of the *Clarion Voice*. It is universally acclaimed for its literary content."

"I daresay it is not universally acclaimed for anything," said Glencairn. "If you expect me to pleased about this, I shall have to disappoint you. However did it happen that you are suddenly to become a published poet?"

Peter tried not to let his brother's disapproval dishearten him. "You see, Glencairn, I was encouraged by your broad-mindedness in allowing me to leave Oxford."

"I am never broad-minded," retorted the earl.

"You seemed so to me," said Peter earnestly. "Why, it was so good of you to not be angry when I spoke to you about my poetry. I decided that I must show my work to someone. I have been writing for ages. I thought of Mr. Baldwin Blair. Oh, do not look so darkly at me, Glencairn. He is a very clever man. He is accounted a good judge of poetry. For a poet to appear in the *Clarion Voice* is considered a great honor."

"So Mr. Blair approved of your poetry?"

"Miss Blair did," said Peter eagerly. "Oh, I know you met her. Why did you not tell me that she was an angel? She is so beautiful! You must think her so."

"I admit she is pretty enough," Glencairn replied gruffly.

"And she was so kind. She thought my poetry was very good. She agreed at once to publish it. I was never so surprised in my life. And then Mr. Blair came in. He is completely charming. I was so honored to meet him."

"I have met him and I cannot share your opinion," returned the earl. "And I have read his damned pamphlet, 'On the Abolition of Titles of Nobility.' I shouldn't be surprised if the fellow would like to see me riding in a tumbril."

Peter laughed despite the seriousness of his brother's expression. "Do not be ridiculous, Glencairn. But how did you meet Baldwin Blair?"

"I had the pleasure of his acquaintance the evening I went to Carlton House. You will doubtless be overjoyed to learn that your hero Blair resides across the square in Fitzwilliam Hewlett's former home."

Peter's eyes opened wide in astonishment. "Mr. Hewlett's home?"

"Yes, indeed. Your champion of the people resides amid the splendor of Hewlett's Chinese drawing room. He and his daughter have come to live with their cousin, a certain Robert Blair."

"Oh, I met Robert Blair yesterday at the *Clarion Voice*. But how did you meet Mr. Baldwin Blair?"

"Two evenings ago, I was returning home when a deerhound ran in front of my horses and was nearly killed. One of the servants knew where the dog lived so I brought the animal back to the Hewlett residence. I had not expected to find Miss Blair residing there. Baldwin Blair and his nephew appeared, and I had the dubious pleasure of meeting them."

"And you did not like Mr. Blair?"

"No, I did not. Nor did he like me. Should he find that you are my brother, he will very likely change his opinion of you as well."

"He knows that you are my brother," said Peter. "He does not hold that against me," said Peter. Seeing his brother's black look, he continued, "That is, he does not hold my being a peer's brother against me."

"How good of him," returned the earl. They rode in silence for a time. Peter was glad that his brother took the news about his poetry as well as he did. In truth, Glencairn was not thinking very much about Peter's revelation. The discussion of the Blairs focused his mind on Athena. So deep was the earl in his reflections that he missed the turn to go to the stables. Finally realizing this, he muttered an oath and turned around. Peter was quite surprised at this for Glencairn was not usually so absentminded.

The earl was greeted enthusiastically by the trainer, Tucker, who appeared very pleased to see his employer. He could scarcely wait for Glencairn and Peter to get down from the curricle before telling them of the colt's progress. "Aye, my lord, your Vulcan is a right one! Wait until you see him! Matthew is warming him up."

Glencairn smiled proudly at the sight of the red colt cantering down the wide dirt track. Another horse was alongside him, a tall white gelding.

"Vulcan is a fine horse," said Peter.

"The finest I've ever had," said the earl.

"Aye, there's none to match him, my lord," said Tucker. "I've seen many horses in my time, but none like Vulcan. And Specter is doing well, too, my lord," he added, referring to the white horse. The men stood watching the horses for some time. The jockeys held their mounts in check for a few laps. "Now you'll see what they can do, gentlemen," said the trainer, signaling to the riders.

The jockeys urged their horses to increase their speeds. Finally given his head, Vulcan raced wildly down the track, leaving the white horse far behind.

"By God, he is a marvel!" shouted the earl. "You are right, Tucker, there is none to touch him." When the race was finished, the jockey rode the colt toward the earl. "Good work, Matthew," said Glencairn.

"Thank you, m'lord," said the rider, patting the horse's neck.

Vulcan snorted as he pulled up alongside his lordship. "Is he not the most splendid creature, Peter?"

"He is indeed," said Peter with genuine admiration.

"Good God, Alex!" said a voice from behind them. "The prince will never speak to you if he sees that horse!"

The earl turned to see Edward Lyttleton. "Ned!"

"I thought you'd be here. I wanted to see this colt of yours in action." He smiled at Peter. "Good day, Peter. What do you think of your brother's horse?"

"He is a fine animal, sir," said Peter. "I do not doubt that he will win every race."

"Indeed, he will," said the earl. "Thanks to Tucker." The trainer beamed at the praise. "I cannot wait for his first race," continued Glencairn.

When the jockeys dismounted and led the horses away to warm down, Glencairn, Peter, and Edward walked along the track.

"You look well, Master Peter," said Edward. "You've grown taller. I have heard you have left Oxford."

"Why should he attend university, Ned? My brother is a poet," said Glencairn. "Peter, you must tell Ned your news."

Edward looked inquiringly at the young man. "News, Peter?"

"I am to have my poetry published in the *Clarion Voice*."

"The *Clarion Voice*? Why, Peter, your work must be very good."

"What do you know about it, Ned?" said the earl sharply.

Edward laughed. "If you were not such a philistine, Alex, you would know that the best modern poetry is published in the *Clarion Voice*. How very ironic, Peter, that your poetry will appear in the same publication that was so unsympathetic to your brother."

"I am not so certain now that I want it to appear," said Glencairn.

Peter appeared stricken. "Not appear? What can you mean, Glencairn?"

"Alex, surely you are not going to forbid your brother from having his poetry published," said Edward.

"And why not? I do not think poetry is the proper occupation for a gentleman."

"That is ridiculous," said Edward. "Why, look at Byron. He is a gentleman and a peer."

"Oh, very well," said Glencairn. "One could not help but want one's brother to emulate Byron."

Edward laughed and Peter smiled in relief. "I shall be eager to read your work, lad," said Edward. "Alex, we must both take subscriptions to the *Clarion Voice*. Especially now that I have met Robert Blair, nephew to Baldwin Blair. I paid a call at the Blair residence yesterday."

"You did what!" said the earl, raising his dark eyebrows at his friend.

"And why not? I was so intrigued with them after your telling me how you met them. I found Mr. Robert Blair quite charming in an unpolished way. I did not have the good fortune to meet the great Baldwin or his daughter."

"Miss Blair is quite lovely, Mr. Lyttleton," said Peter enthusiastically. "It was she who liked my poetry. She is the kindest, most charming lady."

"Why, she has obviously captivated you, Peter," said Edward. "It sounds as if you have a *tendre* for the lady."

Peter flushed. "I have only just met her," he protested.

Edward looked over at Glencairn, but his lordship's face was disappointingly inexpressive. "If you come to my ball on Thursday, I daresay you may have the opportunity to meet her again." Edward felt gratified to see that this remark engendered some response in Glencairn.

"Miss Blair will attend your ball?" said the earl.

"I cannot say with any certainty, but there is a distinct possibility. Why, I invited Mr. Robert Blair, and he was very eager to attend. I urged him to bring Miss Blair and his uncle. I do not doubt that he will encourage them to come. Now I do insist that both of you will come."

"Ned," said the earl, "you know how I detest such

things. And you always have a damnable orchestra and dancing. I abhor such functions."

"Nonsense," said Edward, "you are completely absurd. I shall not forgive you if you do not come. And Peter, you must say you will be there. There will be so many pretty girls about. You must meet my sister Clarissa."

"I should like that very much," said Peter, thinking that he would be very pleased to attend. After all, if there was even the remotest chance that Miss Blair would be in attendance, he would not want to miss the opportunity to see her again.

"Now say you will come, Alex. It would be such a coup for Fanny to have my lord Glencairn attend."

"Now it is you who is absurd, Ned," said the earl, his face breaking into a smile. "Very well, I shall attend."

Edward smiled in return and suspected that Glencairn wished to see Miss Blair again as much as Peter so obviously did.

11

WHEN Athena returned to Regent's Square after her duties at the *Clarion Voice* on Thursday, she was not at all happy to think that she was to attend the Lyttleton ball that evening. Although she usually enjoyed parties, the idea of finding herself among strangers, who were members of London's elite society, did not appeal to her.

Robert, however, was tremendously excited at the prospect of mingling with members of the *ton*. Certain that the ball would be his entrée into the first circles of society, he envisioned himself flirting with elegant ladies of fashion and discussing sport with the leading gentlemen of the kingdom.

Baldwin had been reconciled to the idea of spending an evening at the ball. In fact, although he did not like to admit it, he was rather looking forward it. A gregarious man, Baldwin loved social gatherings. While he doubtlessly preferred the company of his intellectual and literary friends, he suspected that the Lyttleton ball would be very interesting.

Tempted to make excuses about going, Athena decided that it would be better to attend the ball without protest. One sometimes had to suffer evenings of boredom. In all probability she would be ignored. After all, from what she knew of society, its members would hardly be likely to take notice of an unknown lady dressed in an old, unfashionable gown. Athena frowned at the thought of her dress, but silently chided herself at caring about such things. After all, why concern oneself about the opinions of the silly, empty-headed members of society?

When it was time to get ready for the ball, Athena retired to her room. One of the maids had laid out her blue dress on the bed. Athena eyed it gloomily. It was her best dress, and, indeed, she had always thought she looked good in it. Yet she had worn it so many times that she was tired of it. A faint smile crossed Athena's face as she stared at the dress. Well, at least no one at the Lyttleton ball had seen her in it.

"Excuse me, miss," said a feminine voice. Athena turned to see one of the maids, a diminutive girl of perhaps fifteen, enter the room. "Your bath is ready."

"Thank you, Sarah." Once Athena had bathed, the servant returned to assist her with dressing. Unaccustomed to the services of a personal maid, Athena was not sure she liked to have someone fussing about her. However she was pleased to find that Sarah was quite adept at hair styling. The girl had artfully combed and brushed Athena's auburn locks into a modish coiffure with tiny curls about her face and the rest of her hair pulled up into a knot at the top of her head.

"You are an artist, Sarah," said Athena, eying her reflection in the dressing table mirror with approval. "I look quite presentable. Now do help me fasten my pearls."

When the necklace was in place, Athena smiled at herself in the mirror. It was a lovely necklace that had belonged to her mother. "You look beautiful," said Sarah. "Shall I help you with your dress now, miss?"

Athena rose from the dressing table as Sarah took up the gown from the bed. Its numerous tiny buttons occupied the maid some time. "There you are, miss," said the maid. " 'Tis a very pretty dress. You do look lovely."

"Thank you, Sarah." Athena stood regarding her reflection with a critical eye. Perhaps the old blue dress did not look so bad, she conceded. Fashioned of pale blue satin, the gown's hemline was trimmed with delicate ivory-colored lace. The bodice of the gown was cut very low, revealing the voluptuous curves of Athena's breasts, and the sleeves were very short and ornamented with knots of blue ribbon.

"And here are your gloves and fan, miss," said the maid, handing them to Athena.

"Thank you again for all your help, Sarah," said Athena gratefully. "You have done wonders with my hair. You may go. I should like to stay here for a time."

The maid bobbed a curtsy and was gone, leaving Athena to stand there before the mirror, a thoughtful expression on her face. Turning away from her reflection, Athena walked over to the window and gazed out at the square. She could see Glencairn's imposing residence through the trees.

Since the earl's visit, she had thought of little else but his ungentlemanly conduct toward her. The idea that Glencairn might be at the Lyttleton ball crossed her mind, but she dismissed it. She had no reason to believe he would be there. There were no end of parties, balls, and other functions members of society might attend, so it seemed unlikely that the earl would turn up at the Lyttletons'.

Athena frowned, telling herself that she hoped she would not see Glencairn again. His behavior had been shocking and inexcusable. It was clear he considered her a bit of fluff, a woman with whom he might amuse himself. He had acted like an unprincipled rake, and Athena knew that he was not to be trusted.

Yet her rational assessment that Glencairn was an unscrupulous and dangerous man did not change the fact that she was still drawn to him. No matter how many times she told herself that she was a fool, Athena still could not shake off her unsettling feelings for Glencairn.

Was she in love with him? Athena had considered this

question numerous times. It seemed impossible. After all, she scarcely knew him and what she knew of him hardly endeared him to her. It was utterly preposterous to think herself in love.

Athena continued to stare out the window. She was not a prude, nor had she been denied masculine attention. For years she had had many admirers who had expressed their feelings with oftentimes embarrassing ardor. In the past she had had no trouble resisting any of these men. While enjoying their flattery, Athena had never been able to conceive of the idea of romantic passion for any of them.

It was very different with the earl. Much to Athena's considerable annoyance, she had found herself lying in bed imagining Glencairn's caresses. She had been amazed and disturbed that such feelings could come to her and that she had so little power to resist them.

While she had heard and read of women abandoning themselves to passion and committing ridiculous follies with unacceptable men, Athena had always thought those stories nonsense. Now she was not so sure. After all, she had come close to committing this sort of folly herself.

"Athena!" Robert's voice came through the door of her bedchamber. He knocked loudly. "Are ye nae ready? Sarah said ye were."

"Yes, Robert, I am."

"I dinna wish tae be late," said her cousin, opening the door. "Come along then."

Catching sight of Athena, Robert grinned. "Why ye look sae bonnie, lass! Nae man will be able tae keep his eyes frae ye."

"Do not be ridiculous," said Athena, turning to her cousin. "Why, Robbie! You look splendid. Indeed, you are undeniably a man of fashion. I salute your Mr. Warriner."

Robert beamed at the compliment. He had indeed

been transformed by his new evening clothes and appeared almost handsome. His coat of black superfine was exquisitely cut, fitting his thin frame to perfection. He wore black knee breeches and white silk stockings, and his ungainly feet were shod with elegant patent leather shoes with silver buckles. Robert's red hair had been painstakingly curled in a respectable approximation of the fashionable Corinthian style.

Robert grinned. "I believe we will have ourselves a fine time, Cousin."

Although skeptical of this, Athena smiled and allowed Robert to escort her from the room.

12

EDWARD LYTTLETON had spared no expense on the ball since it was given in his sister's honor. Clarissa Lyttleton had just recently been presented at court, and now that she had the royal stamp of approval, she was ready to take her place among the young ladies of society. The ball was her first foray into the august company of London's first circles and, therefore, Edward wished everything to be perfect.

The spacious ballroom of the Lyttleton residence was brilliantly lit and decorated with pink and white flowers and potted palms. Since the Lyttletons occupied a very lofty place in society, their ball was considered a function not to be missed. The cream of the nation's first families crowded into the ballroom dressed in finery of dazzling splendor.

As host and hostess of this assembly, Edward and Fanny were kept very busy greeting the numerous guests who arrived in a steady stream. There was an atmosphere of excitement and anticipation in the room, and even the young dandies seemed to have exchanged their usual looks of fashionable ennui for more animated expressions.

The Earl of Glencairn, however, did not appear at all pleased to be arriving. Accompanied by his brother, Peter, his lordship surveyed the company with a look of practiced indifference. He detested balls. He did not enjoy the crush of people or the noise of shrill laughter

as the ladies expressed their amusement at the question-
able wit of this or that fashionable buck.

Glencairn was a good deal too cynical and world-
weary to enjoy seeing other people amuse themselves. In
addition to that he was in a devilish bad temper. Indeed,
the earl would not have come to the ball at all if it hadn't
been for the possibility of seeing Miss Athena Blair.

"My dear Lord Glencairn," said Fanny Lyttleton,
greeting his lordship warmly in the receiving line.

The earl bowed over her hand and smiled. He liked
his friend's wife although he thought her frivolous and a
trifle bird-witted. She was warmhearted and she meant
well, and Glencairn knew that she had made his friend
Edward a very happy man. "Mrs. Lyttleton," he said. He
glanced over at Peter, who was beside him. "I do not believe you have met my brother, Peter Moncrief."

Fanny smiled warmly at Peter. "I have not. My husband has told me that you are a poet, sir."

Peter flushed. "I should like to be."

"I do adore poetry," exclaimed Fanny.

"Yes, she does," said Edward, who was standing beside his wife. Having now disengaged himself from a lo-
quacious military man, Edward was pleased to see his
best friend and Peter. "Fan always wishes I would write
her a poem, but I could not bear to so disappoint her
with my abominable attempts at verse."

"My dear Ned, you are too modest. Do you not recall
that poem that you wrote to me before we were wed? I
still remember it," said Fanny, smiling fondly at her husband.

Fearing that she might recite his one poetical effort,
Edward hurried to change the subject. "Peter was at Oxford. Perhaps he knows your nephew, Walter."

Diverted by this, Fanny asked Peter if he had met her
nephew. While Peter was making his reply, Edward took
the opportunity to speak to his friend. "I have not seen
her yet, Alex," he said in a low voice.

"What?" said the earl.

"Miss Blair," returned Edward with a knowing smile.

The earl found himself irked with his friend. "Do not be a sapskull, Ned."

Edward laughed. "Do not think you can fool your oldest friend. I know that your brother is not the only Moncrief to take an interest in the lady."

Glencairn frowned. Luckily the swarm of people around the host and hostess did not allow the earl to linger, and he pressed on into the ballroom. Seeing one of his friends from Eton, Peter took his leave of his brother. Standing alone, the earl surveyed the ballroom with a jaundiced eye. It was the usual assortment of fops and fortune huntresses, he decided. Indeed, he found few of the numerous guests to be worthy of his consideration.

Since he was known to be a very formidable personage, his fellow guests were not encouraged to talk with him. The earl was not well-liked, for he had no love of small talk and did not suffer fools gladly. Few sought his companionship, but those who did received only an impatient nod for their trouble. In short, the earl was living up to his reputation of being a difficult man who thought himself above almost any company.

As his lordship shifted his gaze across the ballroom, he caught sight of Athena Blair entering upon the arm of her father. Behind them was Robert Blair. Glencairn's eyes followed her as she moved toward Edward and Fanny. Dressed in blue and with the bearing of a princess, Athena looked lovely. The earl wondered how Athena had so bewitched him.

Athena looked around the ballroom with interest. She had never seen so many splendidly dressed people at one time. Looking down at her gown, she felt like a plain gray goose among a flock of peacocks. The ladies ball gowns all seemed so grand, and Athena did not fail to note the glittering diamonds and sapphires that adorned the necks of so many of them.

Robert, his confidence fortified by his fine new clothes, greeted Edward Lyttleton as if he was his dearest friend. "Mr. Lyttleton," he said, shaking Edward's hand vigorously. " 'Tis glad I am tae see ye."

Several of those persons standing nearby turned at the sound of Robert's broad Scots accent. Edward grinned merrily at the sight of Robert Blair. Certainly the Blairs would enliven the occasion, not that it needed much enlivening for the company was growing loud and boisterous.

"Fanny, I must present Mr. Robert Blair."

After bowing over Fanny's hand, Robert introduced his cousin and uncle to the Lyttletons. Fanny smiled warmly at them. Noting Robert's fashionable attire, she felt rather disappointed. Young Mr. Blair appeared to be an ordinary gentleman of means, not at all the outlandish person Edward had described to her. Baldwin was a handsome middle-aged man who appeared very distinguished. He had a charming smile and elegant manner.

It was Athena, however, who most interested Fanny. Although Fanny's practiced eye could not help noting that Miss Blair's gown was hardly modish, she was very favorably impressed with her appearance. Athena was a very attractive young lady with a winning smile and striking blue eyes. Fanny could see how the earl could be interested in her.

After exchanging a few pleasantries with Baldwin and Robert, Fanny allowed her husband to occupy those gentlemen. She then turned to Athena. "I have so wanted to meet you, Miss Blair, after hearing about you from my husband."

"Hearing about me, Mrs. Lyttleton?" said Athena in surprise.

Fanny laughed. "Why, yes. My husband has heard about you from Lord Glencairn. The earl is Mr. Lyttleton's dearest friend." Fanny lowered her voice to almost a whisper. "It seems the earl has taken quite a fancy to you."

Athena tried to hide her dismay. So Glencairn was Lyttleton's dearest friend? What an appalling coincidence. Or was it a coincidence? Perhaps the earl had sent his friend to call upon Robert. Athena looked across the crowded room. Glencairn must be here somewhere. What had he been saying about her, she wondered. Athena's blue eyes flashed with irritation, but she tried to appear nonchalant. "I scarcely know the earl," she said.

"You will have opportunity to meet him here," said Fanny. "Why, there he is. Do you see him? Why, he is looking in your direction." Athena glanced in the direction Fanny Lyttleton was indicating. Spotting Glencairn, she frowned. The earl was indeed looking at her, and as she caught his gaze, his lordship bowed slightly. "Yes," said Fanny, "he is very interested, my dear Miss Blair." A woman who loved romantic intrigue, Fanny smiled knowingly. "I believe you have made a conquest. I am so glad to see it, for I had thought Glencairn immune to Cupid's darts. See how he stares at you. It is clear that he has finally succumbed."

Athena did not know how to reply to this extraordinary remark. "I fear you are mistaken, Mrs. Lyttleton," said Athena. Cupid's darts, indeed, she told to herself.

"We shall see," returned Fanny, smiling again.

Athena found her conversation with Fanny Lyttleton disconcerting. Even more disconcerting was the fact that Glencairn continued to watch her. Athena managed to smile weakly at Fanny. She was glad that the press of the other guests made it easy for her to move on.

Athena took her father's arm as Baldwin and Robert began to walk across the ballroom. "There are a good many pretty girls about, Robert," said Baldwin with an ironic smile at his nephew. "You will be kept busy with them."

"Aye," said Robert, "but how does one meet them? I canna just walk up tae a young lady, now can I?"

"That is a dilemma," replied Baldwin, rather amused by the seriousness of his nephew's expression. "Athena, how can your cousin meet all the young ladies when we know scarcely a soul here?"

Deep in her own thoughts, Athena was scarcely attending. "I beg your pardon, Papa."

"Woolgathering, my dear? I said that Robert does not know how he is to meet the young ladies. One does not simply barge up and introduce oneself, not in polite society. Whatever is he to do?"

"I daresay I do not know, Papa," said Athena.

Robert considered his situation for a moment while Athena tried very hard not to look in Glencairn's direction. She would ignore him, she decided. If he tried to speak to her, she would give him a proper setdown.

Two young gentlemen approached the Blairs. Athena recognized one of them as Peter Moncrief. Looking very dashing in his finery, Peter smiled warmly at Athena. Beside him was a short red-faced young man who was inclined to stoutness.

"Miss Blair and gentlemen," said Peter in greeting.

"My dear Moncrief," said Baldwin, shaking Peter's hand. "Why, I am glad to see you. We were just saying that we knew no one here."

"I should like to introduce my friend. Miss Blair, Mr. Blair and Mr. Blair, may I present Lord Charles Ponsonby?" said Peter.

Lord Charles seemed very pleased to meet them. He was a pleasant young man with polished manners. Since Lord Charles expressed his admiration for the literary content of the *Clarion Voice*, both Baldwin and Athena were inclined to regard him favorably.

After conversing with the young gentlemen for some

time, Baldwin turned the subject to a topic of interest to his nephew. "I must say that there are a great number of pleasant-looking young ladies in attendance."

"None can hold a candle to Miss Blair," said Peter, regarding her with undisguised admiration.

"Yes, yes, of course," said Baldwin, "but I suspect you gentlemen know many of the young ladies."

"Indeed so, sir," said Lord Charles. "I have five sisters, three of whom are out in society. And I have more cousins than I can count. I have met all of their friends as well as their friends' sisters and cousins. Yes, I daresay that between Peter and myself, we are acquainted with a good many of the ladies in attendance."

"You are the answer to my nephew's prayers," exclaimed Baldwin. "Why, he is dying to meet some of the young ladies, and we have no one to introduce him. Would you gentlemen agree to present Robert to some of these lovely creatures? I should be eternally grateful."

Peter hesitated. He did not want to spend his time taking Robert Blair about the ballroom. He wished to stay with Athena. He had hoped that they might discuss poetry.

"Indeed, I should be grateful," said Robert.

Peter could only nod. "Very well," he said. "But, Miss Blair, I do hope that you will honor me with a dance later."

"I should be more than happy to do so, Mr. Moncrief," returned Athena. Somewhat mollified, Peter smiled. Then he, Robert, and Lord Charles left Athena and her father. Baldwin noted with a grin that they headed in the direction of a group of young ladies standing together.

"Robert will be well occupied," said Baldwin with a smile. "I do not doubt that we will be attending his wedding before the month is out. Few girls will be able to resist him. I hope he ensnares an heiress. One does not know when one may have to touch him for a loan."

"Oh, Papa," said Athena with a laugh. "Look, someone else is coming toward us. Do you know him?"

Baldwin nodded. "Why, you remember Mr. Jameson. He's Sheffield's cousin."

"Oh, yes," said Athena vaguely as a large, balding man came before them.

"Mr. Blair," he said. "I did not expect to see you here."

"No, indeed, Mr. Jameson," said Baldwin. "I am quite out of my element. I must present my daughter, Athena."

"Your servant, Miss Blair," said Jameson. After Athena replied that she was very glad to meet him, Jameson turned once again to Baldwin. "I have a good many friends who are impatient to meet you, Mr. Blair," said Jameson eagerly. He gestured toward a group of splendidly dressed men and women across the room. "I have been sent to commandeer you. Do come with me, sir, and, of course, Miss Blair."

Baldwin smiled brightly, only too happy to comply. He had not expected to be fondly received at a society gathering. After all, he was Baldwin Blair, and society had little cause to have love for him. It was a happy surprise to see that a good number of people were so eager to meet him.

Glancing in the direction of the well-dressed ladies and gentlemen, Athena tried to keep from frowning. She wished that she had never come to the ball. Indeed, she wished that she might leave at this instant. She most assuredly did not want to stand about listening to the conversation of society members.

"Papa," said Athena, "do go with Mr. Jameson. I think I shall join Robert."

"Very well, my dear," said Baldwin with a smile. "I fear, Jameson, that my daughter is deserting us. But my nephew, Robert, will certainly be glad of your presence."

Athena smiled as her father and Jameson took their leave. In truth, she did not want to join Robert. She could see him with Peter Moncrief and Lord Charles. They were talking to a number of young ladies, and Robert seemed to be thoroughly enjoying himself.

Athena frowned, wishing she could escape from the ballroom. Looking about the room, Athena was surprised that Glencairn was no longer standing there watching her. She could find him nowhere.

Feeling relieved, Athena retreated across the ballroom to what seemed the most inconspicuous location. There in the corner she sat down on a bench. She felt tired and irritated. She had been such a goose to come, she told herself. She might have known that Lyttleton had had some ulterior motive in inviting them to the ball. Glencairn must have put him up to it. The thought was vexing, but at the same time flattering.

The bench's location beside a very large potted palm afforded some protection from the eyes of the company. Athena relaxed considerably as she observed the activity of the ball from her position of relative obscurity. She fanned herself and looked thoughtful.

"Miss Blair," said a deep masculine voice from behind her.

Startled, she did not have to turn toward it to know that the voice belonged to Glencairn. Striving to keep her composure, Athena glanced around to see the earl standing there. His face was strangely grim for the ballroom. "Lord Glencairn," said Athena evenly.

The earl came to stand before her. He was dressed in well-cut claret-colored evening clothes. His white silk stockings fit his well-muscled calves like a second skin. "I did not think you would hide in a corner, Miss Blair. You seem to me the sort who would rather be in the thick of things. Do you not enjoy brilliant company?"

"I am quite tired, my lord," said Athena with a frown. "And I prefer to be alone."

The earl's dark eyebrows arched slightly. "May I sit down, Miss Blair?"

"No, you may not," returned Athena curtly.

The reply caused Glencairn to smile for the first time. He found himself thinking how lovely she looked in her blue dress with her hair arranged so prettily. From his vantage point, his lordship had an admirable view of Athena's charms as revealed by her low neckline. He studied her appreciatively.

"If you have come to apologize, my lord," said Athena severely, "I shall save you the trouble. I do not wish to hear it, nor will I accept it."

Glencairn smiled again. "I had no intention of apologizing, Miss Blair. Indeed, I have no reason for doing so. If it is because I kissed you, I cannot apologize for that, because I am not at all sorry for it. I should like to kiss you again."

Surprised at this impertinence, Athena directed a warning look at the earl, but he ignored it. Instead, he sat down on the bench and continued to study her.

Angered at his presumption, Athena knew that she should rise from the bench and hurry away. Yet she remained seated.

"Are you enjoying the ball, Miss Blair?"

Athena continued to fan herself. "I was, my lord . . . until now." Rather than provoke the earl, the comment caused Glencairn to regard her with amusement. Athena frowned. "I think you should leave, Lord Glencairn."

"I am far too accustomed to doing as I please, Miss Blair, and I am very pleased to sit here beside you. However, if you would do me the honor of awarding me a dance?"

Athena's pale blue eyes grew wide in surprise. "Dance with you? Indeed, I must decline."

"And why? You have nothing to fear. There are enough people about."

"You are perfectly odious." Her eyes narrowed indignantly. "And I do not fear you in the least."

"Then you will dance with me?"

He said this as if it were a challenge. "Very well, my lord," she said. "I shall dance with you."

Glencairn rose from the bench and offered her his arm. Taking it reluctantly, she allowed herself to be escorted toward the dancers.

Feeling rather like an actress playing a role, Athena tried very hard to appear cool and indifferent to the earl's presence beside her. Noting the interested glances of many of the ladies and gentlemen in attendance, Athena felt very conspicuous walking with the earl across the ballroom. She found herself wishing she had refused to dance with him. "Do you enjoy dancing, Miss Blair?" said Glencairn as they neared the other dancers.

She glanced up at him. "I usually enjoy it very much."

"I detest it," said the earl.

"Indeed, my lord, if you so detest dancing, I shall be happy to release you from this unpleasant obligation."

He smiled the faint smile that was now becoming familiar to her. "You will not escape so easily, Miss Blair. You have agreed to stand up with me, and I shall hold you to it."

"Very well, my lord," said Athena mildly.

Joining the others, the earl and Athena took their places for the next dance. It was a lively country dance of some complexity. Glencairn, Athena noted, was not a good dancer, but he seemed quite unconcerned at taking the wrong turn or missing a step.

Observers of the earl and Athena—and there were many of them—were surprised to see his lordship dancing at all. It was well known that the Earl of Glencairn did not deign to dance. A good many eyebrows were raised at Glencairn's unusual behavior in moving inexpertly through the dance. The fact that he fastened his attention so firmly on the pretty young lady in the blue dress was not missed by those who were watching the dancers.

When the music stopped, Glencairn extended his arm to Athena. "I do thank you, Miss Blair. There is your father, the famed Baldwin Blair, glowering at me. I shall escort you to him."

Athena caught sight of Baldwin. While she would not have necessarily described his expression as "glowering," it was clear that her father was not very happy to see her in Glencairn's company. Standing with another gentleman and two ladies, Baldwin frowned as he watched Athena and the earl approach.

Relinquishing his partner to her parent, the earl bowed stiffly to Baldwin and took his leave. The presence of the others prevented Baldwin from voicing his disapproval. He could only present his daughter to them and continue with his conversation.

Glencairn walked across the room, seemingly unaware of the fascinated glances of the company. The earl had for some years been the object of a fair amount of interest. After all, he was extremely wealthy and of high rank, and his past love affairs had been the topic of much lively gossip.

As Glencairn passed by, a feminine voice called out to him. "Glencairn, you must join us."

The earl stopped and looked at the source of this remark, a splendidly dressed lady with henna-dyed hair festooned with ostrich plumes. Approximately forty years of age, the lady had taken great care to retain the advantages of beauty that nature had bestowed upon her. Diminutive and attractive, she wore a gown of ivory satin. A necklace of gleaming diamonds adorned her neck, and diamond earrings dangled from her delicate ears.

Recognizing the woman, Glencairn cursed to himself. Lady Penelope Ingraham was not a person he wished to speak with. Eight years ago they had had a short, unsatisfactory affair.

When they had met, Glencairn had been very young

and Lady Ingraham had been having a spat with her current lover. She had found it amusing to take up with the young man, but when her quarrel with her lover had ended, she had unceremoniously dropped Glencairn.

"Yes, indeed, Glencairn, you must not deny us the pleasure of your company." This was said without conviction by a tall dandy, who raised his quizzing glass in the earl's direction.

Glencairn frowned. He had never liked Sir John Reynolds. That the gentleman had so recently bested him at cards did nothing to endear him to his lordship. However, since the earl could not have ignored these salutations without committing very serious breaches of manner, he reluctantly stopped. "Lady Ingraham," he said, making a slight bow.

She was standing beside an older lady, with whom Glencairn had only a slight acquaintance, and Reynolds. The earl bowed politely to the older woman, whom he knew to be the dowager Marchioness of Lonsdale. She was a formidable and influential personage in society as well as an incorrigible gossip.

"We do want to talk with you, Glencairn," said Lady Ingraham, smiling brightly at him. "You must tell us about the lady who has evidently so fascinated you that you have given up your aversion to dancing." She turned to the dowager marchioness. "Everyone knows that Glencairn does not dance."

"After watching you, my lord," said Reynolds with a sly smile, "I daresay that they still hold that opinion."

The earl looked warningly at Sir John, but the delighted laughter of the ladies gave him encouragement to ignore his lordship's displeasure. "I must say, Glencairn," said the dowager, "that while it is very charitable of you to lend countenance to this young lady, I do not think that such persons should be encouraged in society. Perhaps you are not aware that the woman with whom you were dancing is the daughter of that rogue, Baldwin

Blair. And he is also present here! While Mr. Lyttleton might find it amusing to invite such persons to his ball, I find it quite shocking."

"Yes, it most certainly is," said Reynolds, with a look of mock indignation. "But, Lady Lonsdale, it was kind of his lordship to befriend the young lady. See, she is there dancing with young Milford. She will not lack partners now that his lordship has so honored her."

The baronet's words were spoken with such obvious sarcasm, that it was difficult for Glencairn to hold his temper. Reynolds was clearly baiting him.

"I suppose you think this Miss Blair very pretty," said Lady Ingraham with a tone that implied that she clearly did not. "Perhaps she would be presentable if her dress were not so hopelessly out of fashion."

"Yes," sniffed Lady Lonsdale. "I should wonder at anyone appearing in this company in such a dress."

Glencairn frowned ominously, a fact that Lady Ingraham noted with interest. "I do not doubt Glencairn thought Miss Blair's gown fine enough," she said.

"Is that true, Glencairn?" said Reynolds, taking his snuff box from his pocket and taking a pinch. "Did you admire the lady's dress?"

"If Miss Blair were clad in rags," said the earl testily, "she would still eclipse every lady in this room. Good evening." After glaring at the baronet, his lordship stalked off, leaving Lady Ingraham and Reynolds to regard each other with delighted expressions.

Lady Lonsdale appeared insulted. "What a rude man! He is nothing like his father. He is quite insufferable."

"My dear Lady Lonsdale," said Lady Ingraham, "do not be so hard on Glencairn. Why, it is clear he has become enamored of this Miss Blair. Let me see, I believe his last mistress was that actress . . . I cannot recollect her name."

"Mrs. Thorton," supplied Reynolds. "But that ended months ago."

"Oh, yes," said Lady Ingraham. "It is time he takes another. But look, Miss Blair has another dancing partner. It is Peter Moncrief, Glencairn's brother."

This seemed an interesting development, causing the three of them to walk toward the dancers to obtain a better view.

13

As THE night went on, Athena found herself the object of much masculine attention. She danced with a number of gentlemen, including a very eager Peter Moncrief. Her cousin, Robert, had one dance with her as well. She noted with some concern that Robbie was having perhaps too good a time at the Lyttleton ball. Having imbibed a great quantity of punch, he appeared slightly inebriated. Laughing off her caution to stay away from any more drink, Robert left her to seek out some of the other ladies to whom he had been introduced.

While Athena was dancing with different partners, Glencairn stood apart. He spent most of his time watching Athena, seemingly indifferent to the fact that many eyes were upon him.

Athena tried hard not to think of Glencairn, but no matter how charming the gentleman presently commanding her attention, her thoughts were never far from the earl. Oftentimes she would find herself looking about the ballroom, wondering where he was. She would severely caution herself to forget about the earl, but it did no good.

Glencairn, for his part, found himself torn between seeking out Athena once again for another dance and staying away from her completely. Feeling the eyes of society upon him, he knew that the gabblemongers were eager to have more rumors to spread about. Although Glencairn cared little for what might be said of him, he did not like the idea of causing Athena to be the object of gossip.

As the evening wore on, however, his desire to speak with her once again overcame his better judgment. When a young gentleman escorted a rather tired Athena toward the dancers for yet another country dance, Glencairn intercepted them. "Excuse me," said the earl, "but Miss Blair promised me this dance."

The young man looked at Glencairn in surprise. He had never met the earl, but he knew very well who he was. "I fear you are mistaken, my lord," he said stoutly.

"I am not mistaken," returned the earl, casting a black look at the young man. "I should be most appreciative if you would oblige me, sir."

Intimidated by the earl's formidable appearance, the young man hesitated for a moment, as if considering the idea of arguing with the Earl of Glencairn. "Very well, my lord," he said, thinking better of making the powerful earl his enemy. Bowing to Athena and the earl, he retreated.

Athena turned to Glencairn with a frown. "I think that horrible how you bullied Mr. Russell. You cannot expect me to dance with you, sir."

The earl shook his head. "I do not wish to dance. Making a fool of myself once in an evening is sufficient. Come, sit with me there." He motioned toward a group of chairs not too far from where they were standing.

"I could not . . ." began Athena, but the earl allowed her no time to argue. Taking her arm, he led her to the chairs.

"Do not fear, in a few moments, your father will doubtlessly come to your rescue. He clearly suspects I am a scoundrel."

"And he is incorrect, my lord?"

Glencairn smiled. "What do you think, Miss Blair?"

She shook her head and looked down. "I don't know what to think," she replied.

"Please sit down," he said. Athena knew she should walk away from him, but she sat down in the chair instead. "You should not mind sitting, Miss Blair. You have danced every dance. You are quite a success. Indeed, you are the most popular lady at the ball. I should not be surprised if you will find a steady stream of gentlemen coming to your door." The idea clearly irked his lordship.

"If I am a success at this ball, my lord, it is only because everyone is curious about Baldwin Blair's daughter."

"That is not the only reason. Dammit, you are the prettiest woman here and the cleverest."

Athena looked down, embarrassed. "Please leave me, my lord. I'm certain everyone is staring at us."

"Let them stare," said Glencairn gruffly. "Who cares what these scandalmongers may think?" He paused. "You must know that I have very strong feelings for you. I have been watching you all evening. I could not take my eyes from you."

Athena regarded him questioningly. "We scarcely know each other, my lord."

"What does that signify? Do you think that what I feel for you will diminish with further acquaintance? Why, just being beside you, I can scarcely refrain from taking you into my arms."

"You cannot expect me to listen to you if you say such things, my lord. I pray you be sensible!"

The earl shook his head. "I cannot be sensible where you are concerned, Athena Blair."

Her heart pounding as she met Glencairn's gaze, Athena did not feel in the least sensible herself. "Athena!" Baldwin's voice startled his daughter. She looked up to see Baldwin staring unhappily at them.

Glencairn rose. "Blair," he said.

"Glencairn," replied Baldwin stiffly. "You will excuse

us, my lord. The hour grows late. It is time I took my daughter home."

The earl glanced down at Athena. "Good night, Miss Blair," he said. "I shall look forward to seeing you again."

"Good night, Lord Glencairn," said Athena.

His lordship bowed and took his leave with obvious reluctance. When he had gone, Baldwin eyed his daughter as if she were a wayward schoolgirl. "Athena, I would think you should know enough to discourage that man's attentions. You are no green girl. You have seen enough of the world to know what Glencairn is like. He would have no scruples whatsoever about taking advantage of you. You must take care, my dear. The man is dangerous."

Athena sighed resignedly. She was too tired to discuss the matter with Baldwin. Besides, she told herself, her father was right. Glencairn was dangerous. "I am very tired," she said. "I do wish to go home." She rose from the chair to take Baldwin's arm. They then went off in search of Robert.

While his cousin was sitting with the Earl of Glencairn, Robert Blair was thoroughly enjoying himself talking with an agreeable young lady and her aunt, whom he had met through the kind auspices of Peter Moncrief. After what he considered to be a very short conversation, the ladies claimed that they must seek out the elder lady's husband. Robert thought that the young lady looked particularly regretful at the parting. After bowing low to her, he watched the women stroll gracefully away. Then he turned his attention once again to the punch bowl.

Robert had been very pleased with Lyttleton's punch, drinking several glasses of the strong liquid throughout the evening. He felt rather light-headed as he took another glass and downed it quickly. Then he wandered across the room to stand where he could watch the dancers engaged in an energetic round dance.

"She is Baldwin Blair's daughter." Robert turned his head as he heard his uncle's name. There was a tall dandy talking to a group of gentlemen.

"Baldwin Blair!" said one of the men. "I daresay a man like that should be exiled."

"You are being charitable, sir," said another of the group. "I should think the fellow should be hanged. He has written such unspeakable lies. Oh, I have not read anything he has written, of course, but I have heard he quite despises our class. They say he is another Robespierre."

Robert, fascinated by what his eavesdropping had caused him to hear, moved closer to the group of people. He did not know what a Robespierre was, but, from the gentleman's tone, he suspected it was not a very good thing. Resentment welled up within him. How dare they talk about his uncle!

"He seemed an amiable fellow," commented a gentleman.

"You spoke with him?" cried another.

"Indeed yes. Know the enemy. That is what I always say."

The others laughed. "Well, I should not wish to know him," said the tall dandy. "I might wish to become acquainted with the daughter, however. She is a pretty minx. I'd fancy getting to know her better myself."

"You must stay away from her, Reynolds," said one of the other men. "She seems to be Glencairn's property."

"Is she his mistress?" said another of the gentlemen.

"If she is not," said Reynolds, "I'll lay odds that he'll bed her within a fortnight. She looks willing enough to me. Yes, this Miss Blair appears to be a lusty wench. Glencairn is a lucky man."

Robert stared at the tall dandy in astonishment. He was usually a mild-mannered young man, but these remarks brought his Celtic blood to the boiling point. How dare they bandy Athena's name about in such an infamous fashion!

"Excuse me, sir!" he said, barging into the circle of men to confront Reynolds. "Ye are speaking about my cousin! Ye'll nae say another word about her!"

Reynolds did not appear in the least abashed or intimidated. He eyed Robert with an expression of faint amusement. "I'll say what I please."

"Ye have impugned my cousin's honor!" cried Robert.

"I regret that the Earl of Glencairn has had that pleasure, not I," replied Reynolds. The other gentleman laughed delightedly at his audacity.

Robert's lean face took on a terrible expression. "Ye bloody bastard," cried Robert. He drew back his hand and then struck Reynolds on the jaw with his clenched fist. There were gasps from his companions as Reynolds fell back from the blow, landing in an undignified heap on the ballroom floor.

"Are you mad, sir!" cried one of the men. He and another gentleman lunged toward Robert, grasping him firmly by the arms.

Another man hurried to Reynolds's assistance. "Reynolds, are you injured?"

Reynolds looked at Robert with an expression of astonishment mixed with rage. Touching his jaw tentatively, Reynolds shook his head. Fortunately the blow had not landed with full force on its intended target. The others helped him to his feet.

Robert seemed a trifle unsteady, but he tried to break free from the other men who had pinioned his arms. "I'll teach ye a lesson ye'll nae soon forget," he cried, glaring at Reynolds.

By this time almost everyone in the ballroom was looking in their direction. Edward Lyttleton's servants hurried to assist the gentlemen who were restraining

Robert, and the very unhappy Highlander was soon escorted forcefully from the room.

Baldwin Blair and Athena had not witnessed any of the shocking incident, but they did catch a glimpse of Robert being hustled away by two burly servants in livery. Exchanging startled glances, they hurried from the ballroom.

A rather disheveled Robert was released into their custody. Baldwin took him firmly in hand, cautioning him to be quiet. The three Blairs then hastily left the Lyttleton residence, escaping into Robert's carriage.

14

THE angry altercation between Robert Blair and Sir John Reynolds created a sensation among the guests at the ball. Those lucky enough to be invited to the Lyttleton's had known that they would experience an entertaining evening, for the Lyttleton ball was always an exciting affair. However those assembled that night felt especially fortunate to have witnessed such a scandalous scene. After the Blairs had made their abrupt departure, the guests could talk of nothing else but Robert Blair's shocking conduct.

While Fanny Lyttleton was distressed by the events of the evening, she could not help but be a little pleased by the notoriety she had undoubtedly gained from it. She knew that the ball would provide some lively gossip in many London drawing rooms the following day. Indeed, Robert Blair's misconduct had livened things up considerably, providing a great deal for everyone to talk about.

Fanny's husband was much less sanguine about the incident. Edward Lyttleton could not escape the feeling that the whole thing was his fault, for he had invited the Blairs to the ball. Edward had thought it would be diverting to have the rusticated Robert Blair and his radical uncle there, but now he wished he had not acted so impulsively. To cause a scene at his sister's ball was unforgivable, and Robert Blair's conduct had been quite disgraceful.

Of course, Edward told himself, his primary motiva-

tion in asking the Blairs had been to see how his friend
Glencairn would react to the presence of Miss Blair. Earlier that evening, as he had observed Glencairn and
Athena together, Edward had been convinced that his
friend was head over heels in love with her. Edward had
been delighted, for he had been beginning to doubt that
any lady could win the earl's affections.

After disengaging himself from a garrulous gentleman, who kept talking about Baldwin Blair, Robert
Blair, and the barbarous behavior of Scotsmen, Edward
scanned the crowd for Glencairn. Spotting the earl at the
far corner of the room, Edward hurried to meet his
friend.

Glencairn was standing alone, looking none too happy
at being there. Edward tried to appear cheerful. "Alex,"
he said, "at least it is not a dull party. Your Blairs have
made certain of that."

"What was it all about?" said the earl.

"Robert Blair was in his cups. He is a foolish young
man."

"You must know what Reynolds said to him."

Edward frowned. He knew very well what had been
said, for he had heard several versions of the incident,
but he was not at all eager to relate the story to Glencairn.

"Have you not heard?"

"I have not," said his lordship impatiently. "What did
Reynolds say to him?"

Edward hesitated. "I fear young Blair overheard
Reynolds discussing you and Miss Blair. He implied that
she is your mistress."

"Damn him," muttered Glencairn.

"I cannot abide the fellow," said Edward. "I fear it is
much grist for the gossip mill. Everyone will think the
worst, Alex. Although thinking of the fair Athena as
one's mistress hardly seems 'the worst' in my view."

Glencairn's icy expression caused Edward to remove

his smile. "I'm going home, Ned," said the earl stiffly. "Have you seen my brother?"

Edward looked around the room. "Oh, there he is, over at the punch bowl."

The earl followed Edward's gaze to locate Peter. "I shall say good night to you then, Ned. Express my thanks to Mrs. Lyttleton." He walked away, leaving Edward to regard him with a thoughtful expression.

Fanny soon joined her husband. "Glencairn is leaving? I am not surprised. He did not appear to be enjoying himself. But then I cannot say I have ever seen him enjoy himself, my dear. He is not very amusing company. I must say I do not know why you are so fond of him."

"He is a good fellow, Fan," said Edward. "He does not appear at his best in company. He does not like balls."

"He did dance with Miss Blair. He appears utterly smitten with the girl. I watched them tonight and I daresay, the looks they were exchanging even made me blush. I fear Miss Blair will not be able to resist him."

Her husband frowned. "I have known Glencairn a very long time and this is the first time that I can say that I believe he may have lost his heart. I do not know if any good will come of it."

"My dear Edward, are you worried Miss Blair will break his heart?" Fanny smiled. "At least that will prove Glencairn has a heart. Most of the company do not believe it." Before Edward could reply to this remark, they were diverted by some of their guests, who wished to discuss the scandalous behavior of Robert Blair.

Glencairn and his brother, Peter, sat in glum silence as the carriage made its way toward Regent's Square. Glencairn was too intent on his own thoughts to think much about his brother's sullenness. He was more concerned about his own situation. The evening had been most unsatisfactory, decided the earl. Why had Athena's idiotic cousin chosen to make such a scene? All of society would now think that Athena Blair was his mistress. Surely Baldwin Blair would be outraged. He would do all he could to prevent the earl from seeing his daughter. And what would Athena think of it?

Glencairn's expression softened a bit as he thought of Athena. He remembered how he had danced with her and how she had looked so beautiful. Glencairn decided he would have gladly kept Athena in his arms all night. Indeed, his most fervent desire was to have her all to himself. The earl began to imagine Athena in his bed, her auburn-colored hair loose about her shoulders, her body pressed against his as he showered her with kisses.

When he came to his senses, Glencairn looked at his brother who was seated across from him. The dim light of the carriage made it difficult to see Peter's expression, but the earl sensed his brother's displeasure. "Is something wrong, Peter?"

His brother crossed his arms across his chest. "No, nothing at all," said Peter in an unhappy tone that belied his statement.

Glencairn frowned. "I am in no mood for games. It is clear you are out of temper about something. What the devil is wrong with you?"

Peter gave his brother a glowering look. "I do not approve of your behavior toward Miss Blair."

Glencairn regarded him in surprise. "You do not approve of my behavior? By God, it is not your prerogative to approve or disapprove of me."

"No, indeed," said Peter sarcastically. "I am but the younger brother. I am not entitled to an opinion even if your behavior is utterly disgraceful. You have made Miss Blair the object of scandal! I shall never forgive you."

The earl frowned ominously. "You dare speak to me in such a way, you impudent puppy?"

For once Peter did not appear cowed by his brother's

temper. "I will speak in any way I think fit. I have great admiration for Miss Blair, and I will not have you attempting to make her your . . . your light-skirt! I saw you with her tonight. And I heard what everyone was saying—that you intend to make her your mistress. I warn you, Glencairn, if you harm Miss Blair in any way, you will have to answer to me."

"Answer to you?" Glencairn suddenly had the urge to laugh. "I answer to no one, least of all you."

"You will answer to me if you do not stay away from Miss Blair!"

"Damn you, Peter!" shouted the earl. "If you do not remain silent, I shall toss you from this carriage. You know nothing about me and Miss Blair. You will say nothing further on the subject!"

Peter glared but grew silent. The angry brothers did not exchange another word during the remainder of the journey home.

While Glencairn and his brother were staring unhappily at each other in the earl's carriage, the Blairs were arriving at Robert's town house. Robert had been uncommunicative on the carriage ride home from the Lyttleton's ball, steadfastly refusing to say what had provoked his violent outburst. Robert had stubbornly refused to tell them, only muttering darkly "the fellow is a damned scoundrel."

Athena and Baldwin assisted Robert into the house, for he was a bit unsteady on his feet. They helped him into the drawing room where he slumped down on the sofa, then leaned back and closed his eyes.

Athena and her father exchanged glances. Stewart hovered nearby, regarding his young master with disapproval. "Stewart," said Baldwin, "do fetch Tom to help us get Master Robert to bed."

"Aye, sir," said Stewart, leaving the drawing room.

"But I dinna wish tae go tae bed, Uncle. I just want tae sit here awhile."

Baldwin folded his arms across his chest and regarded his nephew sternly. "You will go to bed at once. Well, Robert, I hope you are satisfied. You have made your great entrance into society. I daresay, you made quite an impression. Planting a facer on a fellow guest is certainly a way of making one's mark."

Robert winced at his uncle's sarcastic words. "Ye've nae need tae lecture me, Uncle. I know I made a fool of myself."

"Come, come, my boy," said Baldwin a bit more kindly. "Tell us what happened to put you in such a lather."

Robert glanced over at Athena and then back at Baldwin. "The fellow made certain remarks I didna appreciate."

"I thought as much," said Baldwin with a slight smile. "But what did he say?"

"He insulted the Blairs!" said Robert hotly, his Highland blood rising to the fore once again.

"Did he now? And what grievous insult did the fellow make?" continued Baldwin.

Robert hesitated. "He said you were a robe's . . ." He paused as if trying to remember. "A robe's pea air, Uncle!"

"What?" said Baldwin.

Athena looked puzzled, but then smiled. "A Robespierre, Papa."

"Aye," said Robert. "He didna mean it as a compliment. I dinna know what it is, but, frae how he said it, 'tis nae good."

"No, it is not," said Athena with a laugh. "Robespierre was a Frenchman who enjoyed sentencing people to have their heads chopped off during the revolution."

"He called ye a Frenchman!" said Robert. "Ye can see why I was angry!"

"My boy, I have been called far worse," said Baldwin. "So, when the fellow insulted me, you lost your temper."

"Nae, Uncle," said Robert, shaking his head.

"What?" asked Baldwin, somewhat startled.

"Och, I wasn't about tae lose my temper over a wee thing like that," said Robert.

"You weren't?" asked Baldwin with such a ludicrous expression that Athena smiled.

"Nae, 'twas what he said next . . . " began Robert, and then he stopped.

"Well?" asked his uncle in exasperation. "What did he say?"

" 'Twas about Athena," blurted out Robert.

"About me?" asked Athena, eying her cousin strangely.

"Aye," Robert said, firmly refusing to elaborate.

"Robert, you will tell me what he said this instant!" commanded Athena.

He looked at her. "Och, very well, I suppose ye should know about it sae ye can be on your guard."

"Be on my guard? Really, Robbie, what is this nonsense about?"

"The damnable fellow said you were Glencairn's . . ." His voice trailed off.

"His what!" demanded Athena.

"His mistress," said Robert miserably. "Or about tae be."

Both Athena and her father appeared shocked. Baldwin was the first to speak. "Damn the fellow's eyes!" he shouted, his face purpling in rage. "He shall answer to me for spreading such false accusations about my daughter!"

Athena still appeared stunned. "But whyever would he think such a thing?" she said finally.

"Och, Cousin, 'tis nae sae surprising after all," said Robert. "They say Glencairn is notorious with the ladies. I saw how he was looking at ye tonight. It's obvious he fancies ye. I daresay he would like tae add ye tae his conquests."

Athena blushed. "Don't be absurd, Robbie."

Baldwin frowned. "I fear Robert is right. Like the rest of his depraved circle, Glencairn is totally unscrupulous where women are concerned. I did not like seeing him paying such marked attention to you tonight, Athena. It requires little imagination to surmise his intentions toward you. The man is a villain. You must keep away from him."

"Really, Papa," said Athena. "I am not a child."

"Forgive me for saying this, Cousin," said Robert primly, "but it did appear tae me that ye showed some . . . partiality for the earl. And ye did dance with him."

"I did not think dancing with him a criminal offense," said Athena.

Baldwin shook his head sadly. "No, my girl, but it shows a surprising lack of common sense on your part. Have you forgotten that the Earl of Glencairn represents everything we despise—the abuse of privilege and the squandering of wealth without regard for others? Do not be blinded by the man. Remember what he is capable of—burning the cottages of his poor tenants, forcing them off his property!"

"But, Papa, he has said that he knew nothing about that . . ." began Athena.

"So he says," said Baldwin archly.

"I believe him," said Athena. "I do not think him capable of doing such a monstrous thing."

"Ye dinna know the Moncriefs, Cousin," said Robert. "The family has a barbarous history. The first earl was a cruel man who enjoyed butchering his enemies."

Athena frowned. "Then he was not so very different from other Highlanders, was he?"

Robert ignored this remark, continuing to recount other examples of the earl's wicked Moncrief ancestors.

"So ye see, Athena," he finally concluded, "the present lord of Glencairn comes frae bad blood. The man is nae tae be trusted!"

Athena frowned again. Both her father and her cousin were convinced that Glencairn was a despicable rake. Indeed, what did she really know of him to contradict this impression? She thought of how he had kissed her. Certainly he had not acted like an honorable man. Athena's cheeks reddened. Perhaps her father and cousin were right about the earl.

As her father spiritedly took up the subject of Glencairn's perfidy, Athena thought of the earl. Perhaps she had lost her senses over the man. His presence did exert a dangerous effect upon her. She thought of him sitting beside her at the ball. Yes, perhaps she could not think clearly where Glencairn was concerned. Feeling very dispirited, Athena looked over at her father as he continued on about the earl's lamentable lack of character.

15

RESTLESS as a caged lion, the Earl of Glencairn paced across the drawing room. After spending a sleepless night thinking of Athena Blair and the Lyttleton's ball, Glencairn had risen from his bed shortly after dawn.

His lordship's servants were surprised to see him up at such an early hour. They knew that the earl and Master Peter had returned late and that the two brothers appeared to be on very bad terms. The earl's valet had informed the others that Lord Glencairn had come back from the ball in an even worse mood than usual, and the staff fortified themselves to weather their master's ill humor.

However, when Glencairn made his unusual early morning appearance, he seemed preoccupied rather than bad-tempered. Heading to his stables, he ordered a horse to be saddled. Then he set off on a ride. Single-mindedly fixed upon Athena Blair, the earl pulled his horse up in front of Robert Blair's town house. There was no sign of life there. Looking at the upper floor windows, he wondered which of them was Athena's room. After several minutes Glencairn rode on, silently mulling over his feelings for Athena.

The earl did not return home to Regent's Square for many hours. He had headed to his racing stables some distance away. There he had spent the morning with his trainer, discussing the prospects of his new racehorse and watching the red colt work out.

Yet the earl could not concentrate entirely on racing, for his thoughts often turned to Athena. His lordship did not fail to note that it was the first time a woman could distract him from what had always been his greatest love.

When Glencairn returned to Regent's Square, he once again passed by the Blair's home. Filled with an almost overpowering urge to see Athena, he resisted stopping and returned to his own residence.

The earl was glad to find that Peter was not at home. The servants were not certain where he had gone, but he had told them not to expect him soon. Glencairn frowned to think of his brother. The lad was impudent and ungrateful. He was allowing him to do as he pleased, and all Peter could do was behave like a sancti-monious parson. His brother was certain he had designs upon Athena Blair. The earl shrugged. Of course he did have designs upon her, but that did not signify. Peter must mind his own business. He was the elder brother and Earl of Glencairn. A young cub like Peter had nothing to say about the matter.

Glencairn called for a servant to bring him some food. He was suddenly hungry. He was also extremely restless and impatient. Retreating to the drawing room, he tried to read the newspapers, but seeing a newspaper just made him think of Athena.

His meal diverted him for a time. When he had finished eating, he once again went to the drawing room. There he took a chair near the window that faced the square where he could see the Blair's house clearly. Solemnly regarding the red-brick structure, he sat for a long time. Like a fox before a rabbit warren, Glencairn waited patiently and expectantly as if hoping to catch a glimpse of Athena. It was ridiculous, he realized. In all likelihood, she was not there.

A familiar high-perch phaeton passed by the window. The earl saw his friend Edward Lyttleton driving the vehicle. Edward was not a great hand at the ribbons, and Glencairn smiled to see the expression of the groom who was riding up beside him.

His lordship smiled again as Edward's rotund form descended from the carriage with difficulty. Moments later the butler entered the drawing room. "Mr. Lyttleton is here, my Lord."

"Show him in."

The servant nodded and returned quickly with Edward.

"Good afternoon, Alex," said Edward, grinning broadly at his friend. "I am glad to find you at home. I daresay I was not sure you would wish to see me. I do hope you were not vexed with me last night."

"I am never vexed with you, Ned," returned the earl, "or not for long in any case," he added. "Sit down."

Edward smiled and seated himself. Glencairn continued to stand. "I do think you should get rid of that ridiculous carriage, Ned."

"It is ridiculous to be sure," returned Edward, "but Clarissa thinks it quite dashing."

"You will kill yourself."

"I shall endeavor not to do so, my dear Alex," said Edward.

Glencairn turned toward the window. "I am glad you are here, Ned. I need your advice."

"My advice?" said Edward. "I daresay I cannot remember you ever asking for my advice before."

"I cannot remember asking for anyone's advice before," remarked his lordship, still staring out the window. "I shall probably not do so again. What am I to do about Miss Blair?"

"Do about her?" Edward grinned despite the perturbed look on his friend's face. "So you *are* in love with her!"

Glencairn turned away from the window. "I only

know that I think of her constantly. I have never felt this way before." He frowned. "It is quite irksome to be sure."

Edward regarded his friend with great satisfaction. "Upon my honor, I believe you are in love! I daresay there are but two possibilities. You must make Miss Blair your mistress, or you must marry her."

The earl raised his eyebrows. "Marriage, Ned?"

"Oh, I do not doubt that tongues will wag if you wed Baldwin Blair's daughter. But then tongues are wagging already so that does not signify. And although some might think Miss Blair beneath your touch, my lord Alex, she comes from a very respectable family."

"Respectable? I should hardly call Baldwin Blair respectable, and his nephew Robert is a bumpkin who brawls in ballrooms."

"But my dear Alex, Robert Blair's father is Lord Blair, a Scottish baron of ancient lineage. The family's seat is very near yours in Scotland. I learned this from Mr. Rutherford only last night. I don't believe you know him, but he is such an expert, you know. He has committed the peerage book to heart."

"You mean to say that Baldwin Blair is the son of a baron?"

Edward nodded. "Yes, but I would not mention it to him. I do not doubt that he is ashamed of his aristocratic origins."

"So Baldwin Blair is the son of a nobleman," said Glencairn with a smile. "That is very amusing considering what he has written in his damned pamphlet railing against our degenerate class."

"You have been reading Baldwin Blair? You astound me, Alex."

Glencairn shrugged. "Everyone else seemed to know who the fellow was. He is certainly a man of strong opinions." Edward Lyttleton grinned. "What is so funny? demanded the earl.

"I was only thinking of Baldwin Blair as your father-in-law." His lordship did not seem to share his friend's amusement at the idea. His expression grew grim, but he made no reply. "I do think you should be very glad to hear about Miss Blair's family," continued Edward. "Even the worst of society's sticklers will have less objections when it becomes known that the Blairs are of the Scottish aristocracy."

"Don't be a jackass, Ned," retorted Glencairn. "Do you think I care about the objections of 'society's sticklers'? I shall marry whom I please."

"My dear Alex, it is quite remarkable hearing you talk of marriage. In the past you seemed utterly opposed to the idea. And although I heartily recommend the institution of matrimony, I do hope you will not act too rashly. You have only just met the lady."

Glencairn smiled. "Have you ever seen me act rashly?"

Edward let out a laugh. "My dear friend, you do not have a reputation for prudence."

The earl smiled again and then offered Edward a glass of sherry.

Athena sat at her desk at the offices of the *Clarion Voice*, rereading Peter Moncrief's poems. She had decided to include two of them in the next issue of the *Voice*, but it was hard to decide which to choose. She thought them all quite good. Indeed, she considered Peter Moncrief a young man of prodigious talent.

Resting her head on one hand, Athena stared off into the distance, her mind wandering. Peter Moncrief was certainly very different from his brother, she thought. Had she lost her heart to Peter, it might have made sense, for he was artistic, sensitive, and considerate. She had always thought that if she ever fell in love, it would be with someone like Peter.

The Earl of Glencairn was not at all the sort of man

she ought to find attractive, Athena told herself. An arrogant and imperious nobleman, he was known for his devotion to racehorses and high living. He was obviously accustomed to having his way, and he enjoyed his medieval privileges.

But what was it that made her think of him with such alarming frequency, and why did she wish to see him again? If only one's heart could act in concert with one's head, Athena decided, but it was all too clear that reason had little part in falling in love.

Thinking about the previous evening's events, Athena frowned. Robert had made such a cake of himself, and it was quite dreadful that society would think her Glencairn's mistress. What would the members of her own circle say if the rumor reached them?

While pondering this question, Athena was interrupted by Ashton, who needed her assistance with an article about new labor troubles in several northern cities. Happy for the diversion, Athena was able to put Glencairn from her mind for a while. She was glad when it was time to leave the office and return home.

As usual, Robert's carriage took Baldwin and Athena back to Regent's Square. Baldwin was in a particularly good mood. He had been hard at work at the office, and his time had been very productive. Although the ball had been the topic of discussion in the morning before leaving home, nothing more had been said about it. Athena was glad her father had ceased his warnings about the evil Earl of Glencairn. Indeed, he probably felt that his admonitions to his daughter had been more than sufficient. As they rode home, Baldwin talked about a number of topics, but avoided mentioning the Lyttleton's ball.

Robert was in the drawing room when they arrived at the town house. Attired in his silk dressing gown, Robert sat dispiritedly on the sofa. At his feet was the deerhound, Mally, looking as dejected as her master. She lay there, her grizzled head resting on her paws, and barely looked up as Baldwin and Athena entered. "Och, there ye are," said Robert. "Did ye have a fine day?"

"Indeed, I did," said Baldwin. "I see you have not spent the day very constructively."

"Ye must have pity on me, Uncle," said Robert. "I've still a miserable headache."

"It serves you right, Robbie," said Athena severely.

"Ye are a harsh, unfeeling woman, Athena Blair," said Robert. "Do ye have nae sympathy for me? What am I tae do now? I'll nae be welcome in society."

"That is for the best. Now you must give up this ridiculous idea of being part of London society," said Baldwin. "It is a pointless waste of time and money."

Robert nodded. "I know ye are right, Uncle, but I was enjoying it sae much. The girls were all sae pretty. And the gentlemen were sae splendid. I'll nae receive any invitations now."

"I daresay you are right," said Baldwin. "I'm told this fellow Reynolds is an influential fellow."

"Oh, cheer up, Robbie," said Athena, sitting down beside him. "There is more to London than the society of the *haute ton*. There are far more interesting people to meet. Why, Mr. Sheffield is having a party tomorrow. All of our friends will be there. You met some of them before. Did you not enjoy that evening?"

Robert nodded, but it was clear that he considered a party at Sheffield's a large step down from mixing with members of the first circles of London's society. Athena did not know whether to be amused or annoyed.

Stewart entered the drawing room and held a silver salver before him. He went to Robert and extended the salver. "There is a caller, sir."

Looking at the card, Robert frowned. "Glencairn," he said.

"Damnation," muttered Baldwin. "I cannot imagine the audacity of the fellow coming here."

Athena summoned all her self-control in an attempt to appear totally indifferent that the earl was cooling his heels at their door. "Should we nae see him, Uncle?" said Robert. "Do ye nae wish tae know why he has come?"

"I know very well why he has come—to see Athena. I do not intend to encourage him. Stewart, tell Lord Glencairn that we will not receive him."

Stewart nodded and went to do as he was instructed. Baldwin turned to his daughter. "Athena, my dear, it is very important that you do not see this man again. In a short time this ardor he seems to feel for you will cool. A man like that loses interest very quickly."

Athena did not disagree. She was sure that her father was right. Doubtlessly Glencairn would lose interest very soon. A frown crossed Athena's countenance as she wondered how soon she would stop thinking about the earl.

In the days that followed Athena busied herself in her writing and editing duties at the *Clarion Voice*. She tried rather unsuccessfully to rid herself of thoughts of the Earl of Glencairn, but since his residence was just across the square, she could not help thinking about him each time she returned to Robert's town house. Oftentimes Athena would look out the window at the earl's residence, wondering whether he was at home. She saw him once driving past in his curricle. He did not look up, and his expression was rather grim.

Glencairn had called at the house two more times, but each time Baldwin refused to allow him to be admitted. Athena was torn between wishing to see the earl again and being relieved at avoiding him. Baldwin, seeming to sense his daughter's ambivalence, took a strong stand. Although he had never been a dictatorial father in the past, Baldwin made it very clear that he would not allow Athena to have any communication whatsoever with the earl. He declared that he would not tolerate the Earl of

Glencairn trifling with the affections of his only daughter.

Fearing that Glencairn would attempt to see Athena, Baldwin became uncharacteristically protective of her. He insisted that she not go out of the house unaccompanied by Robert or himself.

When a week had gone by without Athena having any contact with the earl, Baldwin relaxed a bit, thinking that they had perhaps seen the last of him. They did see Peter Moncrief several times, for he was a regular visitor to the *Clarion Voice*. Peter never mentioned his brother, and Baldwin suspected that the young man was happy to forget about his unfortunate connection.

When two weeks had gone by since the Lyttleton's ball, Athena began to wonder if the earl had ceased to think about her. He had stopped paying calls at Robert's town house, and Athena suspected that he had given up. Although Athena certainly had not stopped thinking of him, she would never have admitted the fact to her father or cousin.

She was glad that her work kept her so well occupied. And in addition to spending so much time at the *Clarion Voice*, Athena was busy with dinner invitations and visits to Baldwin's numerous friends and acquaintances. Robert had seemed to have gotten over his disappointment at being rejected by society. He contented himself with accompanying Athena and his uncle to evenings at their friends' homes. Robert seemed to enjoy such occasions although his disinterest in literature and politics limited his conversation somewhat in Baldwin's circle of intellectual friends.

Early in the third week after the Lyttleton's ball, Athena was at the offices of the *Clarion Voice*. It was late in the afternoon and Baldwin, Ashton, and Pike had all gone to the White Willow Coffeehouse. Athena was alone except for the presence of Jeremy Cox, a boy they had recently hired to do miscellaneous clerical jobs and to run errands. While Jeremy manned the front office, Athena closeted herself in the storeroom, taking inventory of the print shop supplies.

Engrossed in her work, Athena did not hear someone enter the storeroom. "Miss Blair." A man's voice startled Athena so that she nearly dropped her pencil. Turning around, she was astonished to find the Earl of Glencairn standing before her.

"I did not mean to frighten you," said the earl.

"What are you doing here?" she said, dismayed to see him. He looked very tall and imposing in his fashionable coat of olive superfine, buff pantaloons, and gleaming Hessian boots. He held his beaver hat in one hand. There was a slight smile on his lips, and his dark eyes regarded her intently.

"I bullied your boy into telling me where you were. I could not believe my good fortune that your father was not here. Why was I not received when I called at your cousin's house?"

"I'm certain you know that, my lord," said Athena. "My father does not wish for me to see you. I agree that it is best."

"You do not wish to see me?"

Athena shook her head. "No, sir, I do not."

"I do not believe you," returned the earl. "Do not pretend that you are not glad that I am here."

"I assure you I am not pretending," said Athena in some irritation. The man was infuriatingly presumptuous. She looked down at the paper she held in her hand. "I am very busy, my lord. I fear I shall have to ask you to go."

Glencairn ignored this remark. He placed his hat down on a shelf. "I must talk with you."

"Truly, my lord, I do not know what we can have to say to each other."

"We have a good deal to say, Athena. I thought that I made my feelings known for you at the ball."

"I pray you do not talk about the ball," said Athena. "It was a most unfortunate occasion."

"Unfortunate? I suppose you refer to the incident with your cousin. I am sure that is all forgotten by now."

"Athena, I have thought of little else but you since that accursed ball. I am not a man given to pretty speeches, but, dammit, I am in love with you."

Athena's blue eyes fastened upon his dark ones with a questioning look. She glanced down at her paper in confusion. "I beg you, sir, to leave me." Her voice faltered a bit. "My father will be returning soon."

"Damn your father," muttered Glencairn. "He fancies me to be some sort of monster."

"He is concerned only for me," said Athena.

"God in heaven," said the earl, "does he think I would harm you? I love you."

Athena knew that she was dangerously near to succumbing. The earl's closeness was making her feel very vulnerable. She stepped back from him. "I have no intention of becoming your mistress," she said weakly. "Do leave me. It is quite impossible. There can be nothing between us!"

Glencairn reacted to this pronouncement by stepping forward to enfold Athena into his arms. Feeling strangely powerless, she allowed herself to be crushed in his strong embrace. He kissed her hungrily, imprisoning her with his muscular arms. Athena did not resist. Wanting him as much as he wanted her, she could only respond with the depth of passion that had been long suppressed.

"Good God! Athena!" Baldwin Blair's voice boomed in the storeroom. "What is the meaning of this, Glencairn! How dare you!"

The earl and Athena sprang apart. "Papa!" cried Athena, horrified at the look of fury on Baldwin's face.

Baldwin frowned menacingly at the earl. "You unprincipled scoundrel!"

The earl eyed Baldwin with surprising equanimity. "I apologize, Blair," he said evenly. "I may have been a bit intemperate—"

"A *bit* intemperate?" asked Baldwin angrily. "How dare you force yourself upon my daughter! You contemptible rake!"

The earl frowned at Athena's father. "I can understand your anger, sir," he said, "but my intentions toward your daughter are entirely honorable."

"Honorable!" cried Baldwin. "I am not blind, sir! It was very clear what your intentions are! Now get out!"

Glencairn made no move to go. "I have to speak to your daughter on a matter of some importance."

"You shall swim the Atlantic before you speak to my daughter!" said Baldwin fiercely. "You will never see her again!"

Athena, who had up until now been too stunned to speak, hurried to stand between the two men. "Papa, please! You must calm yourself."

"I am calm," said Baldwin, trying very hard to maintain control of himself. "I will ask his lordship politely to get out of my place of business." Baldwin said the words "his lordship" with obvious scorn.

The earl scowled. "I will go, Blair, but first I have to speak to Athena."

Baldwin shook a fist at him. "You are an insolent fellow, Glencairn! I suppose you think that damned title of yours gives you license to do anything you want. You damned scoundrel! You attempt to dishonor my daughter right under my nose!"

"You are very much mistaken, Blair. I would not do anything to harm your daughter."

"Poppycock!" muttered Blair.

"You will listen to me, Blair," said Glencairn angrily. "I came here to ask Athena to be my wife."

Baldwin's jaw dropped open, and Athena regarded the

earl in amazement. "What?" asked Baldwin. "What did you say?"

"I wish to marry your daughter," said the earl. Both Baldwin and Athena were momentarily speechless. Baldwin was the first to recover.

"Are you totally mad, sir?" he asked, his face still showing his surprise at Glencairn's announcement.

The earl regarded Baldwin with a puzzled expression. "Mad?" he repeated uncomprehendingly.

"Yes, you must be mad, sir, to think that I would let you marry my daughter!" fumed Baldwin.

Glencairn was momentarily taken aback. Although he knew that Baldwin Blair held no love for him, the earl thought his marriage proposal would quickly change matters. Surely Blair could see now that his intentions were honorable. "I do not understand what you find objectionable about my offer, Blair," said the earl stiffly.

Baldwin suddenly laughed. "I daresay you would not. You undoubtedly thought I would be overjoyed at the prospect of having the rich, noble lord of Glencairn as a son-in-law. Well, sir, I am not! I would not have Athena marry someone like you!"

"Because I am a peer?" said the earl incredulously.

"Because you are an unprincipled libertine. You care nothing for Athena save for satisfying your damnable lust. You'd make her life a misery."

"Papa!" cried Athena.

Glencairn's face grew stormy. He could scarcely believe Baldwin's effrontery. "I'll not take that from any man. Were you not Athena's father, you'd regret those words."

"Please, stop this, both of you!" cried Athena, quite distraught.

The earl stopped and looked at her. "I fear your father has a rather bad opinion of me, Athena. I hope you do not share it."

Athena met his gaze, unsure how to reply. She shook her head. "No, I do not."

Glencairn smiled. He then turned back to Baldwin. "I believe your daughter should have some say in this matter. You do think women should have some rights in deciding whom they should marry, do you not? Did you not express such opinions in a book?"

Baldwin resented Glencairn bringing up his advanced views toward women as a weapon against him. He looked over at Athena. "My daughter is, of course, free to make up her own mind. But she is an intelligent woman. She would not agree to such an impossible match. She will not agree to become the Countess of Glencairn." Baldwin's tone implied that becoming the Countess of Glencairn was a terrible thing indeed.

The earl eyed Baldwin angrily. "Would she not?" said Glencairn. "It is you who hates me because of my rank. It is you who rails against the nobility in that absurd pamphlet of yours, not Athena."

The earl was surprised to see a smile form on Baldwin's lips. The older man burst suddenly into laughter.

"What is so amusing!" cried Glencairn.

Baldwin grinned. "It may surprise you, sir, to learn that I did not write 'On the Abolition of Titles of Nobility.' It is Athena's work. She has written many of the pamphlets appearing under my name."

Glencairn appeared startled. "She is simply doing as you request."

Baldwin grinned again and looked triumphant. "If that is what you think, you do not know my daughter very well." Baldwin turned to Athena. "The earl has offered for you, Athena. Will you accept him? Will you become the Countess of Glencairn?"

Athena had been in a state of confusion ever since hearing the earl's unexpected proposal. That he wanted to marry her seemed fantastic to her. How could she become the Countess of Glencairn? It was ridiculous even to imagine such a thing! And yet, as Athena looked into Glencairn's dark eyes, she wavered. To accept him would mean repudiating everything she and her father had worked for.

Glencairn stood looking at Athena with an expression akin to bewilderment. So she had written the pamphlet? If she believed that the nobility was the cause of all the ills of English society, how would she agree to marry him?

"I am sorry, my lord, but I must decline your offer. My father is right. Such a match would be impossible. You would not be happy with me."

"You refuse me?" he said.

Athena nodded. "I can do nothing else."

"Then you feel nothing for me?"

"That is not what I said," returned Athena. While this remark did not please Baldwin, the earl heard it hopefully. She did have feelings for him. It was obvious from how she had kissed him.

"And now, Glencairn, I will ask you once more to leave us," said Baldwin.

The earl looked at Athena. "Forgive me, madam, if I have distressed you. I shall go." Picking up his hat, he made a slight bow and left the room.

Baldwin shook his head. "Damn the gall of the fellow! Imagine him offering for your hand! The very idea that you would be Countess of Glencairn! He must be mad."

Athena did not reply. She felt a wave of conflicting emotions as she thought of the scene that had just transpired. Remembering Glencairn's arms around her, she found herself close to tears. Bravely she tried to maintain her composure as Baldwin escorted her from the storeroom.

16

WHEN Glencairn returned home, he was in an exceedingly bad mood. After scowling at the servant who met him at the door, he went to the drawing room where he sat, sullenly drinking from a decanter of brandy.

Unaware of his brother's ill temper, Peter Moncrief entered the drawing room. He and the earl had been on bad terms ever since the Lyttleton's ball. They had barely spoken to each other for more than two weeks. Such a state of affairs was especially difficult for Peter, a sensitive individual who abhorred conflict.

Peter had stayed out of his brother's way as much as possible. This was not too difficult, for the earl was gone much of the time at his club or with his racehorses. Peter remained at home, writing or reading except when he would venture out on walks or to visit the *Clarion Voice* office.

Peter's anger at his brother over his conduct with Miss Blair had cooled somewhat in recent days. He had spoken to both Baldwin and Athena on several occasions during the past weeks, and both had seemed cheerful enough. Not one word had been said about Glencairn. Peter suspected that if his brother still intended to make Miss Blair his mistress, he would be disappointed. Probably had found more willing feminine company by now, speculated Peter. The idea reassured him and made him willing to make peace with the earl.

As Peter entered the drawing room, he noted that his

brother did not look particularly cheerful. He was tempted to retreat, but Glencairn saw him and grunted a greeting. "Peter, will you have a brandy?"

"No, thank you, sir," replied Peter. "Do I disturb you?"

The earl shook his head. "Sit down."

Encouraged by his brother's tone, Peter sat down in an armchair near him. "Glencairn, I know we have not been getting on very well of late."

The earl regarded him with a strange look. "Haven't we?"

Peter suspected that his brother had had a fair amount of brandy already. He watched him pour some more into his glass. "No, sir."

"Yes, that's right. You thought I was intent upon seducing Miss Blair." The earl took another drink. "And you did not approve of the idea."

Peter reddened. "Indeed, I did not."

"Well, I *was* intent upon seducing Miss Blair, Little Brother, but I have given up the idea."

"I believe you are drunk," said Peter, frowning at him.

"And why shouldn't I get drunk?" demanded Glencairn. "Do you know what I did this very afternoon? I asked Athena Blair to marry me, and she refused."

Peter regarded his brother in amazement. "You asked Miss Blair to marry you?"

"I know it was a damned idiotic thing to do," said the earl. He stared glumly at his glass. "Can you imagine the daughter of Baldwin Blair becoming Lady Glencairn? I was stupid enough to believe she cared for me."

"You wanted to marry her?" asked Peter again. "You cannot mean that you are in love with her!" The possibility of his brother being in love with Athena had not occurred to him. He had assumed that the earl intended only to add her to his conquests.

A wildly romantic young man, he suddenly viewed the earl in a new light. So his brother had fallen in love with Athena Blair! It should not be so astounding. After all, Peter was a little in love with the lady himself. But for his unsentimental brother to be so stricken! "She refused you?" he asked, for the first time regarding his brother with some sympathy.

"Yes. I daresay that should make you happy, Peter. It certainly made Blair overjoyed."

"Mr. Blair was there?" asked Peter in surprise.

Glencairn smiled bitterly at his brother. "Yes, Blair was there. He did not seem to regard me as a proper candidate for son-in-law." He stared thoughtfully at his glass of brandy. "Nor did Athena seem to think I would be a desirable husband. I could not expect the author of 'On the Abolition of Titles of Nobility' to approve of an earl for a husband." He looked over at his brother and smiled at Peter's puzzled expression. "Athena Blair is the author of the infamous pamphlet, just as she wrote that preposterous 'My Lord Tyrant' letter."

"Indeed!" cried Peter. "She is a very talented lady." Glencairn cast a grim look at his brother for this remark. "I am sorry, Glencairn. Perhaps Miss Blair will change her mind. If she cares for you——"

The earl cut him off. "If she cares for me," he repeated thickly.

"But, Glencairn, I saw how she looked at you at the Lyttleton's ball. I was jealous. Indeed that is why I thought she might . . ."

"You thought she might succumb to my evil intentions?" said the earl ironically.

Peter nodded sheepishly. "I am sorry, Glencairn."

"Good God, don't be sorry. I must confess my intentions were not always so sterling toward Miss Blair. But then I realized that I wanted to marry her." The earl frowned ominously and then angrily threw his glass at the fireplace. It shattered noisily.

"Glencairn," said Peter, "You must talk to Miss Blair again. I'm sure that——"

"Dammit, Peter, it is over," snarled the earl. "I do not wish to hear the lady's name again. Now, please leave me."

Peter hesitated. He had never seen his brother in such a state. He decided that Glencairn must be desperately in love with Athena Blair. Peter got up from his chair and left the room, feeling genuinely sorry for his elder brother.

Glencairn was not the only person to feel wretched and dispirited that evening. Athena had returned to Robert's town house with her father. She had said little about the unfortunate episode on the carriage ride home. Baldwin, who had sensed her confusion and unhappiness, had tried to speak of other things.

Athena had had a hard time concentrating on what her father was saying, for she had been replaying her meeting with Glencairn in her mind. She could not forget how his face had looked when she had refused him. Although she had convinced herself that she had had no alternative, Athena's heart had told her something quite different.

Athena had chided herself to cease being ridiculous. How could she marry such a man—a peer of the realm who was an intimate of the Prince Regent—a man who was notorious for flaunting his wealth and privilege? Marriage to such a man would have been impossible. And yet, Athena had lingered on the memory of the earl's passionate kisses and how her body had responded in his embrace.

When they had arrived at Regent's Square, Athena was brought out of her daydreams. She tried hard not to look in the direction of the earl's residence as she made her way inside.

Both Baldwin and Athena were diverted from their thoughts of Glencairn by Jock Stewart's expression. "Sir and Miss Blair," he said, "the master has had bad news. He is in the drawing room. Ye must go tae him."

Exchanging a worried look, Athena and her father hurried to join Robert. They found him sitting on the sofa near the fireplace looking very grim. "Why, Robbie, whatever is the matter?" cried Athena.

"Och, Athena, Uncle, I fear I have had unfortunate news frae home." He handed her a folded piece of paper. " 'Tis a letter frae my mother. She says my father is verra ill."

"Oh, I am sorry, Robbie," said Athena.

"Yes, that is bad news," said Baldwin, shaking his head. "And what is my poor brother suffering from?"

Robert scratched his head. "My mother is nae exactly clear on that, Uncle. She says he has complaints of the heart, lungs, and liver. Och, and headaches, too." He shook his head. "It sounds verra bad, indeed." He folded up the letter and stuck it back in his coat pocket. "Mother says she wants me tae come back home and I do think I should."

"Yes, my boy," said Baldwin kindly. "It is your duty to go back home with your father so ill. It is a dashed shame, though. It seems you have scarcely arrived in town. But what will you do with the house?"

"Och, there is nae call tae worry about that, Uncle," said Robert. "I shall nae stay in Scotland. I'm too fond of London to be content in Kinlochie. While I am gone, ye must stay here."

Baldwin appeared relieved that he would not have to vacate the house on Regent's Square. He was rather enjoying his luxurious new surroundings.

"Oh, Robbie, we will miss you," said Athena, leaning over and kissing her cousin on the cheek.

He smiled. "Thank ye, Cousin. I shall miss ye both terribly. But wait!" Robert looked as if an idea had suddenly occurred to him. "Athena, ye may nae have tae be missing me at all."

Athena regarded him curiously. "Whatever do you mean, Robbie?"

Robert looked from Athena to Baldwin. "Could nae Athena come back tae Kinlochie with me, Uncle? I know my family would be pleased tae see her again. And it would be a comfort tae me to have company on the long journey."

"Go to Scotland?" said Athena. "I don't see how I could with my duties at the *Clarion Voice* and with looking after father."

"But I do not need looking after," said Baldwin. "I am not in my dotage. Indeed, I think it might be a good idea for you to accompany Robert."

"But the *Clarion Voice*," protested Athena.

"The *Voice* will carry on somehow," said Baldwin. "I have rather enjoyed doing my part again. Indeed, I have for too long allowed you to shoulder the burden. I do not mean that it will be easy to do without you, my dear, but I shall work very hard."

"But, Papa, I do not want to leave my duties. I should worry about you and the *Voice*. Kinlochie is very far away."

"It is not so far as that," said Baldwin. "It would do for you to have a rest and see your kindred in Scotland. Yes, I believe it would do you good to leave London, especially in light of this day's unfortunate episode."

Athena frowned. "So that is what this is about. You wish me to leave town."

Robert looked from his cousin to his uncle for an explanation of this cryptic remark. Baldwin knit his brow. "I do not wish you to leave me, Athena, but I cannot say that I would not rest easier knowing you are safe from that man's influence."

"What can ye mean?" said Robert. "What man and what unfortunate episode?"

Baldwin appeared solemn. "The Earl of Glencairn asked for her hand in marriage this afternoon."

Robert was dumbfounded. It took him a few moments to recover himself enough to make a reply to this extraordinary announcement. "He asked for your hand in marriage? The Earl of Glencairn?"

"She refused him, of course," said Baldwin. "The very idea that my daughter would marry such a man is absurd."

Robert seemed to consider the matter. "Och, he is a verra wealthy man."

Baldwin glared at his nephew. "And that is reason enough for Athena to marry him, is it?"

Seeing his uncle's expression, Robert prudently assured him that it was not. He looked at his cousin. "Why dinna ye come with me, Athena? It would be a welcome change for ye. We'd nae stay for long. As soon as my father is better, we'll be back in London and ye'll be back at your work."

"Yes," said Baldwin. "The *Voice* will be here when you return. Would you not like to get reacquainted with your Scottish homeland, my dear?"

Athena paused. Indeed, the idea of traveling to the Highlands held considerable appeal for her. Although her memories of Scotland were, for the most part, vague, Athena had often thought nostalgically of her childhood there. The reappearance of her cousin Robbie had rekindled her curiosity about the home of her ancestors. She thought of the Earl of Glencairn. She had wondered how she could continue to stay at Robert's town house. How could she remain there and not think of him living across the square? Perhaps it would be better to leave London, to go far away. "I think it would be a good idea for me to go, if you feel you could do without me, Papa."

"I shall make do," replied Baldwin. "My dear, I am only thinking of you. You should go to Scotland with your cousin," he urged forcefully. "It is for the best."

Athena hesitated. She then turned to look at her

cousin. "Well, Robbie, it appears you will have a traveling companion."

"Splendid!" he said. "We must leave as soon as possible. 'Tis a very long journey. Can ye be ready tae start tomorrow?"

"Tomorrow?" said Athena in surprise. "I could not possibly go so soon. I must finish my work at—"

Baldwin cut her off. "Nonsense. I shall see to everything at the *Clarion Voice*. You must not worry at all about that."

"Very well," she said. "I shall be ready."

Baldwin and Robert appeared delighted with Athena's decision. Now knowing that his cousin would accompany him, Robert seemed almost eager to go home. He started to talk about Kinlochie. Athena tried to listen, but her thoughts soon turned once again to the Earl of Glencairn.

17

PETER MONCRIEF walked down the busy streets of London, a new volume of Byron's *Childe Harold's Pilgrimage* tucked under his arm. A great admirer of the poet, Peter was eager to read his latest efforts. However, as he continued along through the crowd of people, Peter's thoughts were not on poetry, but on his brother.

It had been a week since the earl had told Peter about his wish to marry Athena Blair and how she had refused him. It had been unusual for Glencairn to confide in his younger brother about such a private matter, and Peter had hoped that their relationship might finally be getting on more equal footing.

Peter realized he had been quite wrong, of course. After their conversation about Athena, the earl had reverted to his role of elder brother, treating Peter as if he were a schoolboy. Peter suspected that Glencairn had regretted revealing his feelings for Athena to him, for when Peter tried to bring up the subject again, his brother had coldly dismissed it.

Peter shook his head. The earl had gone about his usual routine, staying out late drinking and carousing with the Prince Regent and his circle. One difference was that Glencairn was now beginning his drinking much earlier in the day. And although the earl had always been known for his temper, during the past week he had been in an especially foul mood, raging against any unfortunate servant who happened to be near him.

Peter himself had not been immune from Glencairn's ill humor, so he was trying to stay out of the earl's way as much as possible.

It was obvious to Peter that his brother had taken Athena Blair's rejection very badly. This only confirmed Peter's opinion that the earl was desperately in love with the lady. He worried that his brother would continue on the ruinous path he was on and wondered if there was anything he could do to help him.

Peter stopped at a street corner to wait for a rumbling wagon to go by. He was on his way to the office of the *Clarion Voice*. Peter had not been at the newspaper for more than a week. Although he had wanted to see Baldwin and Athena, he did not want to make a pest of himself. It also seemed prudent to allow some time to elapse since his brother's extraordinary proposal of marriage to Athena.

As he continued down the street, Peter glanced at the volume he was carrying. How exciting to think that one day soon his own poetry would be contained in such a book! It was hard to believe that he was now a published poet. The *Clarion Voice* has published three of his poems, and Miss Blair had assured him that two more would appear in the next issue. Peter had been quite thrilled at seeing his poems on the pages of the newspaper. Of course he had thought it wise to refrain from showing the newspaper to Glencairn.

Peter found himself wondering what Athena Blair thought of his brother. Perhaps he could go and talk to her and find out how she really felt. But no, he rejected the idea. One did not simply ask a lady about her feelings for a gentleman. And, indeed, if she did care for Glencairn, why did she not accept his proposal?

Peter was mulling this over as he arrived at the newspaper. Entering the office, he greeted the now familiar figure of Mr. Ashton. Ashton rose to meet him. He liked young Mr. Moncrief very much. "Good day, sir."

Peter smiled warmly. "Good day, Mr. Ashton."

"Have you brought more poetry, Mr. Moncrief?"

"None of my own," replied Peter. "This is Byron. His latest work. I am eager to read it."

"I am certain Mr. Blair would be interested in more of your work, sir," said Ashton. "He has already received some favorable comment on it from several literary gentlemen of his acquaintance."

Peter looked surprised. "He has?"

Ashton smiled at the young man's expression. "Indeed, Mr. Moncrief."

Peter looked like a small boy who had just been given a large, wrapped present. "Thank you, Mr. Ashton. That is most gratifying!"

Ashton was amused by Peter's excitement. "I am certain that Mr. Blair would be happy to tell you about the gentlemen's comments himself."

"Is he here?" said Peter, looking about the office.

"Yes, sir. He's in with the printers. He'll be out soon."

"And Miss Blair? Is she in?"

Ashton raised his eyebrows slightly. He had heard the gossip about Athena and the Earl of Glencairn. He wondered if the earl's young brother was also interested in Baldwin Blair's daughter. "I am sorry, Mr. Moncrief," he said, regarding Peter curiously. "But Miss Blair is not here."

Peter looked disappointed. "Do you know when she will be back?" he asked.

"I cannot say, Mr. Moncrief. Miss Blair has gone away. We do not expect her back for some time."

"Gone away?" asked Peter in dismay.

Ashton nodded. "She is visiting relations."

At that moment Baldwin Blair came into the office from the back print shop. He spotted Peter and immediately walked over toward him. "Moncrief, my boy! How good to see you again. I must tell you that your poetry has received praise from some very illustrious quarters."

Peter shook his head. "That is wonderful, sir. You and Miss Blair have been so kind to me—"

"Poppycock! Kindness had nothing to do with it. My daughter has an eye for talent, and she was quick to recognize it in you."

Peter blushed. "Mr. Ashton said that Miss Blair has gone to visit relatives."

"Yes, she has," said Baldwin. "We are on our own here trying to survive without her. It is not an easy task."

"Will Miss Blair be gone long, sir?"

Baldwin shrugged. "I cannot say. I miss her very much already."

"But where did she go?"

Baldwin hesitated, wondering if it was wise to reveal her whereabouts to Glencairn's brother. She was safely away in Scotland by now, so there seemed no harm in telling him. "She has gone to Scotland with her cousin Robert."

"Scotland!" cried Peter.

"My nephew received word that his father is quite ill. It was necessary for him to leave for Scotland at once. Athena agreed to accompany him. I must say, it's deuced difficult not having her about the place, but under the circumstances, I am glad she is gone."

Peter frowned. "I assume, Mr. Blair, that by 'under the circumstances,' you mean the matter of my brother asking for her hand in marriage."

"The less said about it the better, young man," said Baldwin. "I am fond of you, Moncrief. You are a talented poet and, from what I know of you, a good and decent fellow. You are not at all like your brother."

"But, Mr. Blair, I do think you have the wrong opinion of my brother," began Peter, but Baldwin cut him off.

"I understand that blood is thicker than water, Mr. Moncrief, and you feel obligated to defend Glencairn.

But I am afraid I will never change my estimation of
your brother. Do not speak of him to me, I pray you."

Knowing that it was useless to say anything further,
Peter dropped the subject. Baldwin turned the conversation to poetry and they spoke of Byron for a time. When
Peter finally took his leave of Baldwin, he felt discour-
aged. It seemed Baldwin was determined to despise
Glencairn. Peter admired Baldwin Blair tremendously,
and it was hard knowing that Baldwin so disliked his
brother.

While Peter stood in front of the *Clarion Voice* office,
reflecting upon the situation, two gentlemen approached.
Stopping before the door, one put his hand on the other's
arm. "Now remember what I say. Do not mention anything to him about Miss Blair."

Although Peter did not like to eavesdrop, Athena's
name made him strain his ears to hear what they said.
Taking up his book of Byron's poetry, he pretended to be
reading it. "Give me credit for some sense, Colling-
wood," said the other gentleman, who was quite rotund
and wore an exceptionally tall beaver hat. "But I find
your story quite absurd. Miss Blair in love with this
earl?"

His companion, who was tall and lanky, clucked his
tongue. "That is why Blair packed her off to the Scottish
wilderness—to get her away from him. He is afraid of
what she might do."

The rotund gentleman laughed. "Damned good idea,
I'd say. I wouldn't want the fellow hanging about my
daughter."

The lanky man nodded, and the two of them proceeded to enter the office of the *Clarion Voice*. Peter
watched them until they disappeared, and then clutching
his Byron under his arm, he hurried away.

Some time later, Peter rushed up the steps to his
brother's house. He handed his hat, gloves, and Byron to

the butler. "Is Lord Glencairn at home, Evans?" he asked.

"Yes, Master Peter," replied the servant. "His lordship is in the library." Evans was tempted to tell the young gentleman that his lordship was also in a vile humor and that he might want to avoid him, but he knew his place and kept silent.

Peter nodded and hurried off to the library. He found his brother sitting reading, a glass and a bottle on a table next to him.

"Good afternoon, Glencairn," said Peter.

His brother looked up at him. "Peter," he said gruffly. He reached over and took up his glass.

"What are you reading?" asked Peter curiously.

Glencairn held up a slim pamphlet. " 'On the Abolition of Titles of Nobility' by Miss Athena Blair."

"I thought you had read that already, Glencairn."

"I have," returned the earl, taking another drink. "It is damned nonsense, of course. If the lady believes what she has written, it is small wonder that she would hold me in contempt."

"Hold you in contempt? I doubt that, sir."

"Then you are a fool," said the earl. "And cease looking at me like that. I am not drunk!"

Peter wondered if he should take his leave. Deciding to stay, he sat down beside his brother. "I went to the *Clarion Voice* today," said Peter. "I saw Baldwin Blair." He paused. "I had hoped to see Miss Blair, but she was not there."

"Dammit, Peter," growled Glencairn, "Do not mention that lady's name."

"She has gone away," said Peter, ignoring the earl's warning looks, "to Scotland."

"Scotland?"

Peter nodded. "She went to Scotland with her cousin. You remember her cousin, Robert Blair?"

Glencairn scowled. "Of course I remember the blasted

fellow." He put his glass down. "She had gone to Scotland?"

"I heard her father 'packed her off' there to get her away from you," said Peter innocently.

The earl sat up sharply. "What the devil do you mean?"

"Oh, it was just something I heard from some friends of Baldwin Blair's. They seemed to think that Miss Blair was in love with you."

Glencairn slumped back in his chair. "Then they are misinformed."

Peter shook his head. "Don't you see, Glencairn? Why else would she have gone to Scotland? If she cared nothing for you, would she not have stayed? I daresay her father knows her feelings, and fears what she might do. Glencairn, can you not imagine how difficult it is for her? Would it be easy for the authoress of that pamphlet to admit that she is in love with an earl? How could she marry you with her father feeling the way he does about you?"

Glencairn stared at his brother. At first his expression seemed uncomprehending, but then he appeared thoughtful. "She has gone to Scotland?"

"Yes. Come, Glencairn, I daresay you won't help matters sitting about sulking. If you love Miss Blair, you must not give her up so easily."

The earl glowered at him. "And what do you suggest, Little Brother? That I follow the lady to Scotland?"

Peter smiled. "Precisely, Brother."

Glencairn looked at him a moment and then smiled. "You surprise me, Peter. So you think I should go to Scotland?"

Peter grew serious. "I do. I know that you are in love with Athena Blair, Glencairn. And I think she is in love with you." He stopped and considered his words. "You must go and find out, or you may live to regret it."

The earl looked at him for a long moment. "I very

likely will live to regret going to Scotland," he said, smiling again.

"Then you will go?" asked Peter.

"Yes, I will," said Glencairn firmly. "Perhaps it is about time I got a look at my Scottish estate. I have never heard from that damned factor of mine at Glencairn Castle. It will give me the opportunity to investigate Miss Blair's accusations." The earl got up from his chair. For the first time in a week, he seemed enthusiastic. "You will go with me, Peter?" he asked.

The young man regarded his brother in surprise. "You wish me to go with you, Glencairn?"

The earl clapped him on the back. "Damned right I do. Don't forget, this is all your idea, Peter."

Peter smiled at his brother but suddenly had a sinking feeling. He wondered if he had been colossally stupid to encourage his brother to race off to the Scottish Highlands to pursue Athena Blair. Despite his misgivings, Peter listened to Glencairn as he began to make plans for the journey.

18

"WE'RE almost there now, Athena," said Robert, peering out the window of the coach. "Nae much farther."

Athena smiled at her cousin. "I must say, Robbie, I shall be very glad to get there."

"Aye," replied Robert, nodding. He said nothing more, but continued to stare out the window. He was seated across from Athena. The dog Mally was curled up on the seat beside him, fast asleep. The other inhabitant of the coach was Robert's servant, Jock Stewart. Dour and solemn, he sat beside Athena, watching his young master with a serious expression.

It had been a long and arduous journey. They had come nearly six hundred miles—a good many of them over narrow, rutted roads. Oftentimes they had been jolted and tossed inside their vehicle, and they had endured days of rain and storms.

Athena, although growing exceedingly weary of traveling, had found the journey to be a great adventure. Crossing the breadth of England and then passing into Scotland, she had marveled at the changing landscape of Britain. Athena had observed many fascinating and beautiful sights along the way, all of them dutifully recorded in a journal she was keeping.

Having had little memory of Scotland, Athena could not help but be struck by the stark beauty of the Highlands with its mountains and shimmering lochs. In the early mornings the mountains would be shrouded in mist, and there would be an unearthly quality about the place. It was a land of rock and waterfalls and icy streams running down from the mountains.

"There is the house," said Robert.

Athena eagerly searched the landscape. "Yes, there it is! Just as I remember it." It was a gray stone structure standing in the narrow glen. Not large by the standards of country homes, it was nonetheless an impressive house. Built in the seventeenth century, it featured numerous chimneys and arched windows.

Catching sight of Ravenscroft, the ancestral home of the Blairs, stirred Athena's childhood memories. She had had many happy times there and remembered the house fondly. Her stay had been marred by the arguments between her father and her uncle. Ultimately the two men had nearly come to blows. Her uncle had ordered Baldwin from the house.

"I do hope that my uncle will not be too upset that I am here," said Athena.

"Why, he will be overjoyed tae see ya," said Robert. " 'Tis uncle he canna abide. He held nae ill toward ye or your mother. Nae, lass. My father often spoke of ye fondly."

Mally awakened as the carriage slowed. Lifting her shaggy head, the deerhound sniffed the air. Athena laughed to see the dog's expression as she sat up suddenly and directed her brown-eyed gaze out the window.

"Aye, ye're home, my lass," said Robert, putting his arm around the animal's neck. Mally's tail beat wildly against the leather carriage seat.

When the vehicle came to a stop, Robert opened the door. Mally jumped over him to descend first. Athena laughed again to see the deerhound race joyfully around in a large circle. "Ye daft creature," muttered Robert fondly. Reaching out to take Athena's hand, he assisted her down from the carriage.

The return of Master Robert caused general pandemonium among the servants at Ravenscroft. They hurried out to see the young gentleman. Robert greeted them with hearty handshakes.

"Is it Miss Athena?" cried one of the servants, a stout woman whose wispy gray hair was partially hidden by an untidy cap.

"Yes," said Athena, "and you are Annie Douglas!"

"Ye remembered me, miss!" returned the servant, quite delighted. "Ye were just a wee lass when we last saw ye, miss. And now what a beautiful lady ye've become."

Athena murmured her thanks. She remembered Annie well, for that worthy servant had had the challenging duty of caring for the Blair children.

"And Mother!" cried Robert as Athena's aunt rushed from the house. He ran to her, enfolding her into a tight embrace. Although Robert had never admitted the fact, he had not been immune to homesickness. He had missed his mother dreadfully.

Lady Blair was a tall, impressive-looking woman. One might have called her distinguished rather than attractive, for her features were a trifle too pronounced for beauty. Lady Blair's hair was red like Robert's, and her fair face was dotted with pale freckles.

Clearly overjoyed to see her son, it was some time before she was aware of Athena's presence. When she saw her niece, Lady Blair hurried to embrace her. "Athena Blair! How good it is tae see ye! Ye must come in. Ye must be hungry and tired after such a long journey."

The baroness led them inside. Athena noted that the house looked very much the same. It was furnished sparingly with no attempt at ostentation. A suit of armor stood in the entry hall, and on the walls hung various artifacts of warfare. Athena eyed the swords and shields that ornamented the entry hall with interest, remembering how as a child she had been rather intimidated by them. Lady Blair escorted them into the drawing room, a rather dismal place decorated with ancestral portraits and a faded tapestry.

"But father?" said Robert. "How is he?"

"Och, he is much improved, Robbie." Athena was very relieved to hear this. She had feared that they would find her uncle on his deathbed.

"I should like tae go tae him," said Robert.

"Robert." A masculine voice made Robert and Athena turn around. There stood a middle-aged man. Tall and gaunt like his son, Lord Blair surveyed them with a sour expression on his face. He did not look at all ill. Athena regarded her uncle curiously. When she was a child, she had always thought there was no resemblance whatsoever between her uncle and father. Now she detected an unmistakable similarity of features.

"Father!" said Robert. "I canna say how glad I am tae see ye looking sae well. I thank Providence for your recovery."

" 'Twas nae sae serious as we thought. Your mother should nae have bothered ye. I didna wish her tae write tae ye. I know that ye didna wish tae leave London. By the look of ye, ye've become an Englishman."

Athena noted that her uncle was regarding Robert's attire with disapproval. Wearing one of his fashionable suits, Robert looked very different than he had appeared when first arriving in London. Lord Blair was dressed in a faded coat and knee breeches that looked as if they had been made in the last century. Noting her uncle's frown, Athena stepped in. "Uncle, I cannot say how glad I am to see that you are well. Robert and I were so worried."

The baron's expression softened as he looked at his niece. "Athena, ye are grown up and verra beautiful. I am glad tae see ye, lass." Athena went to her uncle and kissed him on the cheek. This seemed to improve his humor. "Ye must be tired, lass. Do sit down."

Athena and Robert sat down with Lord and Lady

Blair. Athena sensed that Robert was rather put out to find his father completely well. That was certainly understandable considering the great trouble and expense her cousin had taken to rush to his father's bedside.

Lady Blair looked from her husband to her son. It was her constant sorrow that the two men in her life did not get on very well. Of course the baron was a difficult man. Stern and unyielding, he had never shown his son any affection. Her ladyship had not been surprised that Robert had flown off at first opportunity.

While Robert and his father sat rather sullenly, Lady Blair asked about the journey. Athena was happy to discuss it, and they talked well into the afternoon.

When Athena awakened the next morning, the sun was streaming into her room. After a number of days of gloomy overcast skies, the bright sunlight was very welcome. Rising from her bed, she went to the window. The room was chilly and Athena shivered. How odd to think that she was in Scotland, she thought, surveying the Highland landscape. The hills looked purple in the early morning light, and she could see the mountains beyond them. The tallest of them she knew to be Ben Nevis. An enormous block of red and gray granite, it looked imposing in the distance.

It was a beautiful country, Athena decided, but at the same time harsh and unforgiving much like her uncle. She frowned at the thought of Lord Blair. He had remained very dour throughout the rest of the afternoon and at dinner. Athena had been so exhausted that she had been glad to retire to her room early. She had slept very well despite her lumpy and uncomfortable bed.

Continuing to gaze at the distant mountain, Athena found herself thinking about Glencairn. She had thought of him often throughout the days of the journey. The lengthy ride had given one too much opportunity for reflection.

Turning away from the window, she focused her attention on getting dressed. A maid had unpacked her limited belongings, and she examined the dresses now hanging in her wardrobe. After deciding upon a somber gray muslin dress as suitable, she sat down at the dressing table and began to brush her thick auburn hair.

Breakfast that morning was not the joyful occasion one might have expected on the first day after the return of the only son and heir. Lord Blair seemed in a particularly grim mood. He said little, concentrating only on his food. Athena's aunt was much more cheerful. Athena kept the conversation going by asking about Robert's sisters and their families. Lady Blair was only too happy to talk about her daughters and grandchildren, although the baron seemed completely indifferent to what was being said.

When breakfast was finished, Robert and Athena set off on a walk. The deerhound, Mally, was delighted to accompany them. She ran on ahead, stopping now and again to turn and look at them as if wondering why they were so slow. Then she would dash off into the bracken searching for rabbits.

"And now can ye see why I was glad tae be gone frae here, Athena?" said Robert. "Ye see how my father is. I dinna know how long we will be able tae tolerate each other's company. Why can he nae be more like Uncle?"

Athena did not know what to say. She did not think Lord Blair a very agreeable man. She could see why her father and he had come to the parting of the ways. "Your mother is so glad to see you," said Athena. "And the servants."

"Aye," said Robert, " 'Tis good tae see Mother. And 'twill be good tae see my sisters. I have missed them." They walked on for a few moments. "I am sorry for bringing ye all this way, Athena. 'Twas utterly ridiculous."

"I am glad I came, Robbie," said Athena, completely sincere. She found that she was happy to be there. In-

deed, she had worried that she would be concerned
about the *Clarion Voice*. Yet after the first few days of
travel, she had realized that the newspaper would go on
very well without her. It was good to not have to worry
about it for a change. "I do think it very beautiful here."

"Beautiful?" said Robbie. " 'Tis a barren wasteland
tae me. I shall be glad tae return tae London."

Athena nodded thoughtfully. In truth she was in no
hurry to return to town. The Highlands seemed to be ex-
erting a strong influence on her. Everything seemed so
familiar. It was odd, but she sensed that she belonged
there somehow. Perhaps it was the knowledge that so
many of her ancestors had lived in these glens for generations.

They walked along for more than an hour, climbing
from the glen to a higher elevation. Robert had said there
was a splendid view of the surrounding area a short distance ahead where an old woman lived. Her name was
Aggie MacDonald, and Robert was fond of going to visit
her.

The terrain grew rather rough, the ground hard and
rocky, but Athena did not mind in the least. The air was
brisk and cool and the sky clear save for a lingering mist
that hung at the base of the mountains.

Finally they reached their destination, the modest
stone cottage of Aggie MacDonald. "Aggie!" shouted
Robert. "Are ye home?"

His voice brought an elderly woman dressed in a
ragged dress and shawl quickly to the door. "Master
Robert!" she cried, smiling broadly to reveal only two or
three teeth left in the front of her mouth.

"Aggie MacDonald."

The woman appeared delighted to see Robert. She
grinned at Mally who had run up to her and now stood
wagging her tail happily. "And the Lady Mally," said the
woman. "What a bonnie lass ye are."

"Athena, do ye remember Aggie MacDonald?"

"I am not sure," said Athena uncertainly.

"But I remember ye, miss," said Aggie. "Ye are Master Baldwin's lass. How is your father?"

"Very well, Mrs. MacDonald."

"I canna believe I am seeing ye, Master Robert. I thought ye had gone tae live among the English."

"I had indeed, Aggie, but I have come back for a time. I'll nae stay for long though."

This remark seemed to disturb Aggie. "Ye should stay here, sir. Ye are the laird's son. This is your place."

Athena glanced over at her cousin and suppressed a smile. Robert did not seem at all irked by the remark. He only grinned. "If ye could but see London, Aggie, ye'd wish tae come back with me! Perhaps I'll take ye!"

Aggie burst into shrill laughter. "Imagine me in London town!"

Athena smiled and looked out at the panorama stretched out before her. It was a splendid view. Her eyes alighted on a large structure in the distance, a grim-looking building of gray granite. It loomed up alongside the water of the narrow loch that ran through the glen. "Look, there is a castle! I cannot remember seeing it as a child."

" 'Tis Glencairn Castle, miss."

"Glencairn Castle?" Athena repeated the words in a strange voice.

"The home of the evil laird of Glencairn," said Aggie darkly. " 'Tis my ill luck tae have him for my landlord."

"But does my uncle's land not extend this far?" said Athena.

"Nae, Cousin," said Robert. "We have been on Glencairn's land for some time."

"Glencairn," said Aggie, repeating the name distastefully. "Nae one has ever caused sae misery in the Highlands, forcing all his people frae his lands. A curse be on his head and on his descendants."

The old woman spoke with such venom that Athena

was taken aback. "Come, now, Aggie," said Robert, noting his cousin's reaction to this pronouncement. "I have met Glencairn in London and, while he is hardly an admirable fellow, I daresay he canna be as evil as that."

"All I know, sir, is what he has done. Ye may see for yourself." She gestured toward the distance. "Can ye nae see the ruin there on the hill? 'Twas once the home of a family. There are many more tae be found. All the folk are gone. There's nought but sheep and Aggie MacDonald. And now Glencairn's factor has said I must go as well. But as long as there is breath in my body, I'll nae leave here."

Athena scowled, remembering the earl coming into the office for the first time, his face filled with indignation. "I know the earl would not send you away. I shall write to his factor and tell him so."

" 'Twill do nae good, miss. Ferguson will nae listen tae anyone."

"We will see," said Athena.

"But dinna talk of such things any more," said Aggie. "Come in. I must hear all about London."

Only too happy to oblige, Robert escorted his cousin inside.

19

THE Earl of Glencairn had set off for Scotland in his traveling coach, a commodious vehicle that made the long journey as comfortable as possible. Pulled by six horses, the coach's doors were emblazoned with the earl's coat of arms. The splendid equipage never failed to attract attention. As it progressed northward, people would pause to gape at it, wondering what illustrious personage was inside.

No matter where the vehicle stopped, ostlers and proprietors of inns were beside themselves with glee. Not enough could be done for his lordship. His every request was greeted as if it had come from on high.

Although long accustomed to this kind of treatment, Glencairn found himself regarding the obsequiousness of others with cynicism. Surely there was something absurd and faintly distasteful about it.

Accompanying the earl on his long journey was his brother, Peter, and Glencairn's valet. While Peter had been eager to go, his lordship's valet regarded the idea of going to Scotland with horror. A Londoner, the servant thought Scotland was a savage place inhabited by a race of barbarians. Indeed, the valet had considered giving his notice rather than accompany his master to such a place. Finally he had decided to go, but with every mile they went, he wondered if he had made a terrible mistake.

To make matters worse, the earl seemed in a bad temper all the time, growling at his valet and Peter at the least provocation. Peter Moncrief endured his brother's ill humor with admirable stoicism. He knew that the earl was upset about Athena, and he was glad to think that his lordship's testiness meant that he remained steadfast in his affections. Peter found he was enjoying the trip to Scotland despite the uncomfortable inns and unpalatable food. He was eager to see Scotland for he had long thought of going there to visit the ancient Moncrief lands.

As the great coach rumbled along, Peter had so many ideas for poems that he could scarcely get them all down. His pencil scribbled furiously much to the annoyance of his brother. "Must you keep writing?" Glencairn would demand. Peter would stop for a time, only to continue as soon as the earl appeared distracted. Fortunately for the young poet, Glencairn appeared distracted a good deal of the time.

When they reached western Scotland, Peter could not help but feel excited. The land was beautiful and so very different. As they continued north, he was nearly overcome by the grandeur of the Highland lochs and mountains. Although trying to appear indifferent, the earl could not help but be impressed by the scenery appearing in the carriage window. He seemed scornful of Peter's gushing evaluation of what he saw, but Glencairn did not really disagree with his brother.

The earl had never been to Scotland, nor had he ever thought he had wanted to go there. Indeed, his English friends had little regard for the northern country. Glencairn had never considered himself as Scottish despite his father's family being one of the oldest in Scotland. He had always been glad that his mother was English since that seemed to give him increased respectability in society's circles.

When they neared the earl's ancestral lands, the coach stopped in a village so that the driver could get directions to Glencairn Castle. Taking the opportunity to stretch his legs, Glencairn jumped down from the coach. It was a bleak, colorless place with few inhabitants. Some of the villagers stood nearby. The earl glanced at them, noting their pitiful clothes and wan faces. A gaunt man stared resentfully at him.

Glencairn climbed back into the carriage, strangely disturbed. Since they had come north, he had seen sobering, relentless poverty wherever they had stopped. It was not that he was a stranger to the poor. In London one could scarcely travel about as much as he did without seeing ragged beggars and homeless urchins. One grew hardened to such things. Yet the faces of the wretched Highlanders seemed to affect the earl more than he thought possible.

"Did you see that man?" said Peter as his brother seated himself in the coach. "The poor fellow. He must have a very sad life."

"The lives of peasants do not concern me," said Glencairn, hiding his true feelings with a show of hard-heartedness.

Peter sighed. The carriage continued on and the village was left behind. Peter looked out the window and said nothing further.

The earl's first sight of Glencairn Castle filled him with a strange feeling. It was as if he could remember seeing the looming stone castle some time in his distant past. Of course Glencairn knew that was ridiculous. He had never been to Scotland before, and he had never seen Glencairn Castle. He stared at it through the carriage window. Perhaps he had seen a picture of it. Yes, he could vaguely remember seeing a lithograph of the castle. When he was a boy, it had hung on the wall of the library in their house in Sussex. Someone must have removed it, for he had not seen it in ages.

The castle was a forbidding fortress of gray stones situated at the edge of a long narrow loch. Those with a love of the medieval past might have thought it charming, but Glencairn could see nothing to like in the cold granite with its turrets and narrow windows.

"Oh, Glencairn!" cried Peter. "Is it not wonderful?" Peter was imagining knights on chargers and golden-haired maidens waving to their lovers from the castle's towers.

"Wonderful?" said Glencairn distastefully. "It is nothing but a damned ruin. I will not be surprised if it is uninhabitable."

The coach pulled into an overgrown drive that led to the front doors of the castle. When the vehicle came to a stop, the driver jumped down to open the door. Glencairn stepped out and approached the entrance of his castle. Peter hastened to follow him. The long-suffering valet eyed the medieval fortress with even more disfavor than did his master and cursed himself for not giving notice in London.

When the earl reached the door, he stood for a moment examining the lion-headed knocker affixed to the massive wooden door. He then rapped impatiently on the door with the heavy brass fixture. When the door did not open, he knocked again, this time impatiently hitting it with his walking stick. Still there was no answer. "God in heaven," muttered the earl. "Are they deaf?"

"What is the racket about!" The door creaked open to reveal a short, wiry man with a red face and gray hair. He viewed the newcomers with infuriating surliness.

Glencairn shoved him aside and entered the house. "Where is Mrs. Cameron?" he demanded.

The man who had opened the door regarded the earl in bewilderment. He had no idea who this English gentleman might be. What business could the man have at Glencairn Castle? "And who might ye be, sir?" the man said churlishly.

"I am Glencairn." The earl said these words with such

aristocratic hauteur that the man was completely taken aback.

He bowed low. "I beg your lordship's pardon. I am Gordon, your lordship's butler. Do come in, my lord. I shall fetch Mrs. Cameron at once. Do come in tae the drawing room."

The earl and Peter followed Gordon while his lordship's valet turned his attention to the unloading of his master's luggage. Glencairn sniffed distastefully as he walked through the entry hall. Glencairn Castle was damp, dark, and musty.

As they entered the vast, drafty drawing room, the earl suspected that the room's furnishings dated from the Middle Ages as well. There was a massive table that was stained and nicked and several tall armchairs with high straight backs. The chairs were upholstered in velvet so faded now that the color of it was indistinguishable. On the walls were swords, spears, and the heads of game animals so moth-eaten they appeared ghoulish.

Peter, however, viewed the dingy room with appreciation. The castle seemed fabulously romantic to him despite its dilapidated condition. His imagination was such that it was easy to envision his medieval ancestors there.

A woman wearing a black dress and white cap entered the room. About sixty years of age, she was a large, stout woman with gray hair and unsmiling countenance. She made a low curtsy to the earl. "I am Mrs. Cameron, my lord," she said. " 'Tis an unexpected honor having your lordship at Glencairn Castle."

The earl looked at his housekeeper. He had never met the woman before although he had had some correspondence with her. He had not been pleased with the condition of his property. The dust on the drawing-room table appeared to have accumulated over many months. Cobwebs clung to the heavy draperies, and the windows were so grimy that a gray film made it appear as if there was a perpetual fog.

"If your lordship had let me know that ye were coming, I might have prepared things properly," said the housekeeper.

"I suggest you begin to prepare things now," said the earl sharply. "Start by having this room cleaned. And my brother and I will expect decent bedchambers. And an edible supper. I'll not tolerate slovenly housekeeping, Mrs. Cameron. You will be seeking another position, if you do not have things in order."

Mrs. Cameron assured the earl that she would see to everything. When Glencairn dismissed her, she curtsyed again and then retreated hastily from the room. "Poor old girl," said Peter, rather amused by the situation. "She's terrified of you, Glencairn."

"As well she should be," muttered the earl. "Look at this place. It is disgusting. I expect all my homes to be in instant readiness."

"But it has been thirty years since an Earl of Glencairn visited here. I daresay that is a very long time to keep things in instant readiness. What a terrible shock to find the laird of Glencairn appearing without a bit of warning."

Glencairn shrugged. His brother did have a point. Of course the castle could be expected to be in woeful condition. It had been ignored all these years both by his lordship's father and then by Glencairn himself. "Come, Glencairn, let us allow Mrs. Cameron some time for her preparations. I should like to walk about the area."

"I should think she would need several weeks," said the earl. "Very well, I have no desire to stay in here."

Outside the castle the air was cool, but the sun had broken through the clouds, and the bright sunlight was beginning to dispel some of the gloom of the place. The brothers walked to the loch. "Is it not beautiful, Glencairn? And the air is so clear! Were you not tired of the smoke and grime of London?"

"We will not escape smoke and grime here by the look

of this place," said the earl, casting a glance at the huge castle edifice. Yet even as he said these words, Glencairn seemed less ill-humored. The area around the castle was spectacularly beautiful. The hills stretched purple in the distance. The loch's clear water reflected the blue sky. The earl realized with some surprise that he felt a strange affinity for the place. Once again he had a feeling that it was somehow familiar. As they walked along the edge of the water, the brothers grew silent. They continued on without speaking, each lost in his own thoughts.

By the time Glencairn and Peter returned to the castle, the servants had made some headway in the drawing room. It had been dusted and swept, and the worst of the cobwebs had been cleared away. Supper was served at six o'clock. While hardly a culinary delight, the meal featured some decent mutton so Glencairn was somewhat placated. He and Peter sat in the cavernous dining hall for a long time, talking and drinking. The earl's mood was much improved once he had eaten, and Peter was thoroughly enjoying himself.

They returned early to their hastily prepared bedchambers. The earl's room was spartan in its furnishings. There was a bulky oaken wardrobe and an ancient canopied bed with worn, moth-eaten curtains. A threadbare rug covered a small portion of the cold stone floor.

When Glencairn finally lay under the rather musty bedclothes, he found himself thinking about Athena Blair. This was not unusual since that young lady was hardly ever far from his thoughts. After deciding that he would seek her out as soon as possible the next day, the exhausted earl fell into a deep sleep.

When he awoke in the morning, he was surprised that he had slept so well. The earl's valet greeted him warily, but was soon reassured by his master's unexpected good humor. The worthy servant delighted Glencairn by announcing that he had arranged baths for the earl and Peter. Considering the primitive state of the accommodations at the castle, this was a happy surprise to the earl.

Once bathed and dressed in his fine clothes, his lordship joined Peter in the drawing room. Peter appeared rested and cheerful. After eating a hearty breakfast, the earl's mood was so good that he astonished Mrs. Cameron by complimenting her on the food and on the much improved state of the castle. He gave her leave to hire additional servants to assist with the cleaning and necessary repairs to the living quarters.

Mrs. Cameron then informed the earl that his factor, Ferguson, was there. Glencairn was eager to see the man. He had written to him weeks ago after his first meeting with Athena, but had received no response before leaving London.

The factor came into the drawing room where the earl and Peter were sitting. Glencairn eyed him appraisingly. He was a big, burly man with sandy hair and beard and a pale complexion. After bowing to the earl, Ferguson made a short speech about how pleased he was to hear that his lordship had come to Scotland. Glencairn took an instant dislike to the man. There was something slippery and insincere about him, and he had a way of smiling nervously after he made a remark that the earl found very irritating.

Glencairn did not ask him to be seated. "Did you receive my letter, Ferguson?" said Glencairn. "What is this matter of these clearances?"

"Indeed, my lord. I wrote to your lordship more than a year ago informing you about that. Your solicitor wrote me frae London saying I had your authority tae proceed. A number of tenants have been removed, my lord. But they were scarcely able to make a living here. 'Twas a kindness tae have them leave. They'll do better elsewhere."

Glencairn glared. "Your concern for their welfare is touching," he said sarcastically. "You are not to do anything further with this until I have looked into the matter. Is that understood, Ferguson?" The factor nodded vigorously. The earl waved him away and Ferguson took his leave. The earl looked thoughtful. He had never been overly concerned about his tenants on any of his estates. Having always left the management of his properties to others, he had never thought much about abuses that might have been carried out in his name. He imagined Athena's disapproving gaze.

Noting his brother's expression, Peter felt it wise to make no comments about Ferguson. "So what will we do now, Glencairn? Will you call on the Blairs?"

The earl nodded. "We must get directions from Gordon."

"I daresay Miss Blair will be very surprised to see you," said Peter.

"Yes," said Glencairn, nodding again.

The earl had brought two of his best saddle horses with him. He and Peter mounted the horses and started off. Peter tried to keep up a conversation, but after a time, he gave up. His brother's good mood had vanished, and the earl seemed to prefer his own thoughts.

The village of Kinlochie was on the way to the Blair estate. When the two horsemen entered it, they excited much interest among the inhabitants. Kinlochie was a small village of gray stone houses and shops lining narrow streets. Visitors considered it a quaint, picturesque place, but Glencairn seemed immune to its charm. As they rode through the street, he was more aware of the people on the street. He knew that they were staring at him. Indeed, that was understandable, for doubtlessly well-dressed strangers on blooded horses were not commonplace.

Glencairn would have been surprised to know that the villagers watching him were well aware of his identity.

A servant had come from Glencairn Castle early that morning. He had delivered the astounding news that the laird of Glencairn and his brother had come from England. Most who heard about it were thunderstruck, for no one had ever thought that the earl would return to Scotland. It had been general knowledge that he had abandoned his Scottish heritage, preferring to be English.

Of the onlookers who viewed the earl and Peter's progress along the street, one stared at him with undisguised hatred. Angus MacPherson was a grim young man who looked far older than his twenty-six years. His face was weatherbeaten and his hands were callused from years of hard work.

MacPherson had been a tenant on Glencairn's land, eking out a tenuous existence on a farm. The rocky soil had long been exhausted, and life had been hard for MacPherson and his wife and young children. MacPherson had been one of the farmers forced from the land. Ferguson and his men had tossed their meager belongings from their cottage and had taken their only cow. Having had no place to go, they had slept in sheds and had had very little to eat. MacPherson's wife had not been robust, and she had soon taken ill. She had died, leaving MacPherson with three small children and a consuming hatred for Ferguson and his master, the Earl of Glencairn.

His lordship had not seen MacPherson, and he was completely unaware that any person in the village was harboring black thoughts about him. He and Peter continued on, passing through the village and into the countryside beyond it.

"Did you not think Kinlochie a fine village?" said Peter.

"What?" said the earl. "I thought it had little to commend it."

"I liked it," said Peter. "Indeed, I have liked everything I have seen here. How I love Scotland!"

Glencairn looked over at his brother, frowning at the young man's exuberance. Turning his attention to the road ahead of him, he saw a horse and trap approaching. There were two ladies in the vehicle. "Good God!" said the earl. "I think that is Athena!"

Peter strained his eyes, but could not recognize anyone at such a distance. The earl kicked his horse into a gallop and hurried to meet the trap.

Athena, who was indeed in the vehicle, seated beside her aunt, had not thought much of seeing two riders approaching on the road. When one of them began to run toward them, she regarded him in surprise. "Who is that?" said Lady Blair. She was driving the trap, keeping her horse to a decorous walk.

When she recognized Glencairn, Athena was astounded. She was too stunned to speak. "What is it, my dear?" said the baroness. "Do you know him?"

The earl pulled his horse up sharply as it came alongside the trap. "Athena!" he said.

"Glencairn!" Stopping her horse, Lady Blair looked from Glencairn to her niece with a questioning look. Athena stared at the earl for a moment, then somehow regained her composure. "Aunt, this is Lord Glencairn." By now Peter had come up to join then. "And his brother, Mr. Peter Moncrief. Gentlemen, may I present my aunt, Lady Blair?"

Both of the men tipped their hats politely. "Lady Blair," said the earl.

Peter smiled brightly, "Your servant, ma'am," he said.

"What are you doing here, my lord?" said Athena.

"Can you not guess the answer to that question, Miss Blair?" said Glencairn, fastening his eyes upon hers.

Athena stared at him. It was utterly incredible that he would be there. It had never occurred to her that he would follow her to Scotland.

A discerning woman, it did not take Athena's aunt long to figure out that there was something between her

niece and the gentleman before her. The Earl of Glencairn and Athena! The baroness thought this a most interesting piece of news. When her niece and the earl
seemed oblivious to anyone else's presence, Lady Blair
felt it necessary to remind them that she was there, too.
"Lord Glencairn, I must say that this is a great surprise.
Where ye on your way tae Ravenscroft?"

"I was, madam," returned the earl, reluctantly tearing
his eyes from Athena.

"Then we must go back at once," said Lady Blair.
"My husband will be very glad tae meet ye, gentlemen.
Do come back with us."

"But did you not have to go to the village, Aunt?" said
Athena rather lamely.

"Och, nae, child. I might get that bit of ribbon another
time. Come, gentlemen. 'Tis not very far to Ravenscroft."

The horsemen moved their mounts so that her ladyship could maneuver the trap around. Soon they were
headed back to the Blair estate. Glencairn and Peter rode
alongside.

Athena stole a glance at the earl, who fortunately was
looking ahead and not at her. Her mind was reeling from
the shock of seeing him again, and she was plunged into
a state of confusion. She had been at Ravenscroft for
more than a week, and she had walked and ridden about
the area. She had seen much sad evidence of the clearances, of cottages deserted or burned. She had spoken
with a number of people, and all had been uniform in
their condemnation of Glencairn. Believing the earl far
away in London, it had been possible to think the worst
of him.

Now with him beside her again, her feelings for him
were so easily rekindled. Athena glanced over at him.
Glencairn looked very much the arrogant lord seated on
his splendid horse and wearing his fine clothes. There
was a haughtiness in his bearing that came from a life-
time of aristocratic privilege. Again she told herself that

it was impossible that she should love him, and again she realized that she could not help it.

The Ravenscroft servants were very much surprised to see their mistress and her niece return so quickly after setting out. There were even more surprised to see the elegantly dressed gentlemen accompanying them. Even more astonished was Robert, who nearly gasped to see who was accompanying his mother and cousin. Robert had looked out the drawing-room window at the sound of the horses.

Lady Blair, Athena, and the gentlemen entered the drawing room. The ladies took off their bonnets and placed them on the table. "Robert, can ye imagine?" said Lady Blair. "The Earl of Glencairn and his brother, Mr. Moncrief, are here in Scotland! Athena has told me ye met them in London. I have sent Brown for your father. He will be very eager to meet these gentlemen. Now let us all sit down."

The earl appeared very gracious. On his best behavior, he talked politely to Lady Blair, telling her about Glencairn Castle and assuring her that he was very fond of Scotland already. Peter smiled at his brother's remarks and charmed the baroness by his copious praise of the area's beauty.

Athena said very little, for she was still too taken aback at finding Glencairn there. When Lord Blair entered the drawing room, the earl and Peter rose to greet him. While Athena might have thought that her uncle would disapprove of Glencairn, he seemed more than pleased to have him as a guest. Although Lord Blair did not like the fact that the Earl of Glencairn seemed a good deal too English, he was not indifferent to the honor of having a man of his consequence in his drawing room.

A very traditional man, Lord Blair set great store by rank. He was flattered that the Earl of Glencairn appeared so civil. He was also favorably impressed at the idea that the earl had finally come to Scotland.

Lady Blair spent much of her time watching Glencairn and her niece. Athena was uncharacteristically reticent, but the baroness sensed that she was not at all indifferent to the earl. The baron seemed pleased enough with his guests to show them his most prized possession, a lock of Prince Charles Edward Stuart's hair in a gold locket. Glencairn could not resist raising an eyebrow in Athena's direction after beholding this sacred relic.

Finally Lady Blair began to grow worried that her niece had had no opportunity to speak to the earl. "Why don't ye show the gentlemen the garden, Athena?" she said. "We will be down in just a moment."

Glencairn directed a grateful smile at his hostess and offered Athena his arm. Peter followed them, but once outside, he held back allowing them to speak privately. "Athena," said Glencairn, "I have so wanted to talk to you."

Athena looked down. "You should not have come."

"Dash it, how could I have stayed in London with you here? I cannot live without you."

"That is ridiculous," said Athena.

"I know it is ridiculous," returned the earl, "but it is nonetheless true."

"My lord, you know it is impossible."

"Indeed, I know nothing of the kind."

She shook her head. "I was trying very hard to dislike you. I thought I had succeeded. It is true about the clearances. I have seen so much unhappiness since coming here. There are many who hate you here, my lord."

"I care only what you think of me," said Glencairn, placing a hand on her arm.

"But what of the others?"

"Damn it," said the earl. "How can I speak of others with you beside me? I will concern myself with others later."

"But you must concern yourself with them now. What is to be done? How will you undo all the damage of your loathsome factor? Yes, I have heard stories about him that are quite horrible. Everyone believes he does your bidding. I have visited an old woman who fears that your men will evict her. I wrote to your Mr. Ferguson about the matter, and he did not favor me with a reply."

"It appears he is not a man for correspondence. But have no fear, I have told him to desist from any such behavior. I promise I shall look into this." Glencairn did not want to talk about his factor, nor did he want to discuss such unpleasant subjects as the miserable Highland farmers. He wanted to hold her in his arms once again. He wanted to hear her say that she loved him. "Athena," he said, "marry me."

"Oh, Glencairn, I cannot. I thought you understood that in London. You must know that I could never marry the Earl of Glencairn."

The earl regarded her in frustration. "You are talking nonsense. You will marry me."

"I cannot," said Athena.

"Blast," said the earl. "Do you think your absurd notions about the nobility are more important than your own happiness?"

"They are not absurd!" said Athena, suddenly angry. She pulled her arm from him and walked quickly away. Peter who had been staying back at a discreet distance, appeared alarmed at his brother's expression. Clearly his reunion with Miss Blair had not gone according to plan. Lord and Lady Blair and Robert came into the garden at that moment. Athena, trying very hard to appear as if nothing was the matter, greeted them and began speaking about the flowers.

20

THE reunion with Athena at Ravenscroft put the Earl of Glencairn in a decidedly bad temper. Angry and frustrated by Athena's refusal of him, the earl spent much of the remainder of the day holed up in the castle's gloomy drawing room.

Peter had attempted to find out what had occurred between his brother and Athena, but the earl had been sullen and uncommunicative. Finally giving up, Peter had ventured out on a long solitary walk. On his return he had retreated to his room to write several lyrical verses on the beauty of the Highlands.

The following morning Peter went downstairs to find a harried-looking Mrs. Cameron supervising a motley group of servants cleaning the main hallway of the castle. "Och, Master Peter," she said. "Will ye be wanting your breakfast now?"

"Oh, there is no hurry, Mrs. Cameron. Is Lord Glencairn up yet?"

The housekeeper shook her head. "Nae, sir. His lordship is still abed." As she spoke, Mrs. Cameron thought to herself that she hoped his lordship stayed abed for some time. She was still uncertain what to make of her master and his mercurial moods.

Fortunately for the housekeeper it was quite late when the earl finally did appear. Peter, who had already had a delicious breakfast and an invigorating walk along the scenic loch, was comfortably settled with a book in the library when Glencairn walked into the room. "Good morning, Glencairn," said Peter, setting aside the book.

"Good morning."

"It is a wonderful day. I had a splendid walk."

The earl scowled. "I am gratified that at least one of us is enjoying this accursed place."

"Oh, come, Glencairn. Do not pretend that you detest it here. After all, you told Lady Blair—"

"Dammit, Peter," growled the earl, "I do not wish to hear of the Blairs."

"And one Blair in particular?" asked Peter.

Glencairn eyed him disapprovingly. "I caution you, Peter, your impudence begins to go too far."

Peter hesitated, but continued despite the warning look on his brother's face. "I know your interview with Athena did not go as you had hoped yesterday—"

"That, dear Brother, is a monumental understatement," said the earl sardonically.

"But you must not give up," insisted Peter. "I saw how she looked at you. Athena is in love with you!"

"She refuses to marry me," said Glencairn. "All she could talk of was my poor mistreated tenants and how I must do something about them."

"I daresay she is right," said Peter. "You must look into the matter yourself. After all, you are the laird of Glencairn. It is your responsibility."

The earl regarded Peter silently for a moment. "It appears I am forever to be plagued by 'my responsibility'," he said finally. "Very well, Peter. I shall ride out now and investigate my property. Do you wish to accompany me?" Peter nodded.

The two brothers made their way to the stables. After mounting their horses, they headed across the moorland that surrounded Glencairn Castle.

As they rode along, Glencairn appeared deep in thought. Peter, well aware that Athena Blair was the cause of his brother's pensive mood, tactfully remained silent.

They had ridden a short distance when they came upon a small, dilapidated cottage sitting isolated on the barren moor. Weeds had grown up around the door of the cottage, making it appear even more forlorn.

Dismounting from his horse, Glencairn walked up to the cottage and peered inside the window. Although it was dark inside, he could dimly make out a fireplace at one end of the small abode. Glencairn turned to Peter. "It seems to be uninhabited," he said as he made his way over to the door.

Entering the cottage, the earl glanced around him. The small dwelling was damp and depressing. He noticed there were several chinks in the stone walls that let in some light. Glencairn imagined the gaps in the walls also let in a fair amount of cold during the harsh Highland winter.

The earl took one last look around the place and then retraced his steps to the door. Peter quickly followed after him. Although the deserted cottage had looked quite picturesque to him as they had approached it, the small dingy room bespoke the meager existence of its former inhabitants. As he rode away, Peter thought about the unfortunate people who had resided in the cottage and wondered what had become of them. He would have been surprised to know that his unsentimental brother was thinking much the same thing.

The brothers continued along the barren land that stretched toward the mountains. They passed several more deserted cottages in various stages of disrepair. A few of the cottages had been almost totally destroyed by fire. Glencairn reined in his horse to stop and stare grimly at the blackened structures.

During their ride about the Glencairn lands, they saw few people. There were some bedraggled-looking children playing in front of one neglected cottage. They had stopped playing to stare with wide, frightened eyes at the two men on horseback. When the earl and Peter had pulled up their horses to talk to them, the children had dashed inside the cottage.

The only other person Glencairn and Peter saw on their ride was a lone shepherd on a distant hill. The man was whistling commands to a small red and white dog that was vigorously herding a flock of sheep.

Reaching some steep, rocky terrain, Glencairn and Peter climbed to the top of the rise. Staring down at the stark beauty of the land, the earl found himself thinking of the burned-out cottages and the frightened eyes of the children. His reflections were interrupted by Peter. "Look, Glencairn, there is another cottage on the hill over there. It must be inhabited. There are horses."

The earl followed his brother's gaze to where a small house stood in the vast landscape. Two horses were tethered outside it, one of them harnessed to a cart. Without saying anything, Glencairn started toward the small dwelling with Peter following after him.

As they neared the cottage, Glencairn could hear loud voices raised in an argument of some kind. Pulling their horses up alongside the others, the earl and Peter dismounted. An angry voice came from the open door of the cottage. "I'll have nae more argument frae ye, Aggie MacDonald! I've nae wish tae hurt ye. Go on then. Take that out of here."

Two men came out the door carrying a bed. They stopped to stare at Glencairn. Following behind them was an old woman who looked quite distraught. Close on her heels was the earl's factor, Ferguson.

The factor regarded the earl with surprise. "Lord Glencairn!" Hastily pulling off his shapeless hat, he bowed. "Good day, my lord."

Glencairn was in no mood for pleasantries. He looked at the elderly woman, who wore a ragged shawl around her thin shoulders, and then back at the factor. "What is the meaning of this, Ferguson?" he growled.

"I was just carrying out my instructions, my lord," said the factor.

"Dammit, what instructions?" said Glencairn angrily. "I told you not to proceed with any evictions."

"Yes, my lord, but Aggie MacDonald here was told tae leave this place some weeks ago. Before your last instructions, my lord," he quickly added.

Glencairn's expressions grew dark and ominous. "So you quibble like a lawyer, Ferguson! You knew damned well I did not want any more of these people put out of their homes! You are to leave this woman be."

Aggie MacDonald, who had been quite startled by the appearance of the evil Earl of Glencairn, regarded him with a mixture of surprise and distrust on her lined face. "What? Ye will not put me out?" she croaked in astonishment.

"No, I will not," said Glencairn. He turned to the two men who had removed the bed from the cottage. "Put that back inside! And be quick about it!" The two men hurriedly picked up the bed and began to cart it back through the doorway.

Aggie was momentarily dumbfounded as she watched the earl sternly command the men. "Ye are the Earl of Glencairn, aren't ye?" she asked, clutching her shawl around her. She suddenly appeared wobbly and Glencairn advanced toward her.

"You appear ill," he said, solicitously taking hold of her arm and leading her to a rough-hewn bench that was sitting outside the cottage. "I regret this incident, Mrs. MacDonald," he said, once he had her settled on the bench. "I promise you, you may remain here for as long as you wish." Glencairn turned back to the factor. "So, Ferguson, you would turn a poor, sick woman out of her home?"

The burly factor nervously fingered his sandy beard.

"She is always complaining she's sick, my lord. As I told ye, she was supposed tae leave some weeks back, but she said she was too sick tae move. I allowed her tae stay then, my lord."

"That was kindhearted of you, Ferguson," said Glencairn sarcastically.

The factor, unaware of the sarcasm, quickly nodded. "Aye, my lord. But 'tis not right for Aggie MacDonald tae take advantage of my kindness any longer," he continued self-righteously. "Nor yours neither, my lord."

Glencairn tried to contain his fury. He wanted to throttle the fellow. "How dare you disobey me!" he shouted. "You are dismissed from my employ, Ferguson! You are never to set foot on Glencairn lands again! If you do, I will personally give you the thrashing that you deserve!" Ferguson, seeing the thunderous expression on the earl's face, quickly mounted his horse and retreated down the hill.

Glencairn looked back down at Aggie. "Are you all right, Mrs. MacDonald?"

The old woman was watching the factor's retreating back with considerable satisfaction. "Aye, my lord. Seeing you chase away that scoundrel Ferguson has done me a world of good." She paused and a slight smile appeared on her wrinkled face as she met the earl's glance. " 'Twould appear, my lord, that ye are nae the devil I thought ye tae be."

Glencairn burst out laughing. The old woman laughed along with him.

Peter, who had stood in the background watching the scene, smiled. Immensely pleased by the earl's defense of poor Mrs. MacDonald and his dismissal of the factor, he was rather amused at the sight of his brother sharing a good laugh with the old peasant woman.

Glencairn introduced Peter to Aggie MacDonald, and the elderly woman seemed delighted to meet another member of the once detested Moncrief clan. The earl and his brother then sat down with Aggie, who was only too happy to have the opportunity to speak her mind to the laird of Glencairn. It was some time before the brothers took their leave of the elderly woman, whom they left happily rocking by her hearth once again.

As they rode back to Glencairn Castle, Peter began to praise his brother's chivalry toward the old woman. Glencairn abruptly cut him off. "Do not attempt to place a halo on my head, Peter."

Peter smiled. "I should not attempt to do anything so absurd, Glencairn. But it was good of you to help the poor creature."

The earl looked thoughtful. "Yes, I helped one old woman, but what of the others? As you yourself said, Peter, I am laird of Glencairn—I am responsible."

"But you didn't know of the clearances, of the cottages being burned—"

"It was my duty to know," said the earl firmly, "but I was content to leave all matters pertaining to my Scottish estate to my solicitor." He paused. "And to that damned factor of mine."

Peter did not reply but rode alongside his grim brother in silence. Glencairn suddenly pulled up his horse. "Peter, I am not returning to the castle just yet," he said abruptly. "Would you go along without me?"

His younger brother regarded him curiously. "But where are you going, Glencairn?" Seeing the expression on the earl's face, a light suddenly dawned on Peter. "You are going to see Athena," he said.

Glencairn nodded. "I need to tell her what I've seen today . . . that I understand what has happened here and that I will try to make amends."

Peter smiled. "Good luck, Glencairn." The earl nodded again and then galloped off in the direction of Ravenscroft.

Athena stood perusing the shelves of books in the library of Ravenscroft. She had been left alone to occupy herself that morning with only the dog, Mally, as company. Her uncle and Robert had gone off early to see about a problem with some of their sheep, and her aunt had stayed in bed with a cold.

Recognizing a title from her childhood, Athena pulled out a book from the shelf. The small purple volume proclaimed itself as *A History of the Glorious Reign of the Stuarts.* Opening up the book, Athena saw a familiar inscription, "To my son Baldwin on his sixth birthday."

Athena smiled. Her grandfather would have been quite shocked to learn that his wayward son detested the Stuart monarchs every bit as much as he did the present Hanoverians occupying the throne.

Taking the book, Athena settled in a chair next to a window, the deerhound curling up to sleep at her feet. She opened the small volume and began to read about Robert II, the first ruler of the House of Stuart. However Athena's attention soon wandered from medieval Scotland as she once again began to think about the Earl of Glencairn. Sighing, Athena closed the book and walked over to the window. Mally awoke with a start and quickly followed after her.

Staring out at the lovely grounds of Ravenscroft, Athena thought about the earl's sudden, unexpected appearance in Scotland. It was quite remarkable that he had followed her there and that he had still wanted to marry her. Athena frowned. Surely his pride would not allow him to continue his suit now that she had turned him down a second time.

This thought depressed her, and she quickly turned away from the window. She looked down and found that Mally was watching her with what appeared to be an expression of deep concern. Athena crouched down to pet the dog fondly. "You are a good girl, Mally. Would you like to go for a walk?"

The dog's worried expression was quickly replaced with an expression of pure joy. Mally ran toward the door and then hurried back to Athena and stopped in front of her. Athena laughed. "All right, girl. Just let me get my bonnet."

Although Athena knew Robert and the baron would be displeased by her going out alone, she felt she had to get away from the house and the memory of the Earl of Glencairn's visit there. Quickly donning her straw bonnet, she led an exuberant Mally out the front door of the house.

Deciding that she was too unfamiliar with her surroundings to risk getting lost on the moor, Athena walked along the road. Mally ran eagerly ahead of her, stopping occasionally to sniff along the way. Athena began to feel better as she walked briskly along the country road. The sun had broken through the clouds above her, casting a shimmering light on the pale green moors.

They had gone but a short distance when Athena noted the clouds were darkening overhead. Deciding it prudent to return to Ravenscroft, she called for Mally. The dog came flying back to her with a huge grin on her canine face. Athena patted the dog. "I fear we should go back, girl." Mally continued to grin at her and then mischievously took off again. "Mally!" cried Athena. As she watched the dog in exasperation, she suddenly noticed a horseman on the road ahead of them.

As the horse got closer, Athena recognized the rider as the Earl of Glencairn. "Mally!" she called, and the dog reluctantly made her way back to her.

Spotting Athena on the road in front of him, Glencairn could not believe his good fortune. He had wondered if Athena would even receive him once he arrived at Ravenscroft. Now it appeared she would have to see him.

He pulled up his horse in front of her and promptly jumped down. "Athena!"

"Glencairn," she said, attempting to sound calm despite the wild pounding of her heart.

Mally gleefully bounded up to Glencairn. Reaching down to pet the dog, the earl smiled. "I am glad to see that you are in such fine fettle, my girl." Mally grinned and continued to gaze adoringly up at the earl.

Glencairn advanced toward Athena. "I wanted to talk to you, Athena."

"Please, my lord," said Athena, "Talking will serve no purpose. I do not think it wise for us to see each other again."

The earl scowled. "Dammit, Athena. I'm in love. You cannot expect a man in love to be wise." A slight smile appeared on her face and he was somewhat heartened. "I had to see you again, Athena," he continued. "You see, I did as you wanted. I looked into the matter of the clearances."

She fixed her blue eyes upon him. "You did?"

He nodded. "You were right. It was monstrous how my tenants were treated, forced from their homes, their miserable cottages burned." He paused. "Today I came upon my factor, Ferguson, attempting to throw a poor, sick woman out of her home."

Athena's expression turned indignant. "The villain! I have heard some horrible stories about him. What happened?"

"I dismissed Ferguson. That was hardly punishment enough for the fellow; he deserved a good horsewhipping." Glencairn stopped and looked away. "But, I am hardly one to lecture another man on his behavior. My own has been reprehensible."

Athena's eyes widened in surprise. "What do you mean?"

"I neglected my responsibility. I allowed this to happen." He smiled somewhat ruefully. "I confess I have been a selfish man, Athena, caring only for my own pleasures. But I swear to you, I deeply regret what has happened here. I will do what I can to atone for it." He drew closer to her and gazed down solemnly into her eyes. "I only hope that I can somehow prove to you that I am not a total wretch."

"I do not think that, my lord," she said smiling at him. "Indeed, I have not even thought of you as a tyrant for some time."

Glencairn needed little encouragement. "Darling Athena," he murmured, quickly pulling her to him. However the sound of a horse approaching behind them caused him to quickly release her. "Damn," he muttered, turning to glare at the intruder.

Athena, who despite her better judgment, had been unable to resist falling into the earl's embrace, was dismayed to find the rider approaching them was her cousin Robert. That gentleman quickly pulled up beside them. "What the devil are ye doing here, Glencairn?" he demanded in a belligerent voice.

The earl regarded Robert with his usual aristocratic hauteur. "I was speaking to Athena."

"Speaking was it? It didna look like speaking tae me." Robert's face grew red. He turned to Athena. "Are ye daft, Athena? A man like Glencairn canna be trusted with a woman alone and unprotected."

"Really, Robert, don't be a block!" said Athena sharply.

"See here, Blair," said the earl angrily, "you know that my intentions toward your cousin are honorable. I have asked for her hand in marriage."

"Aye, and ye've been refused. I'll nae allow ye tae force yourself upon my cousin. Ye are tae leave here at once, my lord!"

The earl looked up at Robert with such a furious expression that Athena feared for a moment that the two of them would come to blows. She quickly intervened. "It is best that you go, Lord Glencairn."

The earl hesitated for a moment. "Very well," he said finally. Mounting his horse, he rode quickly off.

Robert got off his horse. "Athena, ye must have better sense. Ye've said ye will nae marry him. Good heavens, what would Uncle Baldwin think if he knew Glencairn was here?"

Athena reddened. She was very irritated with her cousin, although she knew that he was right. It was fortunate that Baldwin knew nothing about Glencairn being there. Robert took her arm and led her toward the house, his horse and Mally trailing behind them.

21

WHEN Athena reached the house, she left Robert and proceeded to Lady Blair's sitting room. Having caught a slight cold, the baroness had remained in her rooms to rest. Entering the sitting room, Athena found her aunt seated in a chair, a thick woolen shawl around her shoulders. She was reading a ladies' magazine.

The baroness appeared delighted to see her niece. "Athena, my dear," she said, putting down the magazine. "How good of ye tae come and see me." She dabbed at her nose with her handkerchief.

"Are you feeling any better, Aunt?"

"Och, 'tis only a wee cold. I'll be better in a trice. I was looking out the window, Athena. Was that nae Lord Glencairn?" Athena nodded. The baroness cast a shrewd look at her niece. "It appears that the earl is nae one tae give up easily. I know that 'tis none of my affair, lass, but Robert has told me the earl has offered for ye. I canna help but wonder why ye have refused him. 'Tis clear as day that he loves ye. And unless I am very much mistaken, I think ye love him."

Athena frowned. "I shall try to explain, Aunt," she said. "You see, it has to do with a person's convictions. Can one give them up simply because she falls in love?"

"I dinna understand."

"My father and I have worked very hard, writing and speaking against injustice. I do not suppose you have ever read the *Clarion Voice*?"

"Och, nae, child, my husband would never allow that, although the minister once mentioned tae me that a friend had sent him a copy frae London. I would have liked to see it, but, knowing how my husband would feel, I didna dare."

Athena nodded understandingly. "My uncle despises my father for his opinions. But my father and I believe firmly in the equality of men. We think that it is wrong to establish artificial distinctions of class and rank. Indeed, I have written a pamphlet advocating the abolition of titles of nobility."

The baroness regarded her niece as if she did not quite comprehend her. "Abolition of titles? Och, my dear!" Lady Blair appeared appalled at the outrageous suggestion. "And your own uncle a laird!"

"Oh, I can understand how shocking the idea may be for you, Aunt. But I have given the matter serious consideration for some time."

"I pray ye dinna speak of such a thing tae your uncle," said the baroness. "I'd never hear the end of it. And is that why ye will nae have Glencairn? Because he is a peer?"

"Believing as I do, how could I marry an earl? How could I, Baldwin Blair's daughter, become the Countess of Glencairn? I should be the worst hypocrite. And my father would disown me!"

Lady Blair shook her head, trying to digest her niece's preposterous remarks. Her husband had often raged against his brother, saying that Baldwin was a disgrace to the family. The baroness found herself in agreement. How dreadful of Baldwin to have given his daughter such nonsensical ideas. "I dinna know what tae say, Athena," said her ladyship.

"There is nothing to say, Aunt," said Athena. She smiled fondly at the baroness. "I did not mean to distress you. I shall leave you. You must get your rest."

Lady Blair watched her niece retreat from the sitting

room, a worried expression on her face. It was clear, she told herself, that her radical brother-in-law had much to answer for.

After dinner that evening at Ravenscroft, the baron and Robert were called out to one of their tenant's farms. There was a crisis with a prized cow, and it was well known that no one knew more about the bovine than did his lordship.

Athena and Lady Blair went to the drawing room. The baroness seemed to be feeling better, although she sneezed several times, prompting Athena to insist that she retire early. When she was alone in the drawing room, Athena tried to keep from thinking about Glencairn, but she had little success. She was glad when the Blair family butler provided a diversion by entering the room.

"Excuse me, miss, is her ladyship nae here?"

"No, Brown. She has retired. I do not think she should be disturbed. Is something wrong?"

"Och, nae, miss. 'Tis only that we have heard that Aggie MacDonald is nae well. I thought her ladyship may wish tae send some things tae her."

"Oh, I am certain that she would," said Athena. "You may do so on my responsibility, Brown."

"Aye, then, miss. I'll have some things prepared and send one of the lads tae take it tae her."

"I shall go, too," said Athena. "Perhaps Mrs. Mac-Donald will need some assistance. I should feel better if I knew how she was."

"But, miss, the night grows stormy. It may rain."

"It is not very far, Brown," said Athena. "I shall be back very quickly. Indeed, I should be glad of something to do."

"If you are sure, miss," said the servant, agreeing rather reluctantly. Still, he reasoned, it was not very far to Aggie MacDonald's, and the old woman would probably be cheered by Miss Athena. All of the servants were very fond of their master's niece. In the short time she had been there, she had managed to charm all of them with her unfailing courtesy and kindness.

When a basket had been prepared for Aggie, Athena set out to deliver it. She was accompanied by a youth whom she knew only as Charlie. Charlie was perhaps twelve years old, but he was large for his age. Rather slow and not very talkative, he was not the best of company, but as she rode beside him in the dogcart, Athena was glad for his presence. The night was very dark and the wind was gusty. Athena suspected that the butler had been right to fear a storm. As they arrived at Aggie Mac-Donald's cottage, big drops of rain began to fall.

Athena rapped at the cottage door. "Mrs. MacDonald?" she called, opening the door and going inside. "It is I, Athena Blair."

"Och, Miss Blair! And Charlie! Come sit beside me. What has brought ye here on such a dark night as this?"

Athena smiled, although Aggie's appearance seemed rather worrisome. She looked tired and ill. "We have brought you some things, Mrs. MacDonald. There is soup and some bread and cheese. There is what Brown called a 'wee doch' of whiskey as well."

"That is most welcome," said Aggie.

"Should you not be in bed, Mrs. MacDonald?"

"Och, I thought I'd stay up a bit longer."

"Are you not cold? Charlie, would you see to the fire?" The boy nodded and set about starting a blaze in the hearth.

"You are very kind, miss," said Aggie.

"You must go to bed, Mrs. MacDonald. Now do not argue, ma'am."

Aggie did not argue and was perfectly willing to submit to Athena's orders. When she was tucked into bed, Athena sat on a stool beside her. "Ye are sae kind tae visit me," said Aggie. "I had other visitors today. Ferguson was here."

"Ferguson here!" cried Charlie, his usual reticence vanishing.

"Aye, and he was about tae toss me frae my home, but who should arrive, but the laird of Glencairn himself! He put a stop tae it." A look of revelation came to Athena's face. So Aggie was the old woman the earl had mentioned. "Ye know, miss," continued the elderly woman, "his lordship seemed a good, kind man. Sore surprised I was tae find him sae! I had always thought him a devil. I may have been wrong. He was very kind tae me. And his brother is a good, handsome lad."

"I think you should rest now," said Athena. "I'll sit with you for a while."

Aggie seemed pleased to hear this. She fell quickly to sleep. Her breathing seemed labored, but regular. Athena turned to Charlie. "I am worried, Charlie. I do not think she should be left alone. I shall stay here with her. You must take the dogcart and go back to Ravenscroft. Tell Mr. Brown to send someone out who can stay the night with Mrs. MacDonald. And perhaps the doctor should be consulted."

Charlie nodded and did as he was told, leaving Athena sitting beside Aggie. Athena stared thoughtfully into the fire while the old woman slept. A few moments later, the door opened suddenly, startling Athena. She looked over to see two young men she did not know. Wrapped in ragged cloaks and wearing tartan caps, they eyed her with suspicion.

Athena rose from the stool and went to them. "Who are ye?" demanded the taller of the two young men.

"I am Athena Blair come from Ravenscroft to see Mrs. MacDonald. She is not well. I have sent someone to get more help."

"I am James MacDonald and this is Angus MacPherson," said the tall man.

"How do you do?" said Athena. She nodded to the other man, but he only frowned darkly.

"The old woman is my grandmother," said James MacDonald. "How is she?"

"I do not know," said Athena, "but she is resting quite comfortably."

"They say that Ferguson and his men came tae evict her today," said MacDonald.

"Yes," said Athena, "she told me about it, but Lord Glencairn prevented them."

"Glencairn," muttered MacPherson, speaking for the first time. "That was the tale in the village. Och, sae the laird has come back and has done a kindness!" The man's face grew sinister. "Where was he when I was burned frae my cottage? Where was he when my Jennie died frae cold and hunger? And now we are tae be sae grateful tae him. Och, may the laird of Glencairn burn in hell for what he has done to me!"

Athena regarded MacPherson in some alarm.

"MacPherson," said MacDonald, casting a warning look at his companion. "Come, 'tis time tae go." Turning to Athena, he smiled. "Thank ye for your kindness tae my grandmother, miss."

Athena nodded and the two men went out the door. They stood outside talking, their voices loud but incomprehensible. Frightened by the hatred in MacPherson's voice, Athena walked to the door and strained her ears. "Ye must be completely mad!" cried MacDonald.

"Ye are my friend, Jamie. Ye must help me." Athena heard MacPherson's voice distinctly.

"I'll nae help ye murder anyone!" she heard MacDonald say. "Least of all the Earl of Glencairn!" Murder the earl! Athena's head reeled in shock.

"Then ye are a coward!" shouted MacPherson. "I wash my hands of ye!"

The voices stopped. She could hear only the sound of rain that was now falling steadily. Athena leaned against the door and tried to stop the sense of panic that was welling up inside her.

Aggie stirred. "Miss Blair? Are ye here, miss?"

"Yes, Mrs. MacDonald," Athena came alongside her.

"Is something wrong? I thought I heard voices."

"It was your grandson, James MacDonald."

"Jamie," said Aggie. "He didna stay?"

"No," said Athena. "And I must go, too. Someone from Ravenscroft will be here soon." She tried hard to speak calmly. "How far is it to Glencairn Castle?"

"How far, miss? Why, two miles more or less."

"And how would one get there?"

"The path, miss, but why would ye be asking that?"

Athena picked up her cloak and fastened it around her. She then put on her bonnet. "Good-bye, Mrs. MacDonald. Do not worry. Someone will be coming soon. Tell them I have gone to Glencairn Castle."

"Tae the castle?" said Aggie in some confusion. Athena did not linger any longer. Rushing outside, she started walking briskly down the path. The rain continued to fall steadily as she hurried along. She saw no sign of MacPherson. He doubtlessly could walk much faster than she. Fear seized Athena, and she started to run. Was MacPherson on his way to Glencairn Castle? Did he actually mean to kill the earl? It was too fantastic and she would have dismissed it as absurd if she had not heard the way the man had spoken of Glencairn.

It was dark and difficult to see where she was going. Once she stumbled and nearly fell on the stony ground. Her sense of urgency growing stronger with each minute, she continued on.

How she managed to arrive at Glencairn Castle was a mystery to Athena. It had been very difficult to follow the path in the darkness. Yet somehow, Athena had made her way there. Suddenly the castle loomed ahead of her.

There were few lights visible from the great stone edifice. Athena did not know how late it was. She only hoped that she could warn the earl in time. Reaching the doors, she pounded furiously on them with her fists. It seemed an unbearably long time before the enormous door creaked open. "What in God's name is it?" The butler, Gordon, eyed her unhappily.

"Let me in!" cried Athena. "I must see Lord Glencairn!"

Gordon regarded her in surprise. "He has gone tae bed, miss. Ye must come back tomorrow."

Athena pushed him aside. "He is in danger. I must see him at once! Take me to him!"

This imperative command stirred the servant into action. "This way, miss," he said.

"Hurry!" cried Athena. "Hurry!"

Alarmed by her words, the servant raced through the entry hall and then up a vast stone staircase. Athena hurried after him, running up the stairs. When they reached Glencairn's bedchamber, the servant opened the door. Athena rushed in.

She saw the open window to the room first, then the form near the canopied bed. Athena screamed.

The earl had been asleep, but the scream roused him. He saw someone bending over him. Alarmed first by noise and then the shadowy figure, Glencairn instinctively rolled away. As he did so, he felt a sharp pain in his shoulder.

Gordon covered the distance from the door to the bed with remarkable swiftness. He tackled the intruder, and both sprawled onto the hard stone floor. The earl was out of his bed in a second. Coming to the aid of the servant, he fell upon the other man. Glencairn was a brawny man of great strength, and he quickly subdued the intruder.

Athena had witnessed the scene in horror. She stood frozen for a moment while the earl and his butler struggled with the man. The room was lit only by the dying flames of the fireplace, and the flickering light made it hard to see what was going on.

Glencairn got to his feet and pulled the intruder up with him. "Who are you?" said the earl.

The man said nothing. "He had this dirk, my lord," said Glencairn's servant, holding up the dagger. " 'Tis MacPherson. He was going tae kill your lordship! Praise God, the lady came when she did."

"The lady?" Glencairn turned to see Athena standing near the door. "Athena!"

"Oh, Glencairn!" Athena was in his arms in a second, burying her face against his chest.

"My God, Athena," said the earl. "You're soaking wet."

"I don't care," said Athena, hugging him tightly.

"What will your lordship do with MacPherson?" said the servant.

The earl regarded MacPherson strangely. He continued to hold Athena in his arms. Indeed, he did not think he ever wanted to release her. "Why did you want to kill me?" he demanded. "Speak!"

MacPherson remained silent, glowering at the earl in the faint light. "I believe I know," said Athena. "Or I know part of it. He was driven from his farm by Ferguson. His wife died. He blames you."

The earl released Athena and turned to regard MacPherson somberly. "Is this true? You blame me for the death of your wife?"

"Ye *are* tae blame!" cried MacPherson. "Ye drove us frae our land! We had nothing! And my Jennie is dead!" The distraught man broke down into sobs.

"Ye are a fool, MacPherson," Gordon said harshly. "Ye have three wee bairns tae look after. Ye've made them orphans this night. And hanging is what ye deserve!"

"Quiet, Gordon," said the earl sharply. He continued in a kinder voice. "Look here, MacPherson, I can understand that you would blame me for what happened, but, upon my honor, I did not know what Ferguson was

doing in my name. That does not absolve me of guilt."
The earl glanced over at Athena. "As I have been reminded more than once. I shall try to make amends for
the wrongs done my tenants. I shall restore their homes.
And if you will swear that you will never again try to
harm me or my family, I shall let you go. Gordon says
you have children. Think of them."

"My lord!" cried Gordon. "Ye canna mean that ye
would nae see the man punished! Why, he tried tae kill
ye."

"That is up to MacPherson," returned the earl. "You
must swear an oath as a true Highlander that you will
never again attempt to harm me or those of my house."

MacPherson seemed to weigh these words carefully.
Finally he nodded. "I swear," he said.

Glencairn nodded. "Gordon, escort MacPherson from
the castle." The servant eyed his master as if he felt he
had done a very foolish thing, but nodded. "And fetch
Mrs. Cameron. Tell her that Miss Blair will need some
dry clothes. She will stay the night. Send a messenger to
Ravenscroft to tell them she is safe."

"Aye, my lord," said Gordon. He turned to MacPherson. "Get ye gone then, Angus." MacPherson glanced at
the earl, but said nothing before following Gordon from
the room.

When they were alone, Glencairn lost no time before
gathering Athena into his arms again. "My darling,
Athena! You have saved my life! How on earth did you
know about MacPherson?"

"I was at Aggie MacDonald's cottage. He was with
her grandson. I heard him tell James MacDonald that he
intended to kill you! Oh, Glencairn, I was so worried!"

"And you came all that way in the dark and the rain?"

She snuggled against him. "It does not matter. You are
safe!" She pulled back suddenly. "You are bleeding!
Your shoulder! Are you hurt?"

The earl had completely forgotten about his injury, but

a dark stain had appeared on his nightshirt where the dagger had torn the garment. "It is nothing. A mere scratch."

"I shall judge that, my lord," said Athena with mock severity. "Come sit by the fire." Glencairn obediently did as she commanded, lowering himself into a stiff-backed armchair. Taking off her rain-soaked cloak, Athena tossed it aside. Leaning down, she then untied the drawstring at the neck of the earl's nightshirt and pulled it open so that she could see his shoulder.

"I think I shall like this," said his lordship, a roguish gleam in his eye.

"Behave yourself, sir," said Athena, studying the injury. "I must get a cloth and some water. I do not think it is very bad."

"Come here, madam," said the earl, reaching out to pull Athena into his lap.

"My lord!"

Laughing, the earl enfolded Athena into a tight embrace. Happy to have his strong arms around her, she did not protest when his lips met hers. It was some time before Glencairn released her from his passionate kisses. "Athena, my dear. God, I love you."

"Oh, Glencairn," said Athena, hugging him tightly. "What am I to do?"

"You are to marry me, my lass," said the earl. He grinned at her. "You have no choice. After all, you are dreadfully compromised, Athena." He glanced over at the bed. "Although I should like to compromise you a good deal more."

Athena smiled. "You are incorrigible, my lord."

"Say you will marry me."

She regarded him for a moment. "Oh, very well." Glencairn laughed and pulled her to him once again.

22

PETER MONCRIEF had not been aware of the extraordinary events that had taken place at Glencairn Castle. After sleeping soundly, he had risen early. Since arriving in the Highlands, Peter had gotten into the habit of early morning rides. He enjoyed his solitary wanderings very much and found them the source of much inspiration for his poetry.

The morning air was brisk as Peter eased his spirited gray horse into a canter. He felt wonderful. Indeed, he had never felt so well as he did in Scotland. He wished he could stay there forever.

As horse and rider continued on the road beyond the village, Peter spied a man on foot carrying a bulky valise. Coming up quickly behind the man, Peter turned his horse to give the walker wide berth. As he passed the man, Peter nodded in a civil fashion. "Good God!" Pulling his horse up sharply, the young man eyed the walker in astonishment. "Mr. Blair!"

Baldwin Blair stood there regarding Peter in some surprise. "Young Moncrief?"

"Aye, sir," said Peter, jumping down from his horse. "Good heavens, Mr. Blair, I did not expect to see you here!" He shook Baldwin's hand. "Why, who is minding the *Clarion Voice*, sir?"

"I have left it in Pike's hands, although I may regret it. But when I heard that your brother had left town for

Scotland, I knew that I must come. I could not allow him to take advantage of Athena."

"But, Mr. Blair, my brother has the greatest regard for your daughter. He loves her with all his heart. That she has refused to be his wife goes very hard on him."

Baldwin frowned. "I think it monstrous that he has pursued her to Scotland. I would have hoped that you might have tried to prevent him, Moncrief. At least you might have sent me word of this." Peter looked crestfallen. "Oh, I should not blame you," said Baldwin. "He is your brother. You are undoubtedly disinclined to believe the worst of him."

Peter started to defend the earl, but stopped himself. He knew that it would be pointless to try to argue. "But where are you going, sir? To Ravenscroft?"

Baldwin nodded. "I must see Athena. I only hope that my brother does not set his dogs upon me."

Peter grinned. "Take my horse. You must be tired, sir."

"No, no, young man, I could not do that."

"Then allow me to take your bag, sir."

Baldwin did not protest, but allowed Peter to carry the heavy traveling bag. The two of them walked together. Baldwin, despite his animosity toward Peter's brother, was fond of the younger Moncrief. Seeming to forget Glencairn, he turned the discussion to Peter's views on the Highlands. Peter was only too happy to expound on his newfound love of Scotland as they continued on.

All of the Blairs at Ravenscroft had risen early that morning. News that Athena was spending the night at Glencairn Castle had been quite astonishing. Robert had been particularly upset to hear that his cousin was there with Glencairn. He would have hurried to the castle, had the baron not expressly forbidden him to set foot outside. After all, the Earl of Glencairn's messenger had said that the earl would see that Athena returned home, and Lord Blair had declared that he would allow him to do so.

Lord and Lady Blair and Robert were seated at their breakfast table when a servant hurried toward the baron. "Your pardon, my lord," he said, "but ye have visitors."

"At such an hour?" said Lord Blair. "Is it Glencairn with Miss Blair?"

"Nae, my lord," returned the servant. "It is Mr. Moncrief and . . ." The man hesitated before continuing. "And Mr. Baldwin Blair, my lord." The baron blinked uncomprehendingly at the man. "It is your brother, my lord, come from London."

Lady Blair gaped at the servant. "Baldwin here?"

"Aye, my lady."

"My uncle!" cried Robert, very excited. "Och, I shall be sae very glad tae see him! This is a great surprise."

"I'll nae see him," said the baron. "Ye may tell him that!"

"Father," cried Robert, "Ye canna turn your own brother away."

"I can and I will," said the baron.

"Malcolm!" said Lady Blair. "He has come all the way frae London. Do see him. I beg you, my dear. Do this for me! Just see him for a moment!"

"Very well," muttered the baron, "but if we come tae blows, 'twill be your fault, Isabelle."

Lady Blair seemed willing to accept that risk. "Go bring them here at once," she told the servant.

Baldwin and Peter entered the dining room. It had been nearly fourteen years since Baldwin had last seen his brother and sister-in-law. He regarded the baron with a scowl, but smiled brightly at Lady Blair and Robert. Robert had jumped to his feet. "Uncle! What a great surprise!" He pumped Baldwin's hand vigorously.

"Robert, my boy, I am glad to see you." Baldwin smiled at his sister-in-law. "My dear Isabelle, you are beautiful as ever." Turning to his brother, Baldwin nodded gravely. "Thank you for receiving me, Malcolm. I have come to see Athena. Where is she?"

"She is nae here at present," said Lady Blair. "Why don't ye have some breakfast? Have ye eaten, Mr. Moncrief?"

"No, ma'am," said Peter, who was very hungry from his ride.

"Then sit down, gentlemen," said the baroness. "Athena will be here shortly. She is . . . paying a call." The visitors sat down at the table.

The baron regarded his wife questioningly, but since he did not wish to speak in his brother's presence any more than necessary, he remained silent. "Paying a call?" said Baldwin. "Well, I shall be glad to see her. I have been very worried."

"Worried?" said Lady Blair. "Why would ye be worried about Athena?"

"I worry about Glencairn," muttered Baldwin. He looked at Peter. "I know he is your brother, Moncrief, but I do not trust him where my daughter is concerned. When I found out that Glencairn had gone to Scotland, I hurried to come here. He wishes to marry her, you see. Of course, she has refused him, but he has come to Scotland to attempt to change her mind. I am here to prevent that."

Lord Blair eyed his brother with disfavor. Despite his intention to say nothing to him, he shook his head. "Glencairn wishes tae marry my niece? Why, that would be a verra great honor. What have ye against the man?"

"I believe I would rather not discuss that with you, sir," said Baldwin icily.

The baron stared at his brother for a moment, but then a smile crossed his dour countenance. "I wish I had known how ye felt, Brother. I should have been more concerned about Athena spending the night at Glencairn Castle."

"What!" cried Baldwin, turning to Peter. "Athena at Glencairn Castle!"

"Indeed, sir, I know nothing of that!" said Peter. "I did not see Miss Blair. Surely you are mistaken, Lord Blair."

The baron appeared gleeful. "Sae ye were nae aware of it, young Moncrief? Is that nae peculiar? Why, Glencairn himself sent a messenger last evening saying Athena was there and would stay the night." He raised his eyebrows. "Ye had best withdraw your objections tae a wedding, Baldwin."

"Dammit!" cried Baldwin, rising to his feet. "Is this how you protect my daughter, your own niece? By God, if any harm has come to Athena, you will be held accountable!" Baldwin glared at his brother and then hurried from the dining room. Peter and Robert followed after him.

"You must give me your horse, Moncrief," said Baldwin, racing down the corridor and into the entry hall. "I shall go to Athena."

"We will go with you, sir," said Robert. "I'll have the horses mounted."

Baldwin rushed outside. "Hurry then, Robert," he said. "Get the horses."

Robert started away, but was stopped by Peter's voice. "Wait, Blair! There is my brother's carriage!" In the distance was the earl's large traveling coach, lumbering down the narrow road. "I am sure that Miss Blair is with him. I know there will be an explanation."

Baldwin cast a dark look at Peter. At the moment he was not feeling very kindly toward anyone bearing the name Moncrief.

Inside the coach Athena and the earl had no thought of anyone else. Having spent most of the ride locked in Glencairn's embrace, Athena had no wish to arrive at Ravenscroft. The earl was just as unhappy to see the residence of the Blairs appear. His arm around Athena, he stared out the window. "I fear, my love, we are here." Catching sight of the three men standing outside, the earl recognized his brother first. "There is Peter. Who is the man beside him? Good God!" he said suddenly. "Athena, there is your father!"

"My father!" Leaning across the earl to see out the window, Athena gasped. "My father here! I cannot believe it."

Glencairn nodded. "It is he." He cast a sardonic look at Athena. "He does not carry a dagger, does he?"

She laughed despite her uneasiness. How could she tell Baldwin that she was going to marry the earl? Her father would disown her.

When the carriage pulled to a stop, Baldwin seized the door handle and wrenched it open. "Athena!" he cried.

Athena allowed herself to be pulled from the vehicle into her father's arms. "Oh, Papa! Whatever are you doing here?"

"When I discovered that Glencairn had gone to Scotland, I knew that I could not leave you unprotected. Thank God, I did come!" He glared at the earl as he climbed down from the carriage. "What is the meaning of this, Glencairn!" he demanded. "My brother has said that my daughter spent the night at Glencairn Castle."

"Indeed she did, Blair," said the earl. "She spent the night at the castle, but not, I regret to say, with me." Baldwin directed an angry look at Glencairn, who seemed unperturbed by the older man. "Your daughter saved me from an assassin last night."

"What!" cried Peter.

"What nonsense is this?" said Baldwin.

"It is no nonsense, Blair," continued the earl. "Athena walked miles in pouring rain to warn me of a plot against my life. She was barely in time to awaken me. I bear the mark of the fellow's knife. I could hardly send your daughter back to Ravenscroft when she was soaking wet and exhausted."

"Is this true?" said Baldwin.

"It is true, Papa."

"But who was the man?" cried Robert.

"His name is MacPherson. My factor drove him from his home. He blamed me for his misfortunes."

"This is monstrous!" cried Peter. "You were injured?"

"Only a scratch." He smiled fondly at Athena and then turned to Baldwin. "I fear you will blame your daughter for her poor judgment in saving my life, Blair, but she has done so. And she has consented to be my wife."

"What!" cried Baldwin. "Athena, you have not accepted him?"

"I have, Papa. Please do not be angry."

"Angry!" shouted Baldwin. "Of course I am angry! See here, Glencairn, if you think that I shall allow you to marry my daughter, you are a great fool."

Glencairn listened to his prospective father-in-law with admirable composure. "I know that you are not pleased, sir," he said.

"Not pleased? By all the gods! I am livid! Do you think that I will stand idly by to see Athena become your wife so that she may hobnob with royal George and his decadent friends?"

"There is no need to fear that, Blair," replied Glencairn. "The Prince Regent and I are no longer on speaking terms. We have had a falling out over a racehorse. When last I saw him, he favored me with what is known as 'the cut direct.'"

"You see, Papa?" said Athena. "Glencairn is no friend of His Royal Highness."

"Indeed not," said the earl with a faint smile. "I am certain he regards you, Blair, more favorably than he does me."

"Humph," said Baldwin, who despite his anger at the earl, was somewhat pleased by the remark. He turned to Athena. "Are you determined to have this man even if it means losing your father?"

"Oh, Papa!" cried Athena. "You cannot cast me off. I could not bear it!"

"Blair," said the earl, "do not force your daughter to choose between us. You are a reasonable man. I know you find the idea of me as your son-in-law abhorrent, but, God in heaven, it is not easy for me to think of having the famous Baldwin Blair as my father-in-law!"

Baldwin knew he should be insulted, but he could not help but find this remark amusing. "You do have a point, Glencairn."

The earl continued. "I have read your books, sir. You speak eloquently of righting the ills of society. I do not argue that there are many to right and that men like me have done little to change things. I am the Earl of Glencairn and I cannot be anything else. I could not give up my title even for Athena, but with her as my wife, I shall be a far better earl. I shall use my power more wisely that I have done in the past. By my honor, I swear it."

"Papa, please accept Glencairn! I love him! And I love you, too!"

Baldwin looked from his daughter to the earl. He knew well that this was a moment of tremendous importance. Baldwin did not approve of Glencairn although the man did not appear to be as totally bereft of redeeming qualities as he had thought. After all, he had claimed to have read his books, and he did appear to love Athena. Baldwin knew that if he refused his daughter permission to marry the earl, she would most assuredly do so in any case.

Baldwin pondered the situation carefully. He loved Athena more than anything in the world. Was he truly willing to reject her because she was making an improvident marriage?

"Papa?" said Athena.

"Dash it," said Baldwin. "Very well, I have spent a good part of my life not speaking to my brother. I would be a fool to spend the rest of it not speaking to my only daughter as well. I will not withhold my permission, Athena, but why could you not have fallen in love with someone else?"

"Oh, Papa!" Athena threw herself into her father's arms and hugged him tightly.

When Baldwin finally disengaged himself from her embrace, he turned to Glencairn. "And now let us go to Glencairn Castle," he said.

The earl looked surprised. "The castle, sir?"

Baldwin nodded. "I'll not stay with my brother. If you will allow me to take advantage of your hospitality, I shall be most grateful, Glencairn."

The earl exchanged a look with Athena. "Of course, sir."

"And, Athena, I'll not have you staying where I am not welcome. You will come as well."

Very pleased at this development, the earl raised an eyebrow at Athena, who nearly burst into laughter.

"But, Uncle," said Robert. "Ye must nae go. My mother will be sae disappointed."

"No, my lad, but tell your dear mother I am sorry. And I am very tired. I shall be happy to take a place in your coach, Glencairn."

"Certainly, Blair," said the earl. Baldwin got into the vehicle. "Come, Moncrief, ride with me and you, too, Robert. I would like to talk to you. Why don't you ride with us to the castle?"

This seemed like a good idea to Robert, so he climbed into the coach. Peter followed behind him. "Come, come, Athena, let us go away from here," commanded Baldwin rather impatiently.

Athena nodded and started for the carriage door, but the earl took her by the hand and pulled her quickly behind the vehicle out of the view of Baldwin and the others.

"Where are they?" Baldwin Blair's voice came from the carriage window. Neither Athena nor the earl seemed to hear him. Looking down into Athena's blue eyes once again, Glencairn drew her to him and kissed her smiling lips.